About t

James E Mack was born in Sc
childhood abroad, gaining a l
and wildlife. He became a Com   ⌐ᴜᴜ and
a member of a Special Operatio.. ⌐ᴜᴜᴛ, with a 22-year career
serving in many of the world's troubled hotspots. James
subsequently specialised as a Counter-Terrorism adviser
and assisted in capacity building operations in support of
UK and US Government initiatives.

His passion for wildlife led James to assist in the
development of counter-poaching programs in Africa. This
passion remains and James spends much of his leisure time
photographing the very animals that he strives to protect.

When time allowed, James began writing novels based upon
his experiences in Special Operations and conflict zones
around the globe. His first novel, *Only the Dead*, was very
well-received and attracted interest from several
screenwriters.

James lives in Northern Scotland where he enjoys the
surfing and the mountains nearby.

ISBN: 9798573997735

Published by Achnacarry Press

ASSET SEVEN

ACHNACARRY
PRESS

JAMES E MACK

Once again, my heartfelt gratitude to those who support my writing, be you readers, friends or family. Without this support, none of my books would be possible and the dream I had as a young man reading Frederick Forsyth, Gerald Seymour and Jack Higgins, to one day follow in their footsteps would still only be a dream. And as always, my deepest thanks to my biggest supporter in every sense of the word; my amazing partner for her wise counsel and constant faith in me.

James E Mack

Also by James E Mack:

Only the Dead
Fear of the Dark
The Killing Agent
Sins of the Fathers

'By the time we got him, Osama Bin Laden was little more than a boogeyman; someone to scare the children with. There were other, far more effective terrorists we just couldn't reach out and touch....'

'John', CIA Officer, Syria 2019

1

NORTH-WEST IRAN

He watched in his rear-view mirror as the vehicle behind did its best to avoid drawing attention to the fact that it was following him. Which it undoubtedly was. Though whoever was driving it had been trained. They backed off on the long, straight stretches of road but closed up as they approached junctions. Kept back just enough to always have his car in sight without making it obvious that they were tailing him. They had been trained well. But not well enough.

As he changed gears and slowed down in anticipation of the junction, Karim wondered briefly if it was just routine surveillance: His turn to be followed to ensure that he wasn't doing anything he shouldn't, meeting anyone that he had no right to be with. Slowing to a halt at the junction, this forlorn hope was immediately crushed as he spotted the dark saloon parked under the shade of the pine trees further up the road. His mouth felt dry and he could feel the beads of perspiration on his forehead as he negotiated the junction and accelerated along the road. The car that had been following him since Negel took the other direction from the junction and again, for a brief moment, Karim's hopes were raised that he had been mistaken. That his paranoia had made him see things that simply weren't there. As he watched however, he saw the dark saloon pull out from its shaded position and begin following him along his route. He shivered as his suspected predicament became unassailably real:

They know.

Like the other vehicle, this one contained the silhouettes of two men; a driver and a passenger. Karim wondered if he would know the occupants, if he'd worked with them or even met them before. He doubted it. They were usually careful about who they sent to follow those they suspected. Deploying men from outside the Unit that were completely unknown to the target. It was a good strategy, ensuring that there were no connections between hunted and hunters that could be exploited for sympathetic gain while having the added benefit of retaining the followers' anonymity. But Karim didn't need to see their faces to know exactly who they were. Or why they were following him.

They know.

He wound down his window and welcomed the blast of air. Cool enough at this time of year to be refreshing, carrying with it the scent of the mountain trees and shrubs. Glancing up at the mirror he saw the black saloon had dropped back some distance, barely keeping him in sight. Not that there was any need to be closer as they would be well aware that there was nowhere Karim could turn off for at least another ten kilometers or so. He wondered what they knew and how they'd found out about it. They couldn't know everything, otherwise he would have been taken well before now. Would not have been allowed the potential to escape. *No.* They knew *something*, something that they wanted to confirm, and that was why he was being followed. But how had they found out? He'd been careful. Always. Only communicating when necessary and only through the secure channels that had been set up for him. *Betrayed?* Highly unlikely. He was in a circle of two people and that other person wouldn't do anything that might attract attention, let alone harm, to Karim.

He sighed and rested his elbow on the ledge of the open window as he considered his options. As it stood, he was certain that they suspected him but either didn't have enough evidence or wanted to observe him for some time to see if he led them to anything significant. If he was right, this at least gave him some breathing space with which to manoeuvre. Pushing his fear to one side, he reverted to his training, calming his mind and exploring possibilities that might help him escape. There was a checkpoint just before the junction to the dam and, if he got through it, he knew he had a fighting chance. If he could make it to his apartment there was the possibility that he could trigger his extraction plan into motion. It was a small chance but a chance, nonetheless. His home would have been searched by now and probably bugged, along with his phones. He would also be covered by a team to make sure he was under complete surveillance. Could safely assume that his car was fitted with a tracker in the event that if his followers lost him, they would be able to pick him up again easily. But his extraction plan had taken much of this into account, making sure that he only relied upon elements that were unknown to his masters.

He hoped.

As he rounded the bend, Karim slowed the car in anticipation of the checkpoint ahead. He watched as bored soldiers extinguished cigarettes and shouldered their rifles properly before taking up their positions around the barrier. Karim's heart began beating faster and he could hear the blood pounding in his ears. *Just stay calm, watch how they behave. You know the signs.* As he brought the car to a halt, he reached into his back pocket and retrieved his identity documents. When he looked up, one of the soldiers was at his window holding out his hand. He took the documents from Karim, glanced at him briefly, then walked over to the checkpoint building where he passed the papers in through a window. Karim felt sweat begin trickling from his armpits and down his side as the heat in the car built up now that he was stationary. The soldier who had taken his papers slouched against the wall beside the window but straightened suddenly and adjusted his beret. Karim swore under his breath but then saw the black saloon approaching slowly behind him. He realised that the soldier had recognised the saloon as an official vehicle and had reacted as such. Karim knew that if they were going to take him it would be now, while they had him blocked and with the support of the soldiers. He tried not to look in his mirror and feigned boredom, resting his head on his hand and closing his eyes. Hearing footsteps, he looked up to see the soldier returning with his documents. Without fanfare or dialogue, his papers were thrust back in his window and he accepted them, returning them to his pocket as the soldier nodded back at the building. The barrier was raised and Karim put his car into gear and crept forward, rigid in anticipation of being ordered to stop. But the order never came and he was soon through the checkpoint and on the other side, accelerating away and letting out a breath he'd been unaware he was holding.

He didn't see the black saloon for several minutes but then, as he approached the long straight leading into Dankash, he caught sight of it a few hundred feet behind him. But he didn't feel the panic that he had before. He

4

had a plan now and needed to be one hundred percent focussed on its execution. Otherwise his *own* execution, after a lengthy and brutal series of torture sessions, was inevitable. Dropping his speed as he approached the village, Karim looked for any obvious signs of surveillance in the streets. His throat tickled as the dust from the poorly maintained road entered the car. He was rolling his window up against the intrusion when he saw Sayed the baker glance at him, look away, then turn back with wide eyes before rushing back inside his decrepit store. Karim nodded.

They're here.

As he turned into the small street where his apartment was, he saw nothing out of the ordinary. Nothing out-with the normal pattern of life of the sleepy little town that he'd chosen for his home for the last six months he'd been based at the Facility. But then, this was VAJA he was dealing with, his country's most formidable intelligence organisation. Until they wanted Karim to see them, he wouldn't. Or at least shouldn't. As a Quds Force operative, they would take more care with their surveillance of Karim, conscious of his own training and abilities. Well aware that Karim was regarded as one of the best with many international successes under his belt. But VAJA were not without weakness. Their arrogance and pride, particularly when working within their area of expertise, were standard behaviours. Karim was banking on this to assist him in his escape plan.

He turned the engine off and exited the vehicle, grabbing his bag from the boot before locking the car and heading into the building. Entering the stairwell, he noted that it was quieter than usual, the Ghorbani kids nowhere to be seen, their mother's shrill calls absent from the silent entranceway. Climbing the stairs to his apartment he noticed a cigarette butt that had been carelessly tossed into the corner of the landing. Nobody who lived in this small block would dare desecrate the pristine cleanliness that the widow Aria maintained, with such an act. Only a visitor, an arrogant one with no regard for consequence, would commit such an offence. And Karim was under no illusion as to who this visitor would have been.

He drew his keys from his pocket and unlocked the door, stepping inside and closing it behind him. For the benefit of any cameras watching, Karim dropped his bag on the floor and walked over to the small fridge, removing a bottle of pomegranate juice and taking several deep swigs. As he replaced the bottle, he saw that the cover on the interior light was hanging at an odd angle, different from when he had left it yesterday morning. Closing the fridge door, he yawned as he walked towards his bedroom and began undressing. As he threw his clothes into the basket at the bottom of the bed, he took the opportunity to study another tell he had left. The rim on the base of the basket had been moved from the place where Karim had placed it. The rattan curve no longer dissecting the space between the two circles on the rug below. He felt a brief surge of anger at the sloppiness of the search team but reminded himself that their arrogance would not allow them to believe for a second that they were anything less than the best in their field. Which was fine when you were dealing with one of the regime's ever-increasing number of dissenters, but not with a front-line operator like Karim.

Naked, he made his way to the shower and turned on the tap, the feeble trickle telling him that the pump was playing up again. Stepping into the small cubicle, he gasped at the initial shock of the cold water, turning quickly away but studying the toilet cistern as he scrubbed himself. There too, was proof positive that a search had been carried out. Karim had rigged the lid of the cistern to sit at a slightly different angle if it was moved and not replaced in the exact manner that he had designed. Rinsing the shampoo from his hair, he turned the shower off and grabbed a towel from the rail, drying himself with vigorous strokes to warm up after the cold water. He returned to the room and dressed in clean clothes, again, noting that some of his tells had been disturbed. *No matter*. There was nothing here for them to find. He looked out the window and saw that it was starting to get dark and thought about what he had to do next.

They wouldn't come for him yet. They were waiting for something and he could only guess that it was for him to make a mistake and give them evidence of their suspicions. He knew that eventually they would tire of this inactivity and he would be lifted and taken for interrogation. And then he'd talk. *Everybody* talked. It was a simple matter of biology. A human being can only experience so much pain before the brain takes over and gives up whatever it believes will cease the assault on its body. But Karim didn't intend to let it get that far. He looked outside again and nodded with satisfaction at the deepening of the night. The darkness would be his only ally tonight. An ally he would rely on to give him the slimmest of chances but at least a chance. Reminding himself to appear as normal as possible for any cameras, he wandered over to the TV and turned on the set, lowering the volume as the familiar presenters of *Alkawthar* chaired a discussion about the illegal sanctions the USA was implementing against Iran. As he sat, to all intents and purposes riveted by the debate, Karim began running his plan through his mind, visualising each element and the potential for it to go wrong.

He was sure that any cameras that they'd installed would not be of a high specification, with little, if any, night-viewing capabilities. No, he knew the routine here:

A camera to record his waking activities and a physical team to watch his home throughout the night. They would be covering every door and window through which Karim could escape, with a team of thugs from *Hefazat,* the Security Investigation Unit, ready to run him to ground. But Karim, months before, had already prepared for this eventuality. His insider knowledge of the workings of the unit informing his planning and preparation. All for a day that, if he was being honest with himself, he'd never *really* believed would arrive. But it had. Today.

The building was still unnaturally quiet as Karim headed back to the bedroom and undressed. He climbed into bed and turned off the small table lamp, the room now in complete darkness. He'd had the heavy, black shutters made to block out the ambient light and help him sleep better but tonight they served another purpose: To help cover his initial escape. He lay still, pretending to be asleep for several hours before taking a deep breath and holding it for a few seconds. As he released it, he slipped out of bed and opened the bottom drawer of his wardrobe. He didn't need any light to see what he was picking out; everything in this drawer, while appearing nothing more than a general selection of clothing, had been carefully placed. He donned the dark cargo-pants and sweater before pulling the tactical boots from underneath his bed and putting them on. He worked in silence and darkness, not an unusual set of circumstances for him, while he maintained a vigilance for any unusual sounds that might indicate he had been noticed.

Karim stood and waited for several minutes before moving. There were no sounds of any note save the distant mewl of a cat in the street. He moved across the room and opened the small cupboard door, quietly removing the cardboard boxes and outdoor jackets that he kept there before placing these contents on the bed behind him. Next, he removed the shelves, taking care not to make any undue noise, and slid them under the bed. With the cupboard empty, the back wall was now exposed and Karim laid the palms of his hands flat against it. He closed his eyes, took another breath, then pushed firmly against the wall. There was a soft click and one edge of the wall moved away, opening up a small doorway. Karim continued to push until the aperture was at its widest. He waited for several seconds, listening for any sounds, before crawling on his hands and knees into the dark space.

Karim stood and stepped into the corner of the room he now found himself in. He tried to calm his heart rate in an attempt to silence the sound of the blood pounding in his ears but he was finding it difficult. The noises he *could* hear came from the widow Aria in the bed on the other side of the room. Deep, heavy breathing with the occasional gentle snore. Satisfied, Karim pushed the portion of wall back to its original position, giving a slight wince as it clicked into place. The widow Aria however, remained undisturbed. Karim could see more in this room due to the ambient moonlight filtering through the cheap curtains and saw that the floor was clear of any obstacles that might trip him. He made his way silently past the bed and eased himself out of the room and into the small hallway. Wasting no time, he strode along the small passage and entered the living room at the end. Dropping to his hands and knees again, he crawled until he was underneath the large window. Taking care not to expose himself, he pulled the curtain back a fraction and peered out, studying the street and buildings around him. Even though his heart was racing, Karim could feel his confidence growing. When he'd designed his exfiltration plan months before, he'd based it on his knowledge of how VAJA worked. He knew that if he was ever under suspicion he couldn't hope to escape from his home, even at night. But he *could* escape from someone else's.

When he'd first moved to the apartment, Karim had made a big show to the neighbours about his general handyman skills. It hadn't been long before the widow Aria had approached him and asked if could help with a few minor repairs in her own home. Karim, of course, had been only too happy to oblige and carried out those repairs and much more. Including building the escape door that led from his own apartment into hers. He'd had to wait until the old lady had gone on pilgrimage, but it hadn't taken him long and the hatch had been complete and the wall looking as it always had, days before her return. And now Karim was under a window at the opposite end of the building that he lived in. He was relying on the laziness and predictability of the security team to only be observing the exits from Karim's apartment. There was no real reason why they would be watching anywhere else however, a professional would have deployed an outer cordon of watchers, just in case Karim managed to elude the close-quarter teams.

After watching the street for almost ten minutes he decided to make his move. He'd seen nothing to indicate there was any surveillance at this end of the building. Standing, he released the catches on the window and opened it wide, pulling the curtain over his head to give him clear access. Karim lowered himself out of the window until he was hanging full length, from his hands. With a final glance to ensure it was clear below, he pushed away from the wall, turning in mid-air as he dropped, and landed on the small patch of grass that masqueraded as a garden. He rolled several times until he came to a stop under some shrubs, where he lay for a moment, catching his breath and listening for any reaction. Keeping to the shadows, Karim stood and stalked his way along the side of the building, heading for the opposite entrance. He opened the door and closed it quickly behind him, striding down the corridor that would take him to the back entrance of the block. He knew that once past there, his odds of making it out of the village increased dramatically. A noise to his front startled him and a door opened as a tall man entered the corridor, closing the door slowly behind him. He turned just as Karim reached him and his mouth opened in a wide circle of astonishment.

Even as Karim pulled his hand back for the strike, he saw the man recover enough of his wits to reach for the pistol that was concealed beneath his jacket. But he was too slow. Karim thrust the edge of his hand into the man's throat and felt the crunching of the cartilage at the same instant the man's head snapped forward. Stepping to one side to avoid the falling man clutching at his crushed trachea, Karim delivered a powerful punch to the man's temple that slammed the man's head against the wall. The dead body slid to the floor in an undignified heap and Karim reached into the jacket and pulled out a small leather wallet, opened it and studied the contents. The identity card showed the dead man was from the Ministry of Intelligence and Security; VAJA. Karim could smell oily food and traces of perfume on the man and assumed he had used his position and influence to persuade a woman to sleep with him, as he wasn't from the area and wouldn't have known anyone here. Karim shook his head at the thought of the man's arrogance and abuse of power, shoved the wallet back into the jacket then withdrew the pistol and spare magazines. Tucking them into the pockets of his cargo-pants, he stooped and grabbed the body by the ankles, dragging it along the corridor until he reached the back entrance. Karim lowered the legs before opening the door and looking outside. Seeing nothing untoward, he grabbed the legs again and hauled his funereal load outside and into the area where the small trees and shrubs bordered the building. Dropping to his hands and knees, he shoved the body under the overhanging branches of a thick tree that was low to the ground. It would be discovered once the sun came up but by then Karim was hoping that he would be far away from here. With a final glance behind him, he turned and began running towards his next destination.

***

Karim was breathing heavily as he approached the abandoned factory, the three kilometers he'd run from the village taking its toll through the adrenalin and nervous energy he was burning. He'd abandoned caution for speed, knowing for certain that they had not discovered his connection to this location. He slowed his run to a jog and then a walk as he caught his breath and navigated around the wall of the complex. Entering an open doorway near the rear of the building, he winced as his steps echoed around the walls of the cavernous space. He shook his head as he remembered that they didn't know about this place, had no idea of his visits here over the last six months. When he approached the faded radiation-warning symbol on the wall beside another open doorway, Karim stopped. He'd placed the sign there himself to discourage anybody curious enough to be snooping around. There had never been any radiation in this factory, although it had been used at one time for the production of military-grade chemical weapons. But the sign would deter even the most curious of explorers.

Karim entered the passage beyond and stooped, lifting a slab of tiling from the floor. Pushing it to one side, he drew back a thin sheet of wood and retrieved a small, metal box. He opened this and pulled out a set of keys before placing the box to one side and making his way further along the passage. He stopped outside a room where several roof joists had fallen against a heavy door. He dragged each one aside until the door was clear then pulled out the keys from his pocket and unlocked the two locks. The door opened with very little pressure as Karim pushed it, a legacy of his regular maintenance over these past months. He closed it behind him and walked forward to a large counter. Opening a drawer, he pulled out a flashlight, turning it on and wincing as the bright beam shocked his night-sensitive eyes for several seconds. Wasting no time, he primed and lit the lamp, the room now bathed in a warm, yellow glow. Karim stared at the motorbike for a moment and allowed himself a smile. Even though he'd been sure they hadn't known about this place, he'd prepared for disappointment. But it was here. Exactly as he'd left it at his last maintenance visit. He walked over to the machine and ran a quick inventory to ensure it was packed and ready to go.

It was a large bike by Iranian standards but he'd known that it was what he would need if this eventuality had ever arisen; a big off-roader built for the gruelling deserts and mountains and capable of carrying a decent load. And Karim had loaded it with as much as he believed he could take without degrading the bike's capabilities. Extra fuel for the journey ensuring he had no need to stop and expose his position. Water, food, shelter, weapons, ammunition, all packed in a rucksack ready to be man-packed when he had to leave the bike. And infra-red lighting that he'd fitted to give him an added advantage in his escape. The skills that the Quds Force had trained him in over the years were now going to be the only thing to keep him alive and the equipment he was carrying on the bike was going to help with that. His exfiltration was not going to be an easy one. He'd known that from the start. But he also knew what he was capable of and that he had to get his information out. Get it to where it could be used to stop the deaths of countless innocents.

From another drawer he took out a mobile telephone and slipped it into his trouser pocket. Grabbing a heavy jacket that was hanging from the handlebars of the bike, Karim zipped the garment up as he took a look around the room. There was nothing here that would help them; everything was on the bike. Content with this, he pulled out his Night-Vision Goggles from one of the panniers and put them on, adjusting the clasps to secure them to his head. He opened the door wide then returned and took control of the bike, heeling the kickstand before rolling the laden vehicle out of the room and along the corridor. It was a heavy beast but he'd practiced with it fully laden and knew that once he was riding the bike, it would be fine. When he reached the ground outside the building, Karim gave a quick scan of the area before starting the engine. In the still of the night it sounded incredibly loud but he knew that it wouldn't carry too far, certainly not as far as the town. He pulled in the clutch, put the bike into gear and took off towards the road, the land in front of him an eerie green in the glow of his goggles.

The wind was cool on his face but his jacket and gloves kept the cold at bay as he rode along the empty road. After a couple of kilometers, Karim slowed the bike and stopped halfway over a bridge above a raging river. The sound of the river below was loud; a result of the melting snows higher up in the mountains. He peeled off a glove then reached into his pocket and withdrew the mobile telephone, powering up the device until the screen showed it was active. He stabbed out a short message on the keys and waited for conformation that the missive had been sent. The confirmatory tick symbol showed him that it had gone and with that, Karim tossed the phone over the guardrail and into the river below. There was a very good possibility that the electronic signature of his transmission had been registered and would be followed up on. But it had been unavoidable. He'd needed to send it. Needed to tell them that he was coming. That he'd begun his exfiltration. That they needed to be ready for him.

As he put the bike into gear and headed off again, Karim thought about the message and the man he'd sent it to. Thought about how far he had to go and the odds on making it. Thought about how his watchers would now turn to hunters, eager to capture their prey. Thought about how he could never have imagined being in the position he was now in. Would never have believed that one day, he would be running from the very regime he had carried out some of the highest-level operations for. Never have imagined that he'd be hurtling along an empty road in the dead of night, a motorbike packed with weapons and equipment and a package of vital information he needed to get out. Could never have considered that, one day, Karim Ardavan, hero of the Quds Force Western Directorate, would be given another name, another role.

Karim Ardavan, veteran of the Quds Force who had taken the fight to the Western enemies of the Republic, was now running towards those same enemies. Because he was no longer Karim Ardavan of the Quds Force: He was an *Asset*. An agent for the Central Intelligence Agency of the great *shaitan* himself; the USA. And he had sent his Handler the message to tell him that he was coming to them. That his exfiltration was in play. That they needed to be ready to get him out. That Karim was no more. He was now the Asset they'd designated him all those years before.

Asset Seven

2

CAMP PALANG, NORTH-WEST IRAN

It was his habit to rise early and gain a head start on the day. Had been since his fledgling days as a scared young officer, conscripted to fight the Iraqis in the long-running war. Dawn was giving way to daylight, the soft mauves of the mountain peaks now giving way to the blacks of the rock and white snow caps. Sipping his coffee, General Zana Shir-Del leaned forward on the rail of his balcony and took in the view in front of him. He'd always loved the mountains; the freshness of the air, the crisp, clean cold, and their utter neutrality for either side in a conflict. He'd come from a mountain village, and as a boy had become strong and confident as he'd learned to climb and ski before he'd learned to read. It had stood him in good stead when he'd been conscripted; many of the young officers he'd attended the Academy with had been dead within the first year of their service. Sacrificed as martyrs charging impenetrable positions. Leading mobs of terrified young men across mined approaches as the Iraqis mowed them down with machine-gun fire.

But Zana's prowess as a mountain man had been identified before he could suffer such a fate himself and he'd been seconded to the NOHED Brigade; the

Airborne Special Forces of Iran. He'd used his background to lead covert infiltrations through high-mountain passes and take Iraqi targets by surprise. He found he had a real aptitude for unconventional warfare and the successes of his unit soon began to mount. These successes were given high-profile exposure and the young officer soon found himself rapidly gaining promotion, medals and, more importantly, influence. His transition to the Quds Force had been almost a formality given his status. He'd operated in many countries around the globe, participated in some of the Republic's major successes. But as he looked at the peaks around him, Zana felt at home for the first time in many years. At fifty-nine, he was beyond running up the steep slopes with the trainees as they endured their selection course, but he was still strong enough to leave many of them bent double and gasping for air on the high-altitude marches as he strode past them.

When he'd been tasked to set up a facility to train Quds Force operators for the most sensitive overseas missions, Zana had initially turned it down. When they'd told him that it would be based in the mountains and that it was a secret and separate entity that he would oversee directly, the offer had far more appeal. Truth was, he'd been getting a bit long in the tooth for the sabotage missions abroad; still strong but taking longer to recover from the physical exertions of infil and exfil on his aging body. So, designing and directing the training of the Republic's most elite operators in a region that he loved, was now his role in keeping the Republic safe. He'd called his creation Camp *Palang*, after the majestic leopards that he would see from time to time when he was deep in the mountains. Elusive, solitary animals that lived and hunted in the most formidable environment in the world, rarely seen by man. It was a model that Zana felt a close affinity with and one he used as a metaphor when delivering his induction speech to the trainees. The thought of the trainees broke him from his reverie and he looked at his watch. It was still too early for anyone other than the overnight watch to be up and about but that would change in the next half hour as the food hall opened for breakfast. Taking the last mouthful of the coffee, Zana headed back inside and picked up his jacket and hat.

Walking through the camp, Zana cast a critical eye over the ground and buildings looking for any signs of untidiness or disrepair. He took a deep pride in his facility and imbued this upon his staff and trainees alike, clamping down hard on any infringement of his expectations. His breath fogged in the chill morning air as he made his way to the administration building. Passing a huge bulldozer, he made note of the fact that the driver had left his jacket and helmet hanging on the shovel blade. Zana knew that most officers wouldn't even have noticed this, let alone view it as an offence. But he had learned from experience how the little things that didn't seem to matter, soon impacted upon each other to become bigger things that really mattered. He also knew that other officers wouldn't have bothered with this because it was at the hands of the mining crew and not the Palang trainees.

When Zana had begun designing Camp Palang, he'd convinced Tehran that the camp would require a cover story; something that would satisfy American satellites about what activity was being carried out in the remote region. So, every day, a small convoy of heavy equipment moved in and out of camp to dig into the sides of a nearby rock face and then process the rock they had retrieved. Small snippets of disinformation regarding a secret mining operation for cobalt in the mountains had been discreetly leaked around some government offices in Tehran, in the knowledge that this would eventually reach the ears of the CIA. And it seemed to be working. For the past two years the camp had been operating, there was nothing coming back to indicate it been compromised. Zana allowed himself a small nod of pride as this thought came to him and he pushed open the door of the administration building.

Captain Turan Abed looked up as the door to the central office opened and the General strode in. Turan smiled as General Shir-Del stopped to take off his coat and hat and hang them on the rack. Although he knew that the General was in his late fifties, with his long, lean build and piercing blue eyes, he could pass for a man many years younger. The only nod to his age seemed to be the groomed white beard that followed the contours of his jawline. His physical presence and reputation reflecting his name; Shir-Del – the lion's heart. Catching Turan's eye, the General spoke.

'Good morning Captain. Anything to report?'

Turan shook his head. 'Nothing Sir. All quiet.'

'Good. Let's get some coffee and go over the preparations for the final exercise before the others arrive. Just want to be certain everything is covered.'

Turan picked up a series of maps and folders and placed them on a large table in the centre of the room. 'This is all the details for the exercise Sir. Participating trainees, staff, scenarios, equipment required and mapping of all exercise areas.'

Zana unrolled one of the maps and placed paperweights at each corner then studied the depicted terrain. Turan disappeared into the small kitchen before returning with the coffees, one of which he placed beside the General. Zana was quiet as he traced routes and traces on the map, visualising in his mind's eye the trainees running through this exercise. Although he knew the exercise inside and out, having designed it himself, he wanted to ensure that it was nothing less than the best it could be. On the last course, they had lost two trainees who had slipped off a mountain ledge during the infiltration exercise. While the deaths themselves didn't concern Zana, the waste of training investment in these potential operators grated somewhat. The exercise was designed to replicate real-life, operational conditions. A two-week evolution, it tested the trainees on everything from infiltrating a denied area to running agents and sabotage activities. Trusted role players selected from the Quds and Special Forces acted as contacts, agents and enemy forces. Live ammunition and explosives were used to add realism. Dog units and hunter forces provided pressure and a chase element. And all conducted in the hostile environment of the high-mountain passes of north-west Iran.

Zana asked some questions about the logistics and transport elements but, as usual, Captain Abed had everything covered. Zana liked Abed. He was one of those junior officers that took immense pride in carrying out his job and not in throwing the weight of his rank around. Zana had been selective in who he chose to work at the Facility. He'd made it clear from the start that Tehran could have no say in this if they expected it to work. They'd kicked back of course, but in the end, Zana had gotten his way: No sycophantic status-chasers who would report his every decision back to Tehran. Only proven officers with real operational experience and the respect of their men and colleagues. He was training men to be self-reliant, confident and effective and you couldn't achieve that by having a paper-shuffler from Tehran screaming and threatening trainees as they did in the conventional army. Neither did Zana want to work with such men who were always looking for something they could report back to Tehran as anti-regime in order to further their own position. No, he had the men he'd wanted and his work was going well.

One of the aspects that had had drawn Zana to the role of running Palang had been that of Mission Specific Training; bringing Quds operators to the camp to train for their individual missions abroad. Training and preparing the small teams in their exact roles before deployment. It was a bold venture but also an effective one as each team that deployed from Palang had been exposed to every eventuality they could expect to encounter, along with potential pitfalls, on their specific tasks. And it was working, with some very strong feedback already coming in from the field. As he sipped at his coffee, Zana reflected that, all in all, he was proud of his Facility and what that they had achieved. He turned to Captain Abed.

'Good. All under control. What's on the agenda today?'

'Usual physical training before breakfast then they've got a couple of lectures from Major Ardavan on his operations in Lebanon. After that they get the Final Exercise brief and draw equipment.'

Zana looked at his watch. 'What time does Major Ardavan come in?'

'Varies Sir. If he does the night exercises, he'll come in a bit later in the morning but I think he was just instructing yesterday so he should be in within the hour.'

'Perfect, I'll have a word with him when he arrives. Want him to take more of a lead on the infiltration phase of the exercise. He's another mountain man after all so we should make full use of that.'

Turan was about to reply when an agitated Sergeant burst through the door.

'Good morning General. Captain. There're some officers from VAJA at the gate demanding to be let in. I told them that only the General can give that permission.

They told me that they are going to have me and my guards shot for our insubordination.'

Zana raised a hand to calm the wild-eyed Sergeant. 'No-one will be shooting anybody unless I give the order Sergeant. Go back and escort these…*officers* to my office.'

The Sergeant nodded and ran back out. Zana sighed and looked at his Captain.

'Any idea what this is about?'

'None Sir. Like I say, everything's been quiet. Something in the background of one of the trainees perhaps?'

Zana shook his head. 'No, they wouldn't have sent a car full of shiny-arses all this way just to tell us that.' He sighed as he grabbed his coat and hat. 'But I suppose we'll soon find out.' He didn't bother putting them on as his own office was a short walk away and he took deep breaths of the mountain air as he walked. Entering his office, he put his coat and hat in the cupboard and nodded at the aroma of fresh coffee brewing in the pot. The heater had also been turned on and was taking the overnight chill from the room. If he'd known the stamp-lickers from Tehran were coming he wouldn't have bothered with either the coffee or the heater, happy to have the visitors endure as uncomfortable a stay as he could without making it too obvious of course. A staccato rap on his door told him they had arrived. 'Enter.'

Two men walked into the room and Zana dismissed the Sergeant behind them with a wave of his hand. The first man walked over and extended his hand.

'General Shir-Del, I am Colonel Hashemi, Ministry of Intelligence and Security, and my colleague is Captain Dabiri. I'm sorry to have intruded upon your facility without forewarning but we have an emergency that needs to be acted upon immediately.'

As Zana studied the man before him he could see that he was scared. There was none of the arrogance and patronising language that usually accompanied such a visit and Zana sensed that he wasn't going to like what came next. He indicated that the men should take a seat as he sat behind his desk and addressed them.

'So, what's the big emergency and what does it have to do with me?'

The Colonel cleared his throat and leaned forward, fingers drumming on the fabric of the hat he held between his hands. 'It's about one of your staff, General.'

'My staff? Which one?'

'Major Ardavan.'

Zana frowned. 'Yes, he's one of my staff here and a good one at that. What's the problem?'

The two security men exchanged a glance and nodded to each other before the Colonel met Zana's piercing stare.

'I'm afraid General, that your star officer is an American spy.'

3

US EMBASSY COMPLEX, GREEN ZONE, BAGHDAD, IRAQ

When the red light indicated the room was acoustically sealed, Bill Howard leaned forward in his chair and stared hard at his subordinate.

'Okay. In small words so that I'm absolutely clear on what I'm hearing. Go.'

Despite the severe nature of his boss's tone, Vic Foley grinned, the beaming white smile breaking through the matted tangle of his unruly black beard. Bill was one of the best Station Chiefs that Vic had worked for but demanded straight answers from his people and had a famous intolerance for bullshit and jargon. Vic cleared his throat and nodded.

'It's Asset Seven. He's running.'

He watched as Bill blew out a breath and sat back in his chair with his hands behind his head.

'Okay, he's running. We talking organised exfil or beating feet to the border?'

'Nope. His last comm was the exfil trigger code. After that he went dark. Been over eight hours now and still nothing. Last signal put him close to Dankash, presumably on his way out.'

'He give anything up about the target?'

'No. But if I was a betting man, I'd say they were on to him. How or why I don't know, but we'd always arranged that if he thought they knew, he would only pass information via physical means. Their tech capability is too good to risk comms.'

Bill Howard mulled over the information as he studied the man across from him. Vic had worked for Bill for over a year and produced some great results, earning him the Station Chief's respect. He was also a straight talker; you asked the man a question and he told you the truth. Or at least asked if you *really* wanted to hear it. While a lot of the Agency held them in lower esteem, Bill liked the SSOs; the Specialised Skills Officers from the Directorate of Operations, the Agency's clandestine element. Prevalent but unspoken opinion in the genteel corridors of Washington and the ivory towers of Langley was that they were useful to have in the shitholes and sandpits where things might get a bit rough. But Bill had worked with enough SSOs to know that as well as their paramilitary skills, some of these guys were as intelligent as any arrogant analyst in the Agency. And from what Bill had witnessed himself, Vic was certainly a very bright guy.

'So, what have we got and what do you want to do?'

Vic sighed and ran his hand through his thick, matted hair. He really needed to clean up and get a shave and haircut. Five months of operating in the wilds of eastern Iraq and he was starting to feel like he was going native. He looked his boss in the eye.

'Last comms I had with him, Seven was pulling together a mother lode of operational intel from a secret Quds Force program. External targets, sleeper cells, facilitators. He was on to something he recognised as being really big but hadn't pushed anything out before he triggered the exfil. I'm guessing that it was this info he'd been digging into when they rumbled him.'

'He liable to panic? Maybe shit himself and triggered the exfil 'cos he got scared?'

'No way. This guy is *good* boss. I mean, he impresses *me* with how he handles himself and I've seen some very capable guys in my time.'

'Okay. Part two of my question: What do you want to do?'

'Extraction. Pure and simple. He's got some very important shit for us and the only way we'll get it is by pulling him out.'

'This likely to be a goat-fuck?'

Vic laughed and shook his head. 'It has the *potential* to the be the mother of all goat-fucks, but the plan is a good one and he's trained and prepared.'

'Be that as it may, this is Quds and VAJA we're talking about here. They are not just going to let this guy stroll across the border without so much as a by-your-leave.'

Vic nodded in agreement. 'No, they won't. However, this is a very tough extraction for anyone chasing my guy. It's high mountain passes, sub-zero temperatures, altitude complications. It was designed to accommodate Seven's strengths and experience. Anyone else trying to catch him will need the same skill sets.'

'Time-frame?'

'We've set five rendezvous points over about a hundred and fifty clicks. With comms, he checks in at each one and we monitor until he gets to the border. Without comms, we'll send up the bird and look for the Infra-Red strobes he'll leave in place.'

'And you really think this guy will make it through those passes? Memory serves me correct, that's some pretty fucking tough country my friend.'

'We designed this together, me and Seven. There's a lot more to it than what I've described obviously, but he was confident. He knows it's a tough one, but he wanted that to give himself a fighting chance if they were on his tail.'

The room was quiet for several moments as each man considered the implications of the situation. As Station Chief of the Baghdad CIA Station, Bill had to consider political as well as tactical fallout. The Agency was still recovering from its reputational battering over the non-existence of WMDs nineteen years before. The Bin Laden success had won them some ground but there was still a way to go. For Vic, the value of the information that Seven was bringing out justified the risk. As well as that was his commitment to his Asset to do whatever he could to get his man out safely. Vic looked up as Bill moved in his chair and took out a small notebook.

'Okay Foley, give me your wish list.'

Vic nodded. 'I'll need a team. If you're happy to authorise I'll approach GREEN direct. I've done work with this squadron before and they know how we do business.'

Bill nodded. It made sense for Vic to talk to the Delta Force Operators, Task Force GREEN, directly rather than extending the communication chain. 'Done. Next?'

'Usual: Comms, transport, eye in the sky, tech, clean weapons. I'll need a cover story for local units so we can forward-mount from their bases. Will also need something to keep them the hell away from our Ops' Box until it's over.'

'I'll get Trent on to that. He's with the Ministers this afternoon so tell him what you need and that I'll fire the official approval to him in the meantime.'

'Thank you. And I'll need Executive Mission Command.'

Bill looked up, frowning at the request. 'Well, you'll have Mission Command, as always Vic.'

Vic shook his head. 'Nope. I'm going to need authority to act with complete autonomy. If this thing gets close to the wire, there'll be no time to get on the comms to ask for authority or permission to carry out certain activities. If Quds and VAJA are on his tail, I need to act with speed and decisiveness otherwise we could all end up in a stinking basement in Tehran.'

There was a moment's silence before Bill pointed his pen at Vic. 'Remember you said *potential* goat-fuck, Foley.'

Vic laughed. 'Yeah, and I meant it Bill. But I've been here before; once in Georgia and another time in Lebanon. On both occasions I couldn't move as fast as I needed to because Station wanted to push the decision Stateside. Some bad stuff happened because of that and I learned my lessons the hard way.'

'Hey, you know me by now. You're a big boy and as far as I'm concerned, *you're* the boss on your own ops, so Mission Command goes without saying. I can feed the head shed back home the line that it's a soldier's Op and therefore you have Exec Command. This close to the weekend, it probably won't even be questioned. Just be careful what you wish for Vic: An Asset with VAJA on his heels coming through the mountain passes into Iraq? All kinds of wrong just waiting to happen.'

'I know Bill. Believe me, I know. But what Seven's bringing out justifies the risk.'

'I'll have to take you on your word at that but from what I know about him, Seven seems like the real deal.'

There was a moment's silence as each man considered his own thoughts then Bill cleared his throat and closed his notebook.

'Okay Foley, you go tell Trent what you need and I'll get the Executive Request fired back to Langley. Good luck and, as always, keep me in the loop unless you fuck it up then I don't want to hear a damn word from you.'

Vic grinned as he stood, well aware that Bill's gruff indifference was nothing more than an attempt to lighten the seriousness of the situation. Bill was one of the few who still cared. Still gave a shit. That's why Vic liked him.

'No probs, Boss. Anything else?'

Bill looked up and shook his head. 'Nope. Just go. You're boring the hell out of me now.'

Vic nodded and let himself out of the room, making his way to the communications room. He swiped his card to enter and made his way towards one of the soundproofed booths. Once inside, he closed the door and took a seat, reaching for the receiver of a large telephone. He punched in a series of digits and after several seconds spoke into the handset.

'I need to speak with Master Sergeant Kelly.'

4

LAFARGE CEMENT FACTORY,
KOBANI, SYRIA

The returning vehicles threw up a giant plume of dust that was almost crimson in the dying rays of the setting sun. He could see there were at least three vehicles less than when they'd left yesterday morning. *Another tough fight.* Spooning the last of the canned peaches into his mouth, Master Sergeant 'Ned' Kelly wiped the spilled juices from his beard and turned from his vantage point on the roof of the building. Heading back inside, he pushed his sunglasses up on his head as he entered the darker interior. Walking along the metal gantry, he glanced below and saw that some of the returning Syrian Defence Force soldiers had already made their way inside. They looked tired and dirty, their quiet demeanour telling him that they'd had a rough couple of days. Ned grinned as he saw a shock of red hair moving among the darker heads of the Syrian and Iraqi Kurds, its owner clapping shoulders and ruffling hair, spreading morale among the downbeat soldiers. Tossing his empty can onto a rubbish pile, Ned took the stairs down to the ground floor and yelled across the vast concrete arena.

'Hey Red. What the hell you doin' back here? I was told you'd get your ass shot off out there!'

Across the room, the red-haired man turned and gave a wide grin.

'Sorry to disappoint you man. Came close a couple of times but you should know by now these shitheads can't kill me!'

As Ned reached him, they embraced and slapped each other's back with genuine affection. Keeping his arm around the shoulder of the other man, Ned indicated with his head towards the back of the building.

'Come on, Randy, let's get you some coffee.'

As they sipped their coffee, Ned tapped his mug against his fellow operator's.

'So. What went down?'

Randy sighed and leaned back before meeting his Team Leader's gaze.

'Was a lot more of the fuckers than we thought. Air was slow to respond to support request. Because of that they got us with a couple of suicide trucks, and big bastards at that. Took out our whole left flank. Eventually I got some Brit ordnance dropped and we closed for the finish.' He rubbed at his eyes and Ned could see how exhausted his fellow soldier was. 'Tell you what though Ned; those guys all fought to the last man. They really went for it.'

Ned nodded. 'They know the end's coming brother. The glorious caliphate is nothing but a dream anymore so if they can't live in it, they might as well die and receive their reward in *Jenna*.'

'Well, from what I've seen these last couple of days man, they're really looking forward to it.'

'Good. Hopefully we can make the process as fast and as painful as we can for these good folks!'

Randy laughed and raised his mug.

'Amen to that brother.'

There was a moment's quiet before Ned spoke.

31

'Anyway. We're going off the reservation for a little while. Team from B Squadron's gonna take our slot here to cover. We leave tomorrow morning around ten so get cleaned up, get some food in you and get some sleep. Don't worry about the report, I'll throw something together and fire it back. You just enjoy the stand-down.'

'Works for me, man. Where we going?'

'In-country but we may have to scoot over into Apache territory for a look-see. It's for the spooks but I know the lead guy and he's okay. Done some shit for him before and he's a straight shooter, one of their better guys.'

'Okay. What about briefing and prep?'

'Nah, you're good man, going to do all that at the other end. All you need to do is pack tonight or tomorrow but get some warm stuff in there; we're in the mountains for this one.'

Randy stood and stretched, groaning as the tension released in his back.

'Okay. I'm gonna get some chow and a hot shower and sleep like the dead. I'll see you in the morning.'

'Sleep well, Randy.'

As Randy headed back to the accommodation, Ned made his way to the secure area to check that the air assets were still on track for their trip east in the morning. The Boss had cleared the support to the Agency operation and Ned had briefed the rest of the Team so in truth, there wasn't really a whole lot more to do. As he made his way into the corridor, Ned wondered exactly what kind of task Vic Foley needed him and his guys for. In the past, Ned had worked on several Agency tasks and had experienced every level of professionalism he'd thought possible. From an aborted shit-fest of a rendition in China to a great infil Op in Yemen. He and his guys had fought their way out of ambushes, called air strikes in on pursuing paramilitaries, been extracted from hot LZs as bullets pinged off the fuselage of their chopper. They'd had some close calls over the years working with the Agency so Ned was glad that Vic Foley was running point on this.

Ned knew that Vic had cut his teeth on some really tough operations in Afghanistan; straight out from Langley after 9/11 and embedded with the Northern Alliance in the very first engagements with the Taliban. He'd worked with Vic in later operations in that country and liked the man. He was upfront about everything and never held back, making sure that Ned and his Team were as informed as it was possible to be. Vic was no stranger to combat either; Ned had fought alongside the Agency man on two occasions where they'd been caught short on the exfil and Vic was no passenger; he held his own and then some. There were a couple of former Delta Operators who had joined the CIA over the years and Ned would usually reach out to them for a discreet heads-up on whatever Agency guy was running point with the Op that Ned and his Team would be helping out on. The word he got back from the former SOF guys was that Vic was a safe pair of hands, well respected by the soldiers and spooks alike. Unlike some Ned had encountered.

His mind wandered back to the colossal fuck-up in China, where he and his team had only just made it out of the country by the narrowest of margins. All because the spook running the show hadn't thought they needed to know that his Asset hadn't been in contact as often as he should. That a sensitive collection platform had identified movements of a unit of the PLA's Falcon Special Forces that was highly unusual. It was only when their communications were attacked that Ned and his Team began to suspect that their exfil was compromised. And being captured in Mainland China by a Special

Forces unit of the Peoples' Liberation Army was not an option for consideration.

Shaking his head at the memory, Ned knocked on the door and waited a brief moment until it was opened by a tall, rangy individual who nodded and pulled the door wider to allow Ned to access the room. Ned muttered his thanks and made his way towards the Air desk, weaving between the makeshift benches and desks that held the computers and radio systems the Task Force used for communications. He stopped when he reached a large whiteboard and studied its contents, nodding with satisfaction when he identified his Team's scheduled ride for the morning had been confirmed. He turned around and made his way back out of the room and headed for his own bunk. He wanted to pack and be ready to go so that he could get a good night's sleep and be refreshed in the morning.

***

Ned closed the book and rubbed his eyes, feeling tiredness begin to seep in. He placed the paperback down on the floor beside his cot-bed and yawned. Turning off his light, he rolled onto his side and closed his eyes as his mind was drawn once again to the task ahead of them. Vic had told him very little over the comms other than where he and his team needed to be and what they should bring. *Good enough.* Ned's guys were all seasoned operators and had been on this rotation for nearly four months now. In truth, Ned was looking forward to something a little bit different from the daily grind against the last gasp of Islamic State's fight for survival. As sleep eluded him, he thought about how these past two years coming in and out of this country to battle the biggest threat to western civilisation had been some of the strangest times he'd experienced as a Special Forces Operator.

He remembered the surreal moment of watching the downlink from the drone showing hundreds of fighters, artillery and tanks converging on his squadron at the Conoco plant and the Combat Support Intel guy shouting *They're speaking fucking Russian.* The panic and confusion as flustered calls were made to command at JSOC, requests for air support held up until it could be determined if the approaching Russians were friend or foe. But when they'd fired their first bombardment at the plant, the line was crossed. It was one of the toughest fights Ned and his guys had been in, the line between their defensive ordnance and the enemy's non-existent. Thousands of bombs, missiles, rockets and bullets shredded the plant and its meagre defences and Ned and his Team fought for their lives, running from cover to cover, returning fire as well as coordinating the air support and reinforcements from the Green Berets at the Mission Support Site. For over four hours they'd repelled assault after assault until eventually the enemy had withdrawn, having suffered a staggering number of casualties. When the dust cleared and reinforcements arrived, every one of Ned's guys had been wounded in some way, although they were all relatively minor ones. Frag, kinetic shock, burns, blast injuries, temporary deafness. They'd been lucky. Later the report back from JSOC indicated that they had killed over three hundred of their attackers, a large proportion of which had been Russian mercenaries from a Private Military Company called Wagner Group. JSOC's assessment was that Moscow had been aware that American Special Forces had been present at the Conoco plant, had even been *told* this by the Pentagon as the build-up to the assault began. But Moscow claimed that there were no Russians present in the battle space. That the US was mistaken. And that was all JSOC needed to hear to rain down hell on the attackers. Ned had personally listened to the translated telephone intercepts between the surviving Russians and their families back home where they recounted, in high emotion, the slaughter of their comrades by the Americans. Ned had asked why the hell Russia had let this happen. Allowed the mass slaughter of their citizens. The Colonel from the Defence Intelligence Agency had replied that the Pentagon believed Russia had used the situation to test American reactions and appetite for an engagement when they were vastly outnumbered. He explained that Wagner was little more than a front for a deployable force of the Russian military that was used for deniable operations in Syria, Ukraine, Georgia and some African nations. It still shocked Ned that a country would allow such a massacre of its own soldiers merely to test the resolve of their foe. *Cold. Very fucking cold.*

Then there was the Iranians. On one hand still the world's biggest exporter and supporter of terrorism against the west but now working against the same enemy as the US in the same battle space. Ned had never thought he would see the day where US forces and Iranian Revolutionary Guard Corps would be sitting in Joint Operation briefs, deconflicting air moves and troop deployments. Each side wary and mistrustful of the other, giving only the minimal information that was needed to avoid misunderstandings. And tomorrow Ned and his guys would be starting a new operation where the Iranians were, once again, the enemy that they had always been. As his breathing slowed and his mind closed down, Ned's last thought before sleep overtook him was that the world was at its craziest since any time that he could remember.

5

DANKASH REGION, NORTH-WEST IRAN

Karim swept the area once again, his hand steady as the scope on the assault rifle magnified the land to his front. The air was cool and still, no sounds save for the distant screech of a raptor riding on the early morning thermals above him. Changing position, he turned around and conducted the same routine facing the direction he had come. He scanned the area for several minutes but saw nothing to indicate they were close. Leaning back against the rock, he laid the rifle beside him and opened up the side-pocket of the backpack, retrieving the gas canister and cooking equipment. Working with a speed born of practice, Karim soon had the water boiling and the noodles cooking in the small pot. His stomach groaned in anticipation and he chewed on some dried meat to assuage his hunger until the food was cooked. After a couple of minutes, he removed the noodles from the gas and set them to one side to cool a little.

Pulling a map from the pocket of his cargo-pants, he traced his finger along the route he had taken to reach this location. He'd been unchallenged through the dark hours of the early morning, as he'd hoped, and had made good progress. Ahead of him, however, lay the real challenge; the high passes of the Zagros Mountains. Sub-zero temperatures, snow, ice, winds, and of course, the challenge of working at altitude. But that's exactly why Karim had selected this route as his exfiltration. Very few people, even among the Quds Force, were capable of comfortably navigating and surviving in such terrain. Or so he'd thought. When he'd been selected to work at Camp Palang, Karim had been surprised to find the training environment so high in the mountains and even more surprised that the same mountains were used to test the students. But it had also presented him with an incredible opportunity with which to spend time in the mountains conducting a reconnaissance of his exfil route under the guise of designing the training exercises for the Palang students. After a confirmatory look at the location of his first Rendezvous point, Karim stored the map and turned his attention to the hot food.

Spooning the noodles into his mouth, a memory came to Karim of enjoying a meal with General Shir-Del and his staff at Palang not long after Karim had arrived. He'd been praising the facility and what it would achieve when one of the captains had mentioned the security infrastructure in place. Karim had listened, rapt, as the officer waxed lyrical about the sensitive measures they used to ensure the camp and its activities were never compromised. This included a classified monitoring platform that identified all electronic transmissions in the area and a complex algorithm that would classify them as either benign, suspicious or outright malevolent in intent. Karim had not known that this capability existed and had the young captain not mentioned it, would have been caught sending his transmissions to Vic without even knowing how he'd been snared. His mouth had gone dry and his heart raced as he'd been intending firing off a quick missive that night to Vic to give him the camp's location and function. He'd managed, during a logistics run to Tehran, to get a brief message to Vic, letting him know he had important information that he couldn't transmit. He'd given Vic his exfil codeword and told him to standby as the next time he heard from Karim it would be to get him out. And here he was. Getting out.

He looked back along the rocky valley he'd just ridden through, almost expecting to see a convoy of vehicles racing towards him but there was nothing to see other than a dust-devil spiralling its way across the valley floor. Karim didn't think they would look for him in the mountains, at least not to begin with. No, they'd start with the usual: Roadblocks, checkpoints, searches of towns and villages. Aircraft conducting aerial sweeps. This thought drew his attention to the bike but he knew it was safe from view under the camouflage netting. They would already know that Karim had no family, girlfriend or friends beyond his acquaintances in the Quds Force and consequently, no one to torture or interrogate to get information from. Karim could not have done this if he had. His parents had died in a factory fire when he was young and he had no siblings, his mother suffering a complication during his birth that meant she couldn't have any more children. There would still be torture and interrogations. But Karim had no problem with these.

The surveillance teams would be thoroughly beaten and their team leaders executed. Those on the night shift would be tortured and interrogated to identify if they had been complicit in Karim's escape. His neighbours would be questioned thoroughly and given a rough time but nothing too violent. The widow Aria would get a pretty hard time once they discovered Karim's escape route through her bedroom but he'd known for some time she was feeding low-level information on her neighbours back to the bottom-feeders at VAJA so he didn't feel too bad about this.

As he cleaned his utensils and re-packed them, Karim thought about the information he needed to get to Vic and patted the lump of the inside pocket of his jacket. The three small flash drives were padded, waterproofed and encased in RFID shielding to protect them against all invasive possibilities. This is what he was risking his life for. Risking his own life to save those of others. Others he had never and more than likely, would never, meet. But he couldn't let something like this happen. No human being with any sense of morality or responsibility could. But then, the Quds Force and the IRGC were not known for either of these positive traits, existing as they did to sow death and destruction to the western nations through their training and mentoring of proxy forces.

As he packed his gear away, Karim recalled with fondness some of those very operations he had been involved in when he had been a committed servant of his regime. Training members of Hamas in complex bomb-making that would elude the Israeli detection systems. Emplacing limpet mines on American and British oil tankers in the Straits of Hormuz. Kidnapping British sailors and Royal Marines from their own vessel and scoring a tremendous propaganda coup for Tehran for which he had been publicly honoured. But that had been when he was the sharp end of the spear for the regime. When he'd been ruthlessly committed to his country's physically hostile foreign policy. And, of course, that had all been before Vic.

**

Karim had been living and working in Beirut for several months, recruiting and training talented Hezbollah fighters for better things. He'd exercised his usual tradecraft, leaving a sensitive footprint that didn't expose his true identity or nature of his activities. Or so he'd thought. He'd been enjoying a quiet lunch one day in a café off Rue Hamra when a man dropped into the seat beside him, removed his sunglasses and gave him a big grin. Karim immediately knew the man was American; his looks, clothing and confidence giving him away. Karim had returned the grin, put his fork down and raised his eyebrows to indicate his puzzlement. Vic had gone straight for the jugular. He'd leaned forward and with a slight inclination of his head, indicated the locations of two vehicles of athletic-looking Lebanese men staring in their direction. He'd addressed Karim by his real name and informed the Quds Force operator that he knew exactly what he was doing. Karim had started to rise up from his seat when Vic placed a gentle hand on his arm and asked him to take a minute. Karim had smiled and said something about Vic being confused and that he did not recognise the name Vic was saying but sat back down regardless, his pride eager to accept the challenge of dealing with the American. Vic thanked him and spoke for a couple of minutes during which Karim realised that he was either going to work with the American or die fighting in a back street of Beirut. The Lebanese in the cars were Vic's Plan B: Plan A was that Karim recognised an opportunity when he saw it and was smart enough to grasp the time-limited offer. If he wasn't smart enough then Vic had clearly misjudged his man. For the first time in his life, Karim heard the word *rendition* applied to his own circumstances and could feel a box closing around him as any options he'd considered for escape were suddenly closed. And then Vic had slid over a small file.

A couple of pages of a photocopied intelligence report from many years before. Karim had given the American an indulgent grin and read the Farsi-language documents. It had only taken a minute but after that minute, his whole life was changed. He'd suspected, of course, that it could be a ruse; a doctored file used to bait him and snare him, but Karim recognised immediately the wording and phraseology of his own country's intelligence agency. It was genuine. He'd looked up at the American across the table from him and met the calm brown eyes and slid the file back to Vic before addressing him in English.

'Rendition will not be necessary.'

His professional relationship with the CIA officer had developed fast and he found himself both liking and respecting the American. After providing information that stopped a Hezbollah assassination attempt, he and Vic shared a celebratory meal where, in a moment of levity, Karim had asked what his CIA codename was. Vic had grinned almost sheepishly and admitted that it was probably the most banal codename ever. He explained that their initial meeting had taken place on the seventh of July and that as he'd had to push out a report almost immediately after the meeting, he'd designated his lucky number, seven, which was also the day and month, as the first thing to come to mind and hopefully as a good omen for the future. And just like that, Asset Seven was created. Karim had feigned indignation at not having a more exotic codename and both men had enjoyed the humorous exchange.

Karim shook his head at the memory and concentrated on the task at hand. He strapped the backpack onto the motorcycle then pulled the camouflage netting away, rolled it up and stuffed it into the top of a pannier. Placing the assault rifle into its sheath on the side of the bike, he gave a final look back along the valley, donned his goggles and pulled away in a small cloud of dust towards the high mountain passes in the distance.

6

DANKASH, NORTH WEST IRAN

Colonel Hashemi chewed on a fingernail as he stared around the ransacked apartment, blinking rapidly as he attempted to identify a way in which he could be blameless in this situation. The traitor Ardavan's escape route had just been identified and a team was next door interrogating the old widow about her role in the affair. She was proclaiming her innocence, of course, but how could she not have known? No; they were in it together. The surveillance team had been arrested and were also undergoing questioning but he'd already given the order to execute the entire night shift for gross negligence of their duties. While he was satisfied that the punishment befitted their crime, Hashemi hoped that the punitive measure would buy him some goodwill from his superiors in Tehran. He closed his eyes as he imagined what their response was going to be when he attended the formal hearing. Probably the same as General Shir-Del's had been when he'd learned that they had Ardavan under surveillance for over twenty-four hours: *And you still let him escape?*

The General had, at first, refused to believe it was possible that one of his precious Palang instructors could be an American spy but when confronted with the evidence knew that there could be no doubt. Ardavan's search history on the internal database and unexplained electronic transmissions that coincided with him being in the remote areas these were sent from, more than enough to convince the General of his guilt. And even if there had been doubts, the fact that Ardavan was running and a short-burst transmission from a satellite telephone had been identified at the same time, these facts spoke for themselves of the man's guilt. The General had accompanied the VAJA men to Ardavan's apartment and whistled when he was shown the clever escape route. He had been less impressed when informed of the death of a senior VAJA surveillance officer, his body found just after sunrise under some bushes in the rear quadrangle of the apartment block. Hashemi had noticed anger and determination in the older man's glare and knew that the General was now taking this personally. His attitude had changed immediately and he began barking requests for maps and last known locations of the Sat-phone signal and potential escape routes that Ardavan might take. This prompted a renewed flurry of activity as the General and Hashemi's men began the deployment of roadblocks and checkpoints on every road and track that the traitor might use.

Hashemi did not know the area as well as the General and was grateful for the assistance. But he had to be careful that the operation remained in his hands, give Tehran every possible reason to allow him to remain in charge of hunting down the traitor. And every possible chance of staying alive. Some raised voices broke him from his panicked thoughts and he looked up as the General slapped the kitchen table where several maps were unrolled.

'You have already told me where the signal put him. My question, *once again,* is why was he heading in that direction? He *knows* we will put roadblocks out. He *knows* we will reinforce the checkpoints. He *knows* we'll eventually put up drones to widen the search. So, my point again; why would a man who knows all this run straight into it?'

There was silence as the General concluded his rant. Hashemi stepped closer to the table.

'Perhaps, General, he panicked. Somehow identified our surveillance and ran before his extraction could be planned.'

The General glared at him, the ice-blue eyes causing Hashemi to recoil slightly at the intense anger behind them. He stabbed his finger in the direction of the bedroom behind them.

'He evaded a team of surveillance officers who were watching his every move. *That* is not a panicking individual. That is a professional deploying on a planned exfiltration. He knows what he's doing and none of his actions are accidental, there's a reason for everything he is doing. So, once again; why is he running into our trap?'

There was a moment's silence as the men in the room contemplated the question. The General gave a deep sigh and leaned over the table, pointing at the map.

'The last visual sighting of Ardavan is here in his apartment last night. The next *possible* location we have him is here, by the river where the satellite telephone signal was intercepted. That's *if* it was him. I believe it was but we can't be completely certain. But let's say it was Ardavan. How did he get there? What car is he driving? Why don't we know this? Someone *must* have seen or at least heard a car starting up in the early hours of the morning.'

Hashemi shook his head. 'No. We've asked and asked again. Nobody saw or heard any vehicles in the timeframe when Ardavan could have left.'

The General straightened and looked Hashemi in the eye. 'Okay, so how did he get to the river where he made the call? Did he rendezvous with someone outside the village and get picked up?'

'We're investigating that possibility now General, but…' Hashemi paused as the ringing of his phone interrupted him. He answered, muttered several monosyllabic responses then terminated the call, meeting the General's gaze once again. 'That's the second search team. They've found something interesting in the derelict chemical factory just outside of town.'

***

Zana put his sunglasses on as he stepped out of the shade of the old factory. He was silent as he looked at the area around him. It was clear that Ardavan had stored his exfiltration kit here for a reason. The technicians identified several traces of tyre tracks throughout the building and assessed that they had come from a motorcycle. This puzzled Zana even further. Why would Ardavan want to escape on a motorcycle? It would stand out so much more than a car and as he could have easily sourced a car for himself, there was a specific reason that Ardavan had chosen a motorcycle. The General sighed and lowered his head as the thought of Ardavan's betrayal struck him again. He'd liked Ardavan. Saw something of himself as a younger man in the Major. They'd bonded over their shared love of the mountains, their respect for the high places where fitness and courage were attributes that kept you alive. Zana still struggled to believe that he'd got it so wrong, that he hadn't suspected let alone seen through Ardavan's ruse. He turned his head at the sound of footsteps behind him and saw Colonel Hashemi approaching. The VAJA officer was quiet for a moment before speaking.

'What's your thoughts General?'

Zana shook his head. 'It's the motorcycle, Hashemi. I just can't figure out why he chose the motorcycle.'

'Speed? Trying to get some distance before the roadblocks and checkpoints kick in?'

'No. If that was the case, we would have heard back from whatever checkpoints he'd gone through. Which begs the next question; where has he gone that he hasn't passed through a single checkpoint?'

'Maybe he has. Maybe that's what the motorcycle was for: He gets off it and wheels it *around* the checkpoint.'

Zana shook his head. 'No. If he just wanted distance, he would have stolen a car and used his official ID to get through the checkpoints. No, the motorcycle is important. If we figure out the *why*, I think it will lead us to the *where*. Where Ardavan is headed.'

'Yes, I can see the logic in that, but, like you General, I just have no idea why.'

Zana was quiet as he focused his mind on the problem. Ardavan would be trying to leave the country the quickest way he could. That would be by air but could only be achieved if he had access to a private aircraft or was traveling under a false identity. They had grounded all the flights due to leave the country earlier that day and Ardavan was definitely not among the passengers and no-one had been missing from the manifests. There were also no reports from the Air Force relating to any suspicious flights or unidentified aircraft. Zana sighed as he wrestled with the motorcycle question. He thought back again to Ardavan and when the Major had first arrived at Camp Palang. An obvious strong work ethic, significant operational experience and a willingness to provide the benefit of that experience to the newer trainees. Ardavan had thrived on the role of reconnaissance, spending days in the high passes, selecting appropriate areas for the students' final exercise…

Zana snapped his head back and turned to look at the mountain ranges in the distance. *No. That's impossible.* Or was it? He turned to Colonel Hashemi. 'I think I may just have worked out where Major Ardavan is going.'

Hashemi raised his eyebrows in surprise. 'Really? Where?'

Zana pointed to the dark peaks in the distance. 'There.'

***

In the Planning Room at Camp Palang, General Shir-Del compared a list of coordinates with locations on the map. Colonel Hashemi and the other VAJA officers watched in silence as the frown on the General's face became more pronounced. Eventually, the General looked up and beckoned the men closer.

'Look; I've put an overlay on the map with Ardavan's route he was supposed to have taken when conducting the exercise reconnaissance. Now, our operational safeguards required Ardavan to call in every three hours on a satellite phone just to let us know he was alive and uninjured. I asked for the geolocations of the calls Ardavan made during those excursions and, as you can see here, he was calling from an entirely different area.'

There was quiet in the room as the officers digested the information. Hashemi pointed to the geolocation overlay.

'What do you think he was doing there? Meeting his contact? Passing intelligence?'

The General shook his head. 'No. I think he was checking an extraction route. Look at the air photography of the region. Can you see that faint line there?' He waited until the men had leaned in and studied the spot. 'That looks like a track or a path. It disappears from time to time but if you're patient, you can find it again as it winds its way through the mountains.'

Hashemi traced the meandering faint line with his finger. 'I believe you're right General. This looks like a herders' track or an old trading route.'

Zana straightened and looked at the Colonel from VAJA. In truth, he wasn't as bad as Zana had expected; the VAJA officer seemed happy to listen to other people's input and defer to subject matter experts. As he watched, the VAJA man pulled out his telephone and began dialling. Zana threw him a questioning look.

Hashemi raised the phone to his face and met the General's eyes. 'I'm calling Tehran and asking for men to be sent to begin the search for Ardavan.' He raised his eyebrows in surprise as the General reached out and took the phone from his unresisting hands and terminated the call.

'We don't need paper-pushers from Tehran. We've got all the men we need here. In fact, we've got the best trained men for the job right here.' Seeing the VAJA officers' look of puzzlement, Zana pointed to the door. 'Beyond that door are twenty-five of the best trained members of the Quds force who have been training and trekking in these mountains for months now. No-one knows the terrain better than them and no one knows how to hunt down a traitor better than them. Their Final Exercise was due to take place in the very mountains that Ardavan has chosen to use as his escape route. This pursuit of Ardavan will be the students' Final Exercise. The most realistic exercise they will ever take part in: The hunt for an American spy.'

7

CAMP ANGELO, NORTHERN IRAQ

Vic closed the lid on the last box of weapons and laid his clipboard down on the bench beside the stack of boxes and valises that contained the sanitised weapons and ammunition for the GREEN team. They couldn't risk losing any US issued weapons or equipment if they had to cross into Iran so the Delta guys would swap out all their standard weapons and kit for the commercially sourced replacements. It was common enough practice on these missions and both Agency and GREEN were comfortable with the procedure. The GREEN guys would just require a few hours to zero the new weapons and configure the systems to their personal preferences. Again, common practice.

Vic walked over to the window and saw the Camp Commander, Major Faisal, talking to another Iraqi commando. Vic had worked with Faisal before and he was a decent enough guy with a lot of operational experience behind him. But Vic only needed the use of Faisal's camp as a staging area for his Op, so on this occasion Faisal and his men's support amounted to little more than security and administrative duties. Vic had sweetened the deal with a thick envelope of cash for the young Special Forces' Major and had been given the Major's word that everything would be done to support the American mission. A loose cover story involving searching for ISIS fighters hiding out in the mountains had been disseminated to the Iraqi Ministry of Defence and the camps and FOBs in the region to explain the presence and activities of the Americans over the coming days and nights.

Air support assets had been briefed and would arrive within the hour, the pilots and crews from the 160th Special Operations Aviation Regiment, the Night Stalkers, all veterans of sensitive and special operations. Vic turned his attention to his secure phone and nodded as he saw the approvals for his requests had been sanctioned. Bill had been as good as his word; now it was up to Vic to stay true to his own promise that it wouldn't end up as a goat-fuck. But he'd been here before; this wasn't his first extraction getting an asset out of a hostile country. And the Delta guys from GREEN had some experience in this also, so although not taking anything for granted, Vic was quietly confident that as long as Seven stuck to the plan they had a good chance of success. The sound of rotors drew his attention and he stowed his phone and made his way out of the prep room to go and meet the Delta Operators.

***

Vic closed his small notebook and looked up at the men seated around the screen where the aerial mapping and photography was being displayed through a projector. 'So, that about wraps up where we are. Any questions?'

The room was quiet for a moment before Ned spoke up. 'Not from me. Pretty standard so far; get out to the field staging area and wait for the Asset to trip the RV markers then fly him the fuck out of there. That seem about the size of it?'

Vic nodded. 'In a nutshell, yes. Once he trips RV 2, we will forward mount to our staging area and monitor his progress. If he's clear, we let him run and scoop him up at the Final RV. If he's coming out hot, we'll assess on the ground and determine what type of support we give. Basic ground rules on this are if we can avoid going into Iran we will, but we have permissions to cover the action if required. Ned, I've forwarded you a copy of those for your command.'

Ned nodded, quietly pleased that Vic had thought to supply him with the permissions; the legal signoffs, for the operation. A lot of Agency guys wouldn't bother, tell the Delta Team Leaders that they were good, everything had been cleared. The more experienced guys like Ned would usually demand a soft copy of the permissions before doing anything but some of the newer guys could be seduced by the prestige of working for the Agency. And that's how people got into trouble. It wasn't unknown for shit to go really wrong on the ground and at the subsequent wash-up, have the Agency guy deny asking the Delta teams to carry out the actions they had. But at least on this one, they were working with a good guy who did things right. Ned pointed to an area on the map. 'What's the comms like here? Anybody know?'

Vic shook his head. 'We have to be super-careful with comms signatures in the area. One of the things Seven did get to me was that there is a sensitive platform operating in the region dedicated to identifying and locating any and all comms activity. So, we should be okay with our system because as far as we know they still can't detect that but we won't be carrying any other means to avoid the risk of exposure. You good with that?'

Ned looked over his shoulder and was given a thumbs-up from Dwight, his comms guy. He'd figured as much anyway, no real requirement on this Op for different comms platforms. He turned his attention back to Vic. 'That it?'

Vic nodded. 'That's it. Wheels-up at zero two-hundred so if you want to brief the rest, we'll finish up and get on the birds.'

Ned stood and turned to face his Team and the pilots and crew from the Night Stalkers. He gave a comprehensive brief on the load plan for the insertion and the actions that they would take on reaching their objective. He covered several eventualities unique to the Op but was happy that the remainder were SOPs; Standard Operational Procedures familiar to every man in the room. When he finished, he asked if there were any questions and was greeted with none. Looking at his watch he saw that they had half an hour until departure. 'Okay guys let's synchronise watches. On my mark, in thirty seconds it will be zero one-thirty… and five, four three, two, one, mark.' The team adjusted their watches and stood, stretching and yawning as Ned smiled. 'You're getting old guys; anyone would think you've been at war or something! Okay, let's get our shit together, get packed and loaded up and on the pan for oh-one fifty for final check.'

As the Team made their way to collect their gear, the Night Stalkers element headed out to prepare the helicopters. Vic donned his tactical vest, the pouches bulging with ammunition, grenades, strobes and a radio. He then shouldered a large backpack before picking up his helmet, assault rifle and pistol, stowing the latter in a thigh-holster. Ned caught his eye and grinned.

'Hell, Agency man. You look like you might actually know what you're doing!'

Vic returned the grin. 'Don't be fooled Master Sergeant; I was always winning prizes for costume parties in our neighborhood!'

Ned laughed and patted Vic on the shoulder. 'Good to be working with you again Vic.'

Vic nodded. 'You too Ned. Let's get this show on the road, shall we?'

Both men walked out of the room, Vic taking the stairs and Ned towards the preparation room. When the Delta Master Sergeant reached his belongings, he threw on his thick jacket before donning his tactical vest and backpack. Like the rest of his team, he was dressed in comfortable outdoor gear, no uniform or military insignia on their persons. He checked his weapons, ran a hand over his pouches to make sure they were closed then, carrying his helmet in his hand, made his way out of the room and down the stairs. He heard the whine as the Night Stalkers started the engines and immediately smelled the familiar tang of aviation fuel on the cool night air. He walked over to his Team and stood close to them, making his way along the group and looking each man in the eye, waiting for their nod to show they were ready. When he reached Vic, the CIA officer followed the same procedure to show he was also good and Vic made his way over to the crew member standing by the door of the first Black Hawk and gave the man the signal that the Team was ready. The rotors on the helicopters began to turn and Ned walked back to his guys and joined them as they split into their predesignated sections for the journey. After a couple of minutes, the crew member stepped back outside the aircraft and waved his chem-light stick, giving the signal to embark. The soldiers walked forward and boarded the helicopters with Ned acting as last man, making sure everyone was loaded before he entered the helicopter. Climbing in, he pushed his backpack into the centre of the space where the other team members had placed theirs. The crew member secured the packs with a cargo net and strapped them down as Ned took his seat and pulled on the headphones, checking comms with the pilot. The crew member slid the door shut, dulling the sound of the rotor blades somewhat. In the dim, green glow from the internal lighting, Vic saw his guys leaning back into their seats, eyes closed and taking the opportunity to rest for a while. They were tired; all of them having pushed out a major amount of activity in the past three weeks with very little respite. But they wouldn't have it any other way. Soldiers who operated at this level were dangerous animals when bored, prone to making mischief in all kinds of ways guaranteed to piss people off. No, a Delta Operator was far happier when he was exhausted and grumpy than when having nothing to occupy himself with. And this little jaunt promised to be pretty mellow by the sound of it. Even if the Asset came running out hot, they would call in a little air support to cover him and scoop him up when he crossed the border. No real heavy lifting unless it went very wrong. The guys could catch some sleep as they holed up through the day waiting for the Asset to make his way through the RVs. His thoughts were interrupted by the pilot's transmission that they were lifting off. Ned leaned back and closed his eyes as the helicopter rose above the walls of the camp then surged forward into the darkness of the Iraqi night.

8

ZAGROS MOUNTAINS, NORTH WEST IRAN

Karim took deeper breaths as the climb began to take its toll on his legs, the weight of his tactical vest and pack adding to the exertion. He looked up at the ascent ahead, the vague impression of a track snaking its way between boulders and outcrops of rock. In the summer months it would be used by the goatherders from the villages below but it was still too early in the year to take the beasts to the higher pastures. He swapped arms as he cradled the rifle, shaking out the free arm to get the blood flowing back into it. He already missed the motorbike and gave a wistful glance behind him to the floor of the valley where the vehicle was concealed under camouflage netting among the rocks. But this had always been the plan; ride the bike as far as he could to put some distance between him and the hunters then get himself deep enough into the mountains that hot pursuit would be almost impossible.

He stopped, shrugged his pack off and sat leaning against a rock as he took a drink from his canteen, the cool water delicious in his thirst. Looking at the valley below him, he wondered how the search for him was progressing. There was still no sign of any pursuit and he could see the dirt road that led into the valley for a good fifty kilometers. No dust plumes on the horizon to indicate they were on to him. No aircraft in the sky to suggest aerial surveillance. He pulled out his map and plotted his current position with his fingertip and calculated the distance and time to RV 1. If he travelled in a straight line, it was little more than twenty kilometers to the designated point. But these were the Zagros Mountains. And there were no straight lines. Karim knew from experience that he might just make it before nightfall if he took it at a steady pace as he couldn't risk injury; a broken ankle or leg would end any chance of succeeding in his escape. He'd also been thinking hard about his signals at the RVs. His original plan had been to deploy the Infra-Red strobes at each designated spot, leaving no communication signature that Palang could pick up on. But the further he'd progressed on his escape, the more he'd considered the nature of the information he was carrying. The responsibility for getting that information to Vic was Karim's, and his alone to bear. If, for some unforeseen reason, he became injured or died in the mountains, Vic would never know what information Karim was bringing out with him. So, he'd changed his mind. For the first RV at least. He would use one of the sat phones to check in at the RV and pray that the burst would be quick enough and deep enough in the mountains for the signal to be missed. It was a huge risk, but one that he felt had to be taken.

As he replaced his canteen in his vest, Karim felt a small moment of serenity imbue him. He recognised it as the familiar feeling he experienced when alone in the high mountains. The silence, the cool air, the clarity of high-altitude sunshine, the reward of effort. He grinned as he remembered that at any moment a helicopter-load of Quds or NOHED could appear, and would find him relaxing against a rock, enjoying the sunshine on his face like a cadet on a hike. Sighing, he rose and picked up his pack and rifle, adjusting the straps of the pack for comfort, then set off walking along the small, rocky track.

He continued to climb, feeling the burn in his legs as the inclines became steeper, the air thinner. Even though he had removed his jacket, Karim was hot, and the sweat was soaking through his shirt. But he was well aware of his capabilities, knew from experience how hard he could push himself without attracting exhaustion through dehydration. He monitored how much he was sweating, again, well aware that if he wanted to maintain his punishing pace, he would need to replenish those lost fluids. At this time of the year there was enough snow and meltwater around to keep his water bottles filled so he wasn't concerned about running out.

The sun burned high in the cobalt sky above Karim as he climbed, and he could feel the heat on his face. He was glad he'd remembered his UV goggles, protecting his eyes from the damaging rays. As he looked ahead, he could see where the steep slopes he was climbing met the formidable first wall of rock faces that he would encounter. Glancing at his watch, he saw he was making good progress and still anticipated making RV 1 before nightfall. A noise to his front startled him and in one smooth motion, he dropped to one knee bringing the carbine up on aim at the potential threat.

A scruffy boy in his early teens stood in the middle of the small goat track staring back at Karim with wide eyes. He was filthy and his face dark, burned and dry from exposure to the sun. A thick, coarse shirt and woolen waistcoat over torn trousers marked him out as a herder or shepherd. Karim cursed to himself and wondered what the kid was doing up here. Keeping the gun trained on the waif, Karim barked at him.

'Are you alone?'

There was no answer, but he could see the boy was terrified, trembling legs and shaking bottom lip. Karim lowered the rifle a little and softened his tone.

'Boy. Are you alone?'

This time the boy nodded his head slowly. Karim cast a quick glance at the area where he assumed the boy had come from but saw nothing to conflict with the child's assertion. He cursed again as he pondered his predicament. Karim knew the safest course of action would be to shoot the boy and hide the body among the rocks. By the time whatever village the boy came from realized he was missing, Karim would be in another country. The suppressor on the carbine also meant that the sound of the shot wouldn't carry. But looking at the sorry state of the grubby child, he knew in his heart that he didn't possess the callousness required to carry out such an act. Sighing, he stood and lowered the rifle to his side.

'Where are you from boy?'

The boy replied but stuttered over the words. Karim held up his hand.

'I'm not going to hurt you. I give you my word. Where are you from and what are you doing here?'

This time the reply was slightly more confident.

'I am from Gurbuz. We lost some of the flock. I came to look for them.'

Karim nodded. 'What's your name?'

'Affan, sir.'

Karim studied the boy for several moments before coming to a decision.

'Are you hungry Affan?'

***

Karim watched the boy devour the nuts and raisins he'd been given. The waif was ravenous. Had probably trekked a lot further into the hills to try and be the hero of his village. A typical boy. Periodically, when he thought Karim wasn't watching, the boy would cast his eye over the strange man and his weapons and equipment. Karim smiled as he imagined what he must look like to a kid living in a region where very little had changed over the centuries. He knew from his work at Palang that in these remote communities it was unusual to find cell phones or even televisions and radios. He may have seen a soldier at some point, but Karim wasn't in uniform, so the boy was probably trying to figure out *what* Karim was rather than who he was. Keeping his movements slow and deliberate, Karim passed his water bottle to the waif and indicated he should take a drink. The boy hesitated a moment and just stared at the metal cylinder before reaching out and snatching it from Karim. He gulped down the water, choking a little in his rush. Karim laughed.

'Slow down there or you're going to choke to death.'

His humor was rewarded with the briefest grin, a flash of white teeth contrasting with the dark face. The boy replaced the lid on the bottle and handed it back to Karim.

'Thank you, sir.'

'You're welcome. I think you were very hungry and thirsty before I came along. How long have you been out here?'

The boy looked down at his feet, the old shoes worn and falling to pieces.

'This will be my second day sir. I... I became lost in the night so waited for dawn until I could find out where I was. I didn't mean to stay away so long and that is why I brought no bread.'

Karim nodded. 'We all get lost from time to time but you know where you are now. Your parents will be getting very worried I think.'

60

The boy shook his head. 'I live with my uncle. My parents died when I was younger.'

'Well then, your uncle will be worried.'

The boy's voice was quieter when he answered. 'No. I think he will not be worried very much sir.'

Karim now understood the boy's determination to find the missing goats. He had probably been dumped upon his uncle as his only or nearest living relative. In an area like this, another mouth to feed, regardless of familial obligations, was never a welcome situation. He imagined the boy had a very tough existence; an orphan being raised by a grudging uncle who probably took his woes out on the child. Karim felt a small burst of affection for the boy's plight as he recalled his own experiences as an orphan. He leaned over to ruffle the boy's hair. The boy flinched and recoiled until he saw Karim's intention was benign. Now he was closer to the boy, Karim could see the swelling and bruises around the cheek and jaw. He lowered his hand.

'Well, he *should* be worried Affan. Someone as young as you surviving a night so deep in the mountains? You have the courage of a leopard boy. He is lucky to be able to call you his nephew.'

The boy looked up, his eyes moist at the unexpected praise and compassion. He lowered his eyes and gave a shy smile. 'Thank you, sir. It *was* very cold, and I was very hungry, but I never gave up. I never cried. I told myself that my father and mother would be proud of me and that kept me strong.'

Karim leaned over and patted the boy's shoulder, noting that the boy still flinched but didn't pull away. 'They would be very proud of you Affan. Very proud.'

They sat in companionable silence for a few moments, munching on the nuts and raisins Karim had provided before the boy spoke again.

'Who are you sir? Where have you come from?'

Karim looked the boy in the eyes. 'I was a soldier Affan, and a very good soldier. But I found out that the people I thought I was doing good work for were evil and doing very bad things. I am trying to stop them, but I need to get to the other side of the mountains to do that.'

The boy listened and nodded in the direction of the valley below them. 'Are the evil people chasing you sir?'

'Not yet, but they will. Soon, I think.'

'What will they do if they catch you?'

Karim swallowed a handful of raisins before replying. 'They will kill me Affan. They will torture me and kill me.'

The boy met Karim's eyes. 'It is the way of things with evil people I am thinking.'

'Yes Affan. It is the way of things.' He watched as the boy scratched at his thatch of matted hair then shook his head as though trying to come to a decision. He gave Karim a sideways glance before speaking.

'I have not told you everything, sir. I am not here looking for goats. I have run away from my uncle. He tried to… to sell me to some bad men. When I said I wouldn't go with them, he beat me worse than ever before.'

Karim allowed the boy some silence before responding. 'How long have you really been out here Affan?'

The boy met his eyes and Karim saw the pain and fear apparent.

'I have made it through three nights, sir. But today I felt so weak and tired that I didn't know where I was and was just… walking around. Then I met you.'

Karim passed the boy some dried fruit and watched as it was practically swallowed whole. 'Where were you trying to get to Affan?'

The boy pointed in the direction he had been walking from. 'There is another country to the west called Iraq. I thought I could cross the mountains and look for work there.'

Karim shook his head. The boy couldn't be any older than thirteen but was speaking like a much-older man.

'Iraq is too far Affan. The way too dangerous.'

The boy shook his head and Karim saw the defiance in his glare. 'No sir. It is not too far. I just need to eat some more food and I will be strong enough to complete the journey.'

'Affan, I know this country. It is too far and too difficult. You should return home, beg your uncle's forgiveness.'

The boy's answer was loaded with vehemence. 'Never. I will never beg or ask anything from such a man who shames my family name. I will die here before I would even think of returning.'

Karim sighed. 'Affan, if I had not found you today, you *would* have died. You were starving and dehydrated and eventually would have wandered off the edge of the mountain.'

He watched as the boy lowered his gaze, a sullen mask drawing over his features. Karim shook his head. 'You can't stay up here. Go back, go to another village and get some work there.'

The boy shook his head and snorted. 'There *are* no other villages until Laruz, and my uncle is well-known there too. And I won't go to the towns where the police will put me in the boy's prison.' He leapt quickly to his feet and as he did, his shirt and waistcoat rode up, exposing his ribs and stomach. Karim winced as he saw the thick welts that scarred the brown flesh beneath. And there were many of them. Probably from a whip or a stick. The boy walked off into the rocks and a moment later Karim heard the splashing of liquid as the he relieved himself. Affan returned several moments later and sat back down in the same place but avoided eye contact with Karim.

Karim knew he had to get moving if he was going to have any fighting chance of making it to the RV before dark. He rummaged through his pack and pulled out some bags and tossed a couple to his silent companion. The boy looked up in surprise as Karim stood.

'There's some food for you there. Will easily last you till you get back to the valley. Go home Affan. Find a way to survive there. The mountain is no place for a boy.'

He donned his vest and pack and picked up his rifle. The boy was looking at him with a neutral expression. Karim nodded.

'It's been nice to meet you Affan. Have a good life my friend.'

Karim leaned into the hill and began walking. He didn't look behind him to see if the boy was following. He didn't think he would. The waif had already survived a couple of tough nights and would have no appetite to repeat the experience. He shook his head at the memory of the cruel welts he'd seen on the boy. His uncle was clearly a vicious brute and had probably been beating the boy since he'd been under his care. As if being an orphan in rural Northern Iran wasn't tough enough already. Karim opened his stride as the incline flattened out and gave a quick look behind him as the track disappeared behind a rock formation. There was no sign of the boy, meaning the orphan must have made his way below the crest of the ridge towards the valley. *Good.* He didn't know what kind of life the boy was going to have but at least it would be a life.

***

The sun was low in the western sky and Karim stopped, dropped his pack and hauled out a jacket. The cold in the air was discernible now as the sun sank behind the peaks to his front, taking its warmth with it. Removing his goggles and checking his map, he felt a flicker of excitement as he identified that he was very close to RV 1. Grabbing his pack, he shouldered the load once more and strode along the meagre path that was getting harder to see in the dying light. He knew he had an hour of light left at best but was certain he'd be at the RV before that.

Thoughts of the boy came to him as he negotiated his way between huge boulders and rock faces. The waif probably had no real chance, but he was a fighter. And that counted for something. He would have the lowest status in his village; an orphan whose uncle treated him little better than an animal. There would be nothing back there for him. Nothing and no-one. Another time he may have helped the boy, but this was not another time. Karim was aware he was very lucky to not have encountered the hunters yet, but he knew it was inevitable. He'd bought himself a good lead and needed to exploit that as best he could because once they were on his tail, he would be running like a hunted beast.

There was barely enough light making it past the sentinels of the towering peaks for Karim to see the track, although it was hard to lose as it followed the path of least resistance around the rock faces and obstacles. By the time he reached the large monolith that loomed out of the darkness in front of him, night was almost complete. With a smile of triumph, Karim lowered his pack to the floor and arched his back, stretching out and groaning. He took a quick swig of water then swiftly fitted his NVGs to his head but did not lower the ocular tubes to his eyes. From the top-flap pocket of his pack he retrieved one of the satellite telephones and took it out of its protective cover. He laid the phone on a rock ledge beside him then picked up his pack and donned his load once again. He needed to be ready, once he'd sent the transmission, to be moving as far from the spot as fast as he could.

Karim took a deep breath and composed the message in his head. It was a longer missive than he had originally planned, but it was important that he got at least a piece of the information to Vic, in the event that something happened to him. He picked up the phone and turned it on, his face lit by the blue glow from the small screen. It took almost a minute for the signal to kick in and then he stabbed the keys in a rapid staccato, knowing every second he was transmitting gave VAJA a better chance at identifying the signal. Taking one last confirmatory look at his message, he pressed the send key and waited several moments until the beep and green tick showed him the message had gone. He turned the phone around and tore the battery from its housing, hurling it into the darkness in one direction and the body of the phone in another. Grabbing his rifle, he lowered his NVGs, powered them up, adjusted them slightly then strode off into the darkness.

His breathing was soon ragged as he maintained his punishing pace, but he wanted to be as far away from the signal location as he possibly could. It had been a short transmission and there was every chance that it hadn't been picked up, but Karim was too professional to rely on luck to save his life. He knew a drone could be deployed to the area with thermal imaging capabilities and he needed to be far enough from the spot to not be in the drone's cone of capture. The NVGs helped him maintain a good pace, the third-generation devices showing the land in front of him in a clear, green hue but picking out all the details of the terrain. His legs were tiring but it was a familiar sensation, a muscle memory from years of tough training courses and even tougher operations and he was able to turn his mind away from the pain. The thin air was also taking its toll, his breathing rapid and rasping as he tried to suck in as much oxygen as possible to fuel his lactic-heavy muscles.

He had been on the move for some time when he decided it was safe enough to take a small break and check his position. Drinking some water, he had to time his intake between breaths as his body struggled to regulate and calm itself. He used a small flashlight to look at the map and saw he'd made a considerable distance and indeed, was nearly at the half-way point to the second rendezvous. He wouldn't try to make that tonight, there being only a few hours of darkness left and his body needed rest. But it heartened him to see such good progress. His attention lingered on an area of the map that showed a large boulder field ahead of him. He nodded as he recognized that this afforded him a perfect position to lie up and rest for a few hours, giving any drone deployed enough time to see nothing of interest and return to whence it came. He stuffed the map back into his pocket and set off into the darkness once again. Despite the temptation to ease off, Karim continued with his fast pace, content with the fact that the next time he stopped, it would be for a long rest. Soon, all he could hear was his own breathing and the rhythm of his footsteps on the rocky track.

He wondered how the boy was. Had he made it back to the valley floor? Returned to his village? Was, even now, lying sobbing in a shack after another beating? Had the boy said anything about Karim? He didn't think so. The orphan was cut from a very different cloth to that of kids the same age. And he had no love for people who did bad things to others. No, Karim was reasonably confident that Affan wouldn't tell a soul about his meeting with the mysterious stranger in the Zagros Mountains. Unless of course, someone forced it out of him. Karim didn't like to think about that; the picture of the young boy being interrogated by VAJA officers because of Karim, not a pleasant one to imagine. But again, Karim thought this unlikely. It would rely on either Affan telling someone about Karim or VAJA learning that the boy had been in the mountains at the same time. Shaking his head, Karim discarded these thoughts from his head and concentrated on making progress up the steep incline.

He could see the beginning of the boulder field; intimidating monoliths guarding the access to the peak above. He slowed his pace to a gentle walk and took deeper breaths, calming his respiratory rate and lowering his heartbeat. He could feel his quadriceps burning and some chafing on his shoulders from the pack, the thought of rest now a welcome one. Weaving his way around the smooth rock formations, Karim left the track and meandered among the giant boulders until he found a space between two of them that afforded cover from above. Wasting no time, he dropped his pack, removed his tac-vest and began setting his camp for the next few hours. He unfolded the collapsible sleeping-mat and placed it on the ground before unrolling his sleeping-bag and placing it on top. The cold was seeping into him as he took off his jacket and the icy breeze found the sweat on his back. Wasting no time, he shuffled into the sleeping bag, pulled his carbine into his side then zipped the bag up to his neck. The warmth came almost instantly, the heat from his earlier exertions now captured and reflected by the down filling of the sleeping bag. His eyes began to droop and before he could have another coherent thought, Karim was asleep.

***

He could not say what woke him, but he had enough of his wits about him to not react until he had identified the reason. There was silence all around save for the occasional whisper as the breeze caressed the walls of the boulders in a soft melody. *There.* The smallest of sounds, a soft scrape of something across rock. Eyes open wide, Karim listened, determined to locate the source of the noise. He could feel his heart beating faster and the blood pounding in his ears as adrenaline began flooding his system. He forced himself to concentrate on remaining calm then heard the sound again. The same thing; a soft scrape of something moving over the rocks. He frowned as he concentrated. Had they found him so soon? His body heat caught by the thermal imaging cameras of a drone? Had the boy given him up? Another sound reached him, closer this time and he thought about another possibility. *Palang*, a leopard. Maybe the animal had smelled an unusual odor and was investigating the intrusion to its territory. This was entirely possible as Karim had seen the elusive creatures from time to time and knew that this deep in the mountains, they had little to no experience of humans and consequently just avoided them rather than run from them. The sounds and smells that Karim had made however, would probably draw the attention of a juvenile animal.

The sound came again. Very soft, and more akin to a tail brushing against a rock. Karim relaxed and, in slow increments, brought the pistol up from inside his sleeping bag. As quietly as he could, he unzipped the top of the bag one small piece at a time until his arms were free, and he had the pistol pointing out in front of him. He wouldn't shoot the animal, would just scream at it to scare it away. But there was always the chance that the beast would surprise him and leap on him before he could react. His pistol provided a back-up in this eventuality. A louder noise to his front told him the beast was very close. If he'd been wearing his NVGs he would be able to see it clearly. Karim stared into the darkness and began to make out the indistinct shape of the leopard as it flitted between the darker patches of shadow among the boulders. Raising the pistol up, Karim took a deep breath and readied himself to scream before the animal pounced. Just as he was about to release his yell, the animal stood on two feet and took a step towards him.

'Sir, do not shoot. It is I, Affan. Sir, the evil people are coming.'

9

ZAGROS MOUNTAINS, NORTH EAST IRAQ

Vic Foley gasped as the ice-cold water cascaded over his head. Pulling his head out of the stream, he grabbed his small towel and dried off quickly, the freeze of the water and the chill of the air cooling the CIA man rapidly. He pulled on his shirt and down jacket, zipping the garment up and burying his chin into the neck in an attempt to seal the warmth in. He made his way back the short distance to where the remainder of the team were sleeping and saw that Ned and Randy were both awake and brewing up some coffee. He nodded as he passed and stowed his wash-gear when he reached his own pack. He assembled his cooking stove and pulled out his rations, munching on a protein bar as he put some water on to boil. Looking around him he reflected on how beautiful it was in the mountains. The late morning sun painting the cathedral spires of the jagged peaks. When his water was boiled, he made his coffee and took a walk over to the Delta Operators. Randy grinned when he saw him.

'Hey Vic. Sleep well?'

'Like a baby. Must be the mountain air. How about you?'

'Same, man. Great sleep.'

Vic offered over his mug of coffee, but Randy just shook his head and pointed to his own water boiling in readiness. Ned looked up and smiled.

'The Asset make it to RV 1?'

Vic took a sip of his coffee and gave a small moan of contentment before replying. 'Yeah, he did. He also got something else out on the transmission that changes things a little.'

Ned raised an eyebrow. 'Sounds interesting. What is it?'

'The Quds have got a major target being developed.'

'Okay, I'll bite. Where and when?'

Vic paused and shook his head. 'Only got the where, I'm afraid.'

'Okay. Where, then?'

'The US.'

There was a moment's silence before Randy stood and faced Vic. 'Fuck. You got nothing more than that Vic? I mean, that's pretty fucking bare bones to be out here extracting an Asset out of Iran for.'

'Nope, I don't have more. But *Seven* does. He's bringing out a ton of stuff on this attack and a lot more. He could only collect it. Didn't have the time or the capabilities to disseminate but he has it with him.'

Ned nodded. 'This changes everything huh?'

Vic nodded. 'Yep. Now that we know there is a planned attack on Continental US soil, Seven's extraction is priority one; we get him out no matter how hard.'

'He say anything about being followed? Hunted?'

'No Ned, nothing. But then again, he would only risk the quickest of transmissions.'

'Okay, what's the play now?'

Vic took a couple of sips of coffee then pointed to the east. 'He's coming through those mountain passes even as we speak. High altitude, thin air, tough climbs.

As fast as he can. At some point the Iranians *are* going to figure out where he's gone. We need to be ready to pitch in and help our boy the moment he needs us. But not before.'

Randy spoke. 'Why don't we just fly in and grab him now? Quick scoot in and out of apache territory before the Indians even know we're there.'

Vic shook his head. 'I've asked man, but the threat of losing a bird or US troops in Iran is absolutely out of the question. Seven's got to make it as far as he can so that if we have to go in, it's for the shortest distance and quickest time.'

Ned sipped at his own coffee before standing and looking east into the mountains where the sun was now rising. 'So, we wait for the signal from RV 2 then we move?'

'Yeah. I'm anticipating it being pretty quick. Seven wouldn't have hung around RV 1; would've put as much distance as he could between himself and the signal location. By my reckoning he'll have covered a lot of ground towards RV 2 and then probably rested for a few hours.'

'That's what I figured. I assume we're still walking in rather than call up the birds?'

'Affirmative. I don't want the Iranians to see any activity anywhere near this place until we absolutely need to. Since they shot down the Hawk, the Pentagon is squirrelly about putting any more American airframes into their cross-hairs.'

Ned nodded, recalling the shock and surprise when he'd learned that the Iranians had shot a Global Hawk UAV out of the sky. Two hundred and fifty million dollars-worth of American taxpayers' money destroyed in an instant. To say nothing of the propaganda value, and reverse engineering opportunity, for the Iranians. He could understand why the Pentagon was so risk averse to the deploying of further assets into Iranian airspace.

But the Pentagon took risks in other ways: Ned knew there had been at least three serious cyber-attacks against Iranian military targets in the past month alone in retaliation for their seizure of international ships in the Gulf. Essentially the USA was at war with Iran through clandestine means. Deniable operations and non-attributable actions. He had no doubt that one day soon, one side or the other would escalate it into a full-blown physical confrontation, but in the meantime, everyone had to play the game. As he sipped his coffee, he watched Vic walk over to Dwight and transmit his Situation Report back to his people. Ned knew there was a lot riding on Vic's shoulders; now that the target location had been identified as CONUS, the Continental United States, senior figures in Washington would be getting involved. He leaned back against the rock face where he'd laid his rack for the night and felt the rays of the sun as they penetrated the serrated mountain peaks. He enjoyed moments like this; rare snatches of peace in wild, faraway lands. He thought of Cathy and the girls and broke into a smile. When this rotation ended, he had a stint back at Bragg for six months and both he and Cathy were looking forward to some much-needed family time. Cathy and the girls were everything to him outside of Delta. His guys were everything to him inside. Cathy understood that, admired him for it even, the fact that he was a leader to his men in every sense of the word and that they worshipped him for it. But when he'd taken the family to Hawaii on vacation, he'd noticed something that hadn't been apparent before.

Katrina had been talking excitedly about her upcoming summer camp and then a school excursion to DC. She'd been a non-stop chatterbox as she'd regaled them with all the things she was going to see and do.

She'd then started talking about when the trips were and where and when she needed to be and which of her friends she wanted to travel with. And that's when Ned had noticed that this final topic of the conversation had been directed at Cathy; he had not been included in any of it. When he'd interrupted Katrina and said he'd help out, his daughter merely looked at him in surprise and said she just assumed he wouldn't be around. There had been no malice or anger, just a statement of fact but the words had hurt Ned. That his daughter didn't even bother involving him in her plans anymore because he was never around to take part in them.

Cathy had smiled and patted Katrina on the arm and told her to go and play while she and Daddy talked about who would be doing what. Katrina had skipped away smiling, innocent to the heartbreak Ned was feeling, but Cathy had known. She'd always been good at seeing through him and she'd recognized he'd been hurt. Putting her arm around him, she'd kissed his cheek and told him that the girls had come to terms with the fact that he was away from home far more often than he was there and so had begun working around it. They loved their Daddy, and missed him when he was gone, but they had also learned to function without him. She'd nudged him playfully and given him a small smile, telling him they were getting more like him every day. But he didn't want them to be like him. He thought of himself as a good man with a strong moral compass. What he wasn't though, was a good *family* man. Yes, he loved them with all of his heart, and he was a great provider, but he was never there. He'd missed practically every key moment in Elisa's life and caught only a few of Katrina's.

He sighed as he came to the conclusion that it was maybe time to move on; hang up his spurs and enjoy what was left of the girls' young years before it was too late, and he was contending with hostile, unruly teenagers who resented him. That would break his heart. He'd seen it in a few of the older Squadron Sergeants-Major, men who'd dedicated their lives and sacrificed their family harmony to the Unit. Had missed so much of their children's lives that on entering their retirement from the military, they were living with young people with whom they'd had little to no connection with for the bulk of their upbringing. Ned didn't want that, didn't want it to be too late. Maybe when he was back at Bragg, he'd look at his options. Extend his time in Support Squadron while he looked for conventional employment in the private sector. The thought filled him with conflicting emotions of excitement and dread: The thrill of a new start and re-engagement with his family, and a fear of turning his back on a life of intensity that he'd loved for over twenty years. His thoughts were broken as a shadow loomed over him and he looked up. Shielding his eyes against the sun he squinted at Vic.

The CIA man gave him a rueful grin.

'We might have a problem Ned.'

10

GURBUZ, NORTH WEST IRAN

Colonel Hashemi watched as the General addressed his students although Hashemi wasn't sure they could be called students any more considering they were now engaged on a live operation to hunt down the traitor Ardavan. He could see from their attentive faces, straight backs and puffed out chests that they respected the General, their entire focus on his every word. The whine from the rotors of the helicopters behind them underlined the urgency of the hunt. The Reaction Force that had gone into the mountains earlier that morning was already reporting boot prints on an old herders' track. They were close to the location where an unidentified communication signal had been triangulated and the Reaction Force had requested the deployment of the Hunter Force to box their quarry in. Hashemi looked up as the General finished his brief, telling the students that this would probably be the most important task in their career as Quds Force operatives and as such, they could not fail. The zeal and determination not to let their General down was impressive to see and Hashemi reflected that he had rarely, if ever, in his thirty years' service to his country, witnessed such undisguised reverence. The troops broke ranks and ran for their heavy packs and weapons, making their way to the waiting helicopters. He picked his own pack up as the General approached. The focus and determination in the older man's eyes was identical to that of his students and Hashemi felt a surge of hope that they might, just *might*, catch their man. He smiled as the General slapped his shoulder and bent to pick up his own pack.

'Come, Hashemi. Let's show this traitor how the *Palang* hunts its quarry in the mountains.'

Hashemi nodded in response but wondered if he had the stamina to keep up with these super-fit operatives in the challenging mountain environment. He'd kept the weight in his pack to a minimum as had Captain Dabiri but they both recognized they were nowhere near as fit and strong as General Shir-Del's Palang troops. Following the General towards the helicopter, Hashemi hoped that the hunt would be over before his endurance was put to the test.

***

General Shir-Del looked down at the jagged spires of the peaks as the helicopter contoured the tortured landscape. Through the earphones he heard the first helicopter reporting that it was two minutes to its drop-off location. He felt the old excitement spread from the pit of his stomach as the anticipation of dropping into a live operation against a trained and competent adversary became reality. He closed his eyes for a moment as he pictured the thought of the traitor Ardavan hearing the arrival of the helicopters and scuttling under a rock like a cockroach, hiding from the justice and punishment his treason deserved. General Shir-Del felt a wave of rage consume him at the thought of Ardavan's treachery. That he could have respected Major Ardavan, seen positive traits in the man that he compared to those of his own, made his gorge rise. Shaking his head, the

General listened as the call came from the first helicopter that it had dropped the Hunters and lifted off. The next call was from his own pilot giving him the two-minute warning. Zana leaned forward and waved his hand to attract the men's attention and held up his two fingers. One of the helicopter crew yanked the door open and a blast of frigid air and the roar of the rotors invaded their warm cocoon. The helicopter dropped swiftly, and Zana felt his stomach lurch along with a burst of adrenalin, a muscle memory of the many times before when he'd entered a battle or firefight in exactly the same way. He whipped off the headphones and dragged his pack to the side of the door just as the wheels touched down and the aircraft gave a small bounce before settling. He was out of the door with a speed that belied a man of his age, pack over one shoulder as he jogged a small distance beyond the radius of the rotor blades. He threw himself on the ground and lay in the prone position, aiming his carbine into the area in front of him. Around him, the other men from the helicopter did the same as they took up their individual positions. A louder whine from the helicopter and an increase in the dust and debris battering him told Zana that the drop-off was complete and the helicopter lifting off. In the absence of the aircraft the silence was complete. Zana fitted a small earpiece and pressed his transmission switch.

'Palang 1 this is Palang 2. Moving now.'

A young Major led the two sections away from the landing site and along the track that the Reaction Force had identified. Zana looked at the soldiers ahead of him with a sense of pride, their moving, spacing and awareness now a natural extension of themselves. A cackling transmission came through his earpiece from the Reaction Force commander giving his location. They had been dropped further into the mountains, ahead of Zana and his Hunter Force. Their sections were moving towards the Hunter Force, looking to pressure Ardavan to break cover and identify his position. Zana looked up as a hand signal from the Major stopped their progress and each man took a knee, weapons pointing in alternate directions, every possible angle of attack covered. Zana stayed standing and walked past the kneeling men to the young Major who was studying the ground in front of him. He looked up as the General's shadow crossed him. Pointing to some indistinct impressions in the dust, the Major pointed west.

'One day old. Maybe a little more. Carrying weight and moving fast.'

The General nodded. 'Ardavan?'

'Yes Sir. See here, this is the tread from our issued cold-weather boots. Only we possess such items. The length of his stride and depth of the heel shows a man running fast but in control. A trained and physically fit individual. Ardavan.'

The General patted the Major's shoulder and indicated for him to continue leading the patrol. Zana let a couple of the soldiers pass him before he took up his position in the line, scanning the boulders around them. Ardavan could be anywhere in this mess of rock formations but Zana also knew they had ways of smoking the traitor out. The patrol carried on in silence, the men's breathing and the scraping of boots on rock the only sounds. Periodically, Zana answered transmissions from the Reaction Force ahead of him. They did not have a skilled tracker like he had but as their role was to harass Ardavan into breaking cover they didn't really need that capability. A whispered message from the soldier to his front informed Zana that the Major wanted a word. He nodded and made his way to the front of the patrol where the Major was examining the dirt and looking around the general area. When Zana reached him, the Major picked up a small stick and used it to point to the indistinct impressions on the ground.

'Here is Ardavan. You can just make out the heel impression. He's still moving fast, same pace, same stride. Quite impressive at this altitude.' He paused and looked the General in the eye. 'But now, he's no longer alone.'

Zana frowned. 'What do you mean?'

The Major shrugged. 'There's someone with him.'

Zana felt a jolt of excitement. 'American?'

The Major stood and scratched at his chin as he pondered the question. 'I don't think so. The print isn't clear as the ground is hard and his print overlaps Ardavan's. I would say it is someone smaller and much lighter, carrying no weight.'

Zana scanned the surrounding ridges and peaks. *Who the hell is this now?* Who could Ardavan possibly have arranged to meet up here? *A guide?* Zana discounted this possibility almost immediately. Ardavan had recce'd these routes so would be very familiar with them. *A lover?* Maybe. But nothing in his file showed any hint of a relationship with anyone. But then again, his file had also failed to spot any indications that he was an American spy. Zana turned to the Major. 'Good work. Carry on and call for me when you find anything else of note.'

After an hour or so, the tracks became harder to distinguish as the path changed from dirt to hard rock in places. The Major however, was a skilled tracker and always picked up the traitor's trail eventually. At one point, the Major stopped for some time as he interpreted the ground sign to identify the activity. He called Zana forward and with the aid of a stick, walked the General through what he thought had occurred.

'See here Sir; this is where he put his pack down for whatever reason. He then put it back on but did not head off immediately. Instead he walked to the edge of the ridge *here* and then turned around and carried on his way.'

Zana nodded and looked at the coordinates of their current location on his map. 'Yes Major. This is the area that the signal was identified as coming from. There's a good chance that this is the spot and he paused here to call his CIA contact.'

The Major stood and brushed the dust from the knee of his trousers. 'He can't be far ahead General so it's only a matter of time until either the Reaction Force flushes him out or we track him close enough to scare him into giving up his position.'

'Let's get moving then. The sooner we get him panicked the sooner this is ended.' He turned as the Major gave the hand-signal for the troops to follow him and slotted in between two of the front men. They still had hours to go before they lost the light and Zana was determined to close with the traitor before the coming of night aided his escape. He knew that he should have allowed Hashemi to request assistance from Tehran, but Zana wanted this ended on his own terms. He had no doubt that Hashemi would soon be receiving calls demanding updates, as all that his superiors knew was that the traitor Ardavan was being pursued. They probably believed that it was a hot pursuit where they were just behind their quarry and not, as they really were, hunting among the rocks and ridges of the formidable mountain passes.

But Zana had hunted people before. Many times before. And with that experience came a sharply honed instinct; an ability to almost predict his quarry's next move. He had no problem with keeping VAJA Headquarters out of the loop until he had achieved his task, confident that the situation would be resolved by nightfall. As he negotiated his way over a rough rock fissure, a transmission from the Reaction Force made him stop mid-stride as he concentrated on the contents of the message.

'Palang 2, Palang 1. We have visual on Target'

11

ZAGROS MOUNTAINS, NORTH WEST IRAN

Karim looked through the scope and tracked the movements of the men below through the crosshairs of the rifle's optics. He shook his head as he recognized one of the trainees from the Palang Course. This was a very clever move by the General, using troops who were both seasoned to the altitude and cold as well as being familiar with the geography of the mountains. He frowned as the implications ran through his mind. Karim had hoped that Tehran would send squads of ill-prepared VAJA officers to hunt him down, allowing him to maintain his advantage of experience. But the deployment of the Palang troops cut that aspiration dead. These were fit, well-motivated troops and Karim knew he would have to adjust his original plan in order to keep his exfiltration on track. He thought about the possibility of calling Vic and arranging for American assistance to pull him out, but Vic had warned him from the beginning that this would be almost impossible without incurring serious casualties and risk of capture. Karim had known that this would be the case, and that was why they'd planned such a challenging exfil plan that played to his strengths and experience while discouraging those following him. But that was when he'd thought his opponents would be the thugs from VAJA, not the special operatives of the Quds Force. Sighing, he lowered himself behind the rock and glanced at the sleeping figure of the boy.

When he'd arrived in the dead of night to warn him, Karim had wasted no time; pack on his back and moving within the minute. He'd said only one word to the waif; *Follow.* They'd climbed through the night to gain as much elevation as they could before dawn, knowing that any movement after sunrise could lead the hunters directly to them. He had no idea why the boy had chosen to risk his life and warn him. Why the tired, hungry, disheveled orphan had stumbled and skidded his way along precarious paths and sheer drops to find and alert Karim. Wasn't even sure how the boy had found him although when asked, he'd shrugged and said that Karim had left tracks that even a child could follow, dark or not. But he was glad the boy had found him. His timely intervention had enabled Karim to get them higher into the mountains where there was the possibility of skirting around the hunters as they tracked them along the trail below. The boy moaned and shifted in his sleep, retreating deeper into his fetal position on the scrubby patch of moss he'd chosen to lay on. Karim gave a soft smile. The boy was tough. Despite the privations he'd suffered, he'd trekked through the night then climbed hundreds of feet at a blistering pace. Karim had known from his labored breathing that Affan had been exhausted during the climb but not once had the boy fallen behind or asked Karim to slow down. They'd stopped only once, from necessity, for several minutes as Karim left something behind to aid their flight.

Keeping his movements slow and taking care not to silhouette himself, Karim once again studied the movements of the troops below, noting the measured advance and use of cover. With their training and practice, they would not be an easy foe to defeat but Karim had one weapon in his arsenal that gave him at an advantage over the Palang troops: experience. Years of sabotage, ambushes, assassinations, kidnappings, and bombings in countries all over the world had provided Karim with a wealth of operational experience that none of the Palang troops could hope to match. And that's what he was relying on now. Through the scope, he watched as the lead soldier gave a hand signal to the men behind him. The troops began spreading out, encircling the small, rocky rise where Karim had paused earlier that morning. When the lead man reached the base of the natural rock wall that protected the rise, he took cover and waited. From his vantage point above them, Karim could see the leader was waiting for the men encircling the rise to get into position. There was no movement from the soldiers for some time and then, in a flurry of motion, the leader and two others leapt over the rock wall, weapons up on aim as they entered the small crater. Although he couldn't quite see the expressions on their faces, he could imagine they were a combination of puzzlement and disappointment. Puzzlement that the woodsmoke they had been following was from the remains of a dying fire, and disappointment that the flash of color they'd seen from afar had been nothing more than a thermal shirt rammed between rocks. The leader of the troops must have transmitted something over the radio as the remainder of his men stood and advanced up the small rise to join the officer. Knowing what was coming, Karim readied himself and flicked the safety catch of his carbine to the fire position. As he watched, he saw one of the soldiers walking towards the higher rock formation at the other side of the crater and lean over to examine something.

The explosion was louder than he'd expected, and Karim flinched at the noise. The sound ricocheted off the boulders and rock faces, echoing then dissipating through the maze of gullies and passes. Karim nodded in satisfaction; his pressure-pad initiated trap had worked better than expected. The area of the rise was shrouded in a thin cloud of smoke and dust debris that began to clear as Karim retrained the scope back on to the targets. The screams reached him first; agony, fear and anguish manifested in high-pitched vocalizations that bounced off the disinterested rock faces. The men who had not entered the crater began running towards it to aid their colleagues. Karim shot the first man through the pelvis and saw him tumble across the ground, mouth wide and hands clutching at the wound. Turning his attention to the second soldier, Karim fired a burst of rounds at the man's lower body and watched as this soldier too, crashed into the hard ground. He didn't want to kill the men. He needed them wounded and in agony so that they would have to be attended to and evacuated, tying up men and resources as Karim and Affan fled the area. Dropping behind the rock he looked up as the boy, sitting upright with his back against the rock stared at him with big round eyes. Karim grabbed his pack and nodded towards the peak looming above them.

'Let's go.'

12

ZAGROS MOUNTAINS, IRAQ

Ned tabbed some keys on the laptop and the map on the screen zoomed into larger relief. He pointed at an area of compressed contours and looked up at the team.

'Satellite says there's a bunch of activity in this area here. Multiple helicopters and troop movements. Problem for us is that area is in the vicinity of the Asset's first Rendezvous Point.'

Randy spat a wad of tobacco over his shoulder then pointed at the displayed screen.

'VAJA chasing our boy?'

Ned nodded. 'That'd be my guess. Not much more intel than that I'm afraid. Vic's requesting a drone but doesn't think Washington will have the appetite for the risk. So, what we have is an Asset we *need* to get out being chased by a couple of helicopters of hostiles.'

Dwight held his hand up for Ned's attention. 'Hey Ned, I'm getting intermittent comms signatures coming through. Probably person to person as they're really weak but enough traffic to confirm the satellite's observations.'

'Thanks Dwight. Keep on it and see if we can nail down rough estimate of numbers.'

Dwight gave the thumbs-up and returned to his work as Ned stood and stretched, looking around at his team. 'My take on this is that we go in and grab the Asset as soon as he's triggered the second RV. Looking at the map, that's pretty tough country for the birds to land so we may need to locate a drop off some way from the target area.' He watched the men exchange glances. He didn't blame them; none of them were afraid of the fight, but on foot in the mountains of Iran and facing an enemy in their own backyard certainly held limited appeal. 'I get it. It's not ideal but this is the hand we've been dealt so we have to play it. It's nothing we haven't done before it's just this time the combination of altitude and pursuing hostiles is gonna make it more challenging. And who doesn't enjoy a challenge?' He gave a wide grin as he met each man's eyes in turn and saw them smile back in acknowledgement. 'Okay, go get some chow and some shut-eye while Vic and I square the plan away. The Asset should hit RV 2 by late afternoon so make the most of the time between now and then.'

The men walked back to their sleeping areas, some priming their stoves while others crawled into the warm, down-filled bags, keen to grab as much sleep as they could in anticipation of the coming extraction. Randy walked some distance from the camp area and sat on a rock ledge, legs dangling over a drop of several hundred feet. He scanned the mountains around him, taking in the tortured buttresses and spires that dominated the skyline. Like most of the Delta operators, he'd done his share of mountain warfare, but these mountains looked a lot tougher than most he'd encountered. Lots of severe, steep slopes and loose rock. A terrible combination for anyone working in this environment, especially at night. The lack of suitable LZs was also not a welcome fact. Randy and the guys were strong, fit soldiers but if it came to a fighting retreat from a large squad of VAJA troops, this would be put to the test. In addition to that, VAJA would probably call up air support, something that Randy was sure Washington would not allow them to reciprocate. Taking a swig of his coffee, he tilted his head back and allowed the cool air to blow the hair back from his forehead, appreciating the rare moment of quiet and solitude. With a sigh, he opened his eyes and got to his feet, staring at the abyss directly below him. He stepped to the edge and let his toes hang over the enormous drop. He grinned at the memory of Laura yelling at him when he had done the same thing while on vacation in Yosemite. It had freaked her out, but she'd forgiven him soon enough, never able to carry an angry word for long. He thought about her and realized he was missing her a lot more on this rotation than on any other. He pictured her smile and the soft curls of her dark hair, a legacy of the Irish blood of her ancestors, and surprised himself by thinking about marriage. They'd been together nearly three years and she'd accepted Randy's life without complaint or frustration, and he loved her all the more for that. He'd struggle to count the number of relationships he'd seen tank over the years because a wife or girlfriend couldn't cope with the constant separation and short-notice deployments. But Laura had understood it was a fact of life from the beginning and had never been anything but supportive to Randy. Yes, marriage. Definitely. He shook his head and turned back towards the camp wondering what the hell was in the mountain air that could turn a man's thoughts from killing Iranians to getting hitched.

***

Vic unclipped the mic and headphones and rubbed his face with his hands. Washington and Langley wouldn't sanction the drone due to the risk of interception from the Iranians on the ground. The CIA liaison at the

National Security Agency at Fort Meade however, was tasking satellites to collect any available intel that they could to help the Team successfully extract the Asset. While this would help, there was nothing like having a Pred with a couple of Hellfires or the real-time surveillance capabilities of a Global Hawk to provide a comfort blanket on a difficult exfil. He sighed, stood and thought through their options. It seemed to Vic that they were saddled with one available course of action and that was to wait for the RV 2 trigger then go in and grab Seven. Which was all very well in theory but with a sizeable pursuing force and no real-time intel on their locations, it was hardly ideal. Losing troops in Iranian territory was not an option. Yes, the Team's weapons, ammunition and even their clothing had been sanitized so that nothing could be linked to a US Military operation, but they all knew Tehran would make massive capital out of any dead or wounded combatant they recovered from the field. Sanitized or not, the Iranians would know full well that they had disrupted a covert US Military operation in their own country.

He made his way over to Dwight and pointed at the laptop that lay open. Dwight nodded and Vic began looking at the mapping of the area around RV 2. He needed to find somewhere the birds could put down as close to the RV as possible. He wanted the Team to have as little exposure on the ground as possible. Up here, it wasn't just bombs and bullets they had to worry about. Altitude was a factor, and nobody really knew how badly it affected them until they were at height. A fall leading to broken bones would disable a man and tie up a couple of his buddies as they helped him. And between the loose rocks, the snow, and the ice patches they would encounter, there were plenty of ways for a man to fall. His mind wandered to Bill Howard's conversation with him back in the Green Zone. *That's some pretty tough fucking country up there my friend.* Had to hand it to the man, he'd known what he was talking about.

He turned his attention back to the map and studied the contours and relief, transposing a mental picture of the ground based on the representations on the imagery. There was definitely nowhere suitable for the birds within a kilometer of RV 2, so he began looking further out until he'd identified a small plateau, high on a glacier. It was just over three klicks from RV 2 but was the best he could find. Vic checked once again to make sure that he hadn't missed anything but found nothing else. *So be it. If that's all we've got, then that's all we've got.* He looked around and caught Ned's attention, beckoning him over. He wanted the Delta operator's opinion before contacting the pilots with the coordinates. As Ned approached him, Vic reflected that if anything went wrong on this extraction, it was going to go *very* wrong. Fifty klicks inside Iran and with a three-kilometer hike back to the birds? Bill's words came back to haunt him once again. *You said potential goat-fuck Foley.* He looked up as Ned arrived and indicated for him to sit down by the laptop.

'Okay, as you can see, I've struggled to get a good LZ for the birds but what I have found is a small, flat area *here* that looks pretty good. Problem is, it's three klicks from RV 2.'

Ned leaned in and studied the area on the screen before replying. 'Yep. I don't see any other alternatives either.'

Vic traced his finger on the screen as he continued his brief. 'Path of least resistance from RV 2 to our potential LZ. Still pretty tough country but the best we can hope for. Seven should be coming along that route with his heels on fire so hopefully we'll meet him half-way and help cover his ass back to the LZ.'

'Sounds good… in theory. Once we engage with the Iranians, we can expect to see air support and ground reinforcements up there. And what about this side? They got anyone they can call on to come at our six?'

Vic nodded and met the Master Sergeant's eyes. 'Yep. They've bought some major influence in Diyala and some of the other provinces and I know for a fact there are a handful of senior Quds officers a helicopter ride away. So that's something we have to consider.'

'Plan?'

Vic ran his hands through his hair, feeling the resistance from the matted clumps. 'I paid Faisal a pretty big bonus back at ANGELO. At my request him and a bunch of his commandos will run interference on any assholes trying to sneak up on our rear. It'll get very political very quickly after that, but it will buy us enough time to be off this fucking mountain and back at a FOB.'

Ned gave the CIA man a grin. 'Shit Vic, you almost sound like you know what you're doing.'

Vic laughed. 'Just bluffing it like the rest of us brother.' His attention was diverted as he saw Dwight waving his arm at him. He walked over and knelt beside him. Dwight pointed to an area on the screen and began his brief.

'From NSA, there's two groups on this side of that peak and from time comparisons it looks like they're moving towards one another. Also, they think there was an explosion of some kind with dead and or injured.'

Vic frowned. He didn't understand why there would be two groups moving towards one another. Unless… He patted Dwight's shoulder. 'What chatter are you picking up? Does it sound like you've got two distinct groups operating different systems?'

Dwight shook his head. 'Nope. Definitely same comms and I'd say from the patterns, they are talking to each other.'

Vic nodded his thanks and stood, making his way back towards Ned. The Delta operator looked up and raised his eyebrows in response to Vic's return. The CIA man remained standing and pointed to the east.

'Looks like they've got two groups trying to box Seven in. Also looks like our boy is holding his own; Meade reckons there's been an explosion and casualties but no sign of choppers to extract the hunters, which there would be if they'd got their guy.'

Ned folded his arms as he considered the update. 'Sounds feasible. But if there's a group in front of him and a group behind, how the fuck is he going to make to RV 2? Unless he can sneak through their line, he's not going to make it as quickly as we'd thought.'

Vic turned his gaze to the peaks in the east and imagined Seven scrambling among the snow and shattered rocks, being hunted by determined pursuers hungry for blood. He didn't know how Seven was going to make it to RV 2 but did know that it was the Asset's only chance.

And Vic's if he had any hope of halting an attack on the mainland US.

13

ZAGROS MOUNTAINS, IRAN

The rage in the General's eyes was intimidating even to a man of Hashemi's standing. As the last rock was placed on the mound that covered the bodies of the dead Palang students, Hashemi watched as General Shir-Del turned to address the Quds teams assembled in a small huddle.

'The traitor Ardavan has shown us that he cannot be underestimated. Shown us what little regard he has for his fellow soldiers and what love he has for the great *Shaitan* that he would kill his own kind to get closer to the Americans. Every minute we waste, the traitor gets closer to his CIA spymasters. Grieve our dead but grieve them by bringing me the head of this vile snake.'

Hashemi saw the anger mirrored in the hunters' faces and the resolve to carry out the General's bidding. As the General approached him, Hashemi cleared his throat before addressing the senior officer.

'General Shir-Del. I think now might be the time to request assistance from Headquarters. If the traitor Ardavan isn't caught soon, I fear that…' His request was cut short by the intense blue eyes staring hard at his own.

'You have nothing to *fear*, Hashemi. The traitor *will* be caught, and he will be caught soon. He was only a matter of minutes ahead of us before his cowardly attack and we will soon shorten that small advantage.'

Hashemi's eyes widened in surprise as the General turned and walked back to his equipment, donning his pack and weapons with a fixed determination. Doubt was now a permanent companion to Hashemi's thoughts, and he felt his mouth dry at the thought of the repercussions if Ardavan escaped. His masters back in Tehran would be apoplectic at the success of an American coup of this magnitude and Hashemi would be held accountable for the entire situation. As the senior VAJA officer on task, the responsibility for keeping Tehran updated and involved in the manhunt was his alone. However, the punishment would not be meted out to only himself. When a failing as big as this came about, the punishments were wrought upon immediate and even distant family. A trickle of sweat ran down his spine at the thought of his wife and daughters undergoing torture in the dank, stinking cells below Alf Ta, the notorious prison in Isfahan where they would be taken. The General would probably only be executed for his role, due to his reputation and the respect for his position, but Hashemi would suffer much more. He sighed as he picked up his own pack, hoping that the General was right and that this would all be over soon, and they could inform Tehran of their success in halting a CIA operation against their glorious Republic. As he tightened the straps on his pack, it came to Hashemi that he now really only had one weapon in his arsenal with which he had any use for:

Hope.

***

Zana scanned the rocks and peaks around him as they continued to follow the herders' path as it twisted around monoliths and sheer walls of stone. The men were much more alert after the IED trap that Ardavan had lured them into. The small fire and its trail of woodsmoke enticing the hunters to trigger a pressure-pad initiated device, killing two and wounding three others. Zana had ordered the dead men buried on the mountain and the three injured to remain at the site along with a medic and two guards. He'd made it clear to the medic that no outside help would be coming before the traitor had been captured and stared hard at the younger man until he'd seen that his unspoken message had been understood; *do all you can but don't let them suffer.* The soldier with the wounds to his pelvis was in extreme agony and from experience, Zana knew that he was unlikely to survive the afternoon. But the focus had to remain on capturing the traitor. Although killing the swine with his bare hands and parading the body through the streets was what he dreamed of doing, the tortures and interrogations that awaited Ardavan motivated Zana to taking his man alive.

The light was beginning to fade as evening approached and for the first time, a tiny element of doubt began creeping into the edges of Zana's thoughts. He couldn't allow Ardavan the advantage of darkness and he cursed himself for not having the foresight to have brought tracker dogs on the hunt. They would have been of great value in closing the distance with the traitor but then again, Zana would have had to have gone outside the unit for this asset and that would have raised questions of its own. *No*, his own men would bring this to an end and bring it to an end soon. But the thought of tracker dogs had sparked something in his mind that he hadn't thought of before. Quickening his pace, he strode past the soldiers walking in front of him until he reached the signaler and tapped on the man's shoulder. He stated his request and the patrol moved into cover while they waited.

Zana watched as the signaler altered frequencies on the large radio and spoke into his mic. As he was establishing comms with Camp Palang, Zana studied his map and with the stub of a pencil, marked a series of positions on the contours of the document. The signaler looked up at him and Zana relayed a series of coordinates which were in turn, radioed back to Palang. There was some further back and forth before the signaler nodded and Zana smiled, indicating for the patrol to proceed. As he walked, he was happy the thought of the dogs had occurred to him. He might not have been able to get tracker dogs to help without arousing unwanted attention, but from his own unit, he could deploy something almost just as good. Not quite tracker dogs, but close.

Very close.

14

ZAGROS MOUNTAINS, IRAN

The light was beginning to fade as the sun sank below the peaks in the west. Karim scanned the area to the east looking for any signs of movement but had seen nothing for the last ten minutes to indicate his pursuers were close. He lowered the rifle and sank behind the rock, leaning his back against it and pulling the map from his trouser pocket. Fixing his position, he traced his finger to the next objective, an outcrop of rock that he and Vic had agreed would be his second rendezvous point; RV 2. He was less than a kilometer from the location, but it was a lot lower than his current position. Karim was loath to concede the height that he and the boy had worked so hard to gain but he had no choice. He couldn't risk choosing a new location and sending Vic the coordinates; the transmission time would be far too long, and he wouldn't risk the threat of compromise now that he was so close. He'd been fortunate with the IED; the Palang students too confident and eager to please the General to consider Karim as a serious threat. But it would be different now. The troops would be far more alert and less likely to succumb to such traps. They would also be more motivated to capture Karim, nothing getting a soldier's blood up like the killing or wounding of a comrade in arms.

He folded the map and stowed it back in the pocket of his cargo-pants before looking at the boy. The waif was curled up, asleep and still, laying on Karim's mat and covered with a heat-reflective blanket. Although didn't show it, the boy had been exhausted, the night's climb and the fast extraction from their last position taking its toll. Karim still couldn't quite believe that he was dragging the orphan around with him when the challenges to staying alive were so high. But he felt an obligation to the boy; his appearance at Karim's sleeping spot the night before, undoubtedly saving his life. He thought back to his own childhood as an orphan, being passed from distant relative to even more distant relative until he'd been old enough to extract himself from the cycle of abuse and servitude. The boy asleep at his feet had suffered far more than Karim and he knew in his heart that this was as much a reason for helping him as his gratitude. As though hearing his thoughts, the boy stirred and raised his sleep-wrinkled face from the comfort of the mat. He stared at Karim for a moment before running his hands through his black thatch of hair. Karim threw a handful of items to the boy's side.

'Here. Protein bars. Good for energy. Eat them, get a drink, have a piss, then we're on our way again.' He didn't wait for a reply but began devouring his own bar, alternating bites with swallows of water, ensuring he remained hydrated. Grinning to himself as he watched the boy gobble down the bars before he was even half-way through his own, Karim felt in his heart that taking the boy with him was the right thing to do. Once they'd finished their food, Karim packed the gear away as the boy took himself out of sight to take care of his ablutions. He returned as Karim was hoisting the pack on to his back and watched the Quds operative pick up the carbine and meet his gaze.

'We have a small distance to travel but we're descending. Watch your feet on these slopes; the loose rock is treacherous, and you don't want to fall down here. You'll be over the edge before you know it. Follow my footsteps and you'll be fine.' With that he turned his back on the boy and began walking, examining the ground in front of him before taking a step. It would be slow going but better to be late at the RV than suffer the alternative of not making it at all. He glanced over his shoulder to see the boy adhering to his directive and following closely behind. Several times he felt the loose rock begin to slide beneath his feet but managed to recover before it became a full-on fall, his adrenalin kicking in and cursing under his breath. While the decision to gain height had been a sound tactical one given the circumstances, he was regretting it now as he tried to negotiate the treacherous terrain in rapidly fading light.

They'd covered a good distance when Karim heard a hiss from the boy and he stopped, turned, and looked at the orphan. The boy was looking back the way they had come and tilted his head to one side as he concentrated. Karim started to ask what was wrong but was silenced by the boy's raised hand as he continued his solemn vigil. After several moments the boy turned to face him.

'Something is coming.'

Karim wasted no time. He pointed at a clump of large boulders and they ran towards them, skidding on the loose rocks, sacrificing safety for speed. Karim could hear the faint noise for himself now and as they wedged themselves under the cover of the huge boulders, he felt his heart lurch with disappointment. The sound, while faint, was one that could never be confused with

101

anything else. Once heard, never forgotten as the Americans liked to say. Pulling the boy further into the cover of the rock, Karim chided himself for not expecting this sooner. It was inevitable that, at some point, the hunters would request some assistance to give them the advantage over the running man. And the sound that Karim and the boy could hear was certainly a big advantage for the hunters:

A drone.

From his knowledge and experience of the Unmanned Aerial Vehicles, Karim wondered what type of drone they would be facing. He assumed that it would have Thermal Imaging now that night was falling, highlighting him and the boy as glowing figures in the grey and black backdrop to the operator thousands of feet below. Probably armed as well, in the event that the hunters couldn't get to Karim before he made it across the border. But as he listened to the approaching aircraft, he could tell that it was a *khoffash*. A bat. The smaller of the Quds UAVs that was used mainly as a delivery mechanism for equipment. Karim frowned as he tried to work out what it could be that was being deposited. *Medical equipment? Food, ammunition?* In truth, it could be anything but, whatever it was, he knew that it was not good for him and the boy. The drone whined past their location towards the west, in the direction they intended travelling. Karim knew that the hunters were no longer split into two groups after his IED trap and it came to him that whatever the drone was doing might be replacing the capability that had been lost. *Cameras?* That would make sense, giving the hunters a real-time alert system should Karim be picked up by one. But that seemed hit and miss, relying on Karim to cross directly, or very close to, the camera position.

His frown deepened then froze as he suddenly realized what had been deployed. Not the unreliable cameras that he'd been thinking of but something far more effective and a serious threat to Karim's escape: Sensors. Small, sensitive devices that alerted the operator to any sounds or movement within a wide radius. This in turn would provide the ground forces hunting Karim with lock-ons to his position and worst of all, Karim would have no idea that it was happening. The irony of the situation was that one of Karim's colleagues had stolen this technology from the Americans and it was possible that these small devices would end Karim's escape and his efforts to help those very people stop an attack on their home soil.

He had a decision to make. He thought about his options for several seconds before arriving at his conclusion: Speed had to be the priority. He had to make it to RV 2 before dark and get the message out. Then he would worry about the sensors but at least if Vic knew he'd made the RV, there was a chance of some help from his American handler. A small chance, but still a chance. He nudged the boy with his foot.

'I don't have time to explain but we're going to move and we're going to move fast. Do what you did before, and you'll be fine, but we need to get somewhere very quickly, and we don't have time to waste. Ready?'

The boy nodded and Karim wriggled his body out from the cover of the boulder and stood up. When the boy joined him, he indicated with his head towards the darkening sky in the west.

'Let's go.'

15

ZAGROS MOUNTAINS, IRAQ

Dwight pulled his down jacket on and zipped it up as he addressed Ned and Vic. 'My guess would be small to intermediate drone. Signature seemed to indicate something of that size. Made four incursions into the mountains in the area of the coordinates I gave you. First site looks close to where the troops and helicopter activity was happening. They're only rough locations but still, better than nothing.' He turned and made his way back to his sleeping area leaving the CIA officer and the Delta Master Sergeant to digest the new information. Vic spoke first.

'Four incursions? That's not a thermal overflight looking for body heat. Think they've got spotters guiding the drone into likely areas of cover?'

Ned shook his head. 'Nope. That's the wrong pattern for that as well. My guess would be a depositor; it's dropping something ahead of the hunter force.'

'Okay, that actually sounds right. What would they drop though? Gotta be a small payload if it's carrying four of whatever the fuck it is.'

Ned was quiet for several moments before replying. 'If it was me, I'd probably drop a TUGS screen ahead of the guy I was hunting.'

Vic cursed and closed his eyes. That would make complete sense, but also bad news for Seven. TUGS, the Tactical Unattended Ground Sensors, were used by Special Forces to relay movement, noise, chemicals and gas signatures back to their controllers. In this case, it was more than likely the Iranians were trying to get a fix on Seven's location and were using the sensors to narrow that down. Without knowing where they were, this meant that they could also pick up the noise and movement from Vic and the Delta operators on their ingress route. Vic nodded back at Ned.

'That would explain the first incursion into the area of the troop activity; they were dropping the receiver to the hunter force.'

'That'd be my guess too. Getting more interesting by the minute this little caper, huh?'

Vic laughed. '*Interesting* is a nice way of putting it. What bothers me though, is why haven't they flooded the entire area with troops? They've got the manpower and don't give a shit if they all survive or not. This is a really small pursuit force for such a hunt, and they must know they run the risk of losing Seven once night kicks in.'

'Must have their reasons Vic. Maybe they want to stay off *our* radar; keep it low key so that no US platforms pick up on their activity. I mean, they won't know about our tech capabilities, not to any accurate level anyway, so maybe they're trying to get this done quietly.'

Vic shook his head. 'Nope: Not their way. They must have identified Seven is working for us and so they should be stopping at nothing, *nothing*, to catch their guy. No, there's something else at work here but I just can't work out what it is.'

The men were quiet for several moments and Vic pulled his zip up on the down jacket, the evening cold of the mountains starting to bite. He exhaled and watched his breath fog in the cooling air. He called over to Dwight.

'What's the Met for tonight?'

He watched as Dwight raised his head from the hood of his sleeping bag.

'Clear and cold initially, possible snow later but not too heavy.'

Vic nodded his thanks. With any luck they would have Seven safe in a FOB by the time the weather changed. He looked at his watch then pulled the Sat-phone from his pocket, checking the screen for any activity but there was still nothing from Seven. He wondered how close the Asset was to RV 2 and imagined Seven scrambling among the peaks and boulders trying to make the RV before nightfall. In his shoes, that's what Vic would be trying. But night was almost here. Looking around him, Vic noted that it was now difficult to see much beyond the radius of their temporary camp. He left Ned to his rest and walked over to his own area, sitting cross-legged on his sleeping bag while he opened up the lap-top and studied the area around RV 2 once again. He made some rough calculations in his head based on how fast he assessed that Seven could travel in the challenging terrain and how quickly he and the Delta guys could hoof it from their LZ. The contours displayed on the digital mapping system told him that the terrain was steep and littered with all sizes of rock formations, passes and boulder fields. Progress would be slow but slow was better than the alternative of injured or dead operators.

Vic closed the computer down and crawled into his sleeping bag, zipping it up and feeling the warmth begin to envelope him. He closed his eyes and felt the tiredness seep in, his breathing deepen, and his thoughts run together. He was almost completely asleep when the buzzing in his thigh pocket brought him crashing back to reality. He tore open the sleeping bag and pulled out the phone, looking at the screen and giving a grunt of triumph. *Seven.* Vic read the brief message twice before leaping to his feet and yelling.

'Okay, Asset has reached RV 2 and is running gentlemen. Confirmed pursuit by hostiles numbering twenty-plus, a couple of klicks behind. Dwight, get the birds inbound, Ned, let's run the play one more time then brief the team. The rest of you guys get packed and ready.'

Without waiting for an acknowledgement, Vic packed his own equipment away and was tightening the straps on his pack just as Ned approached. Both men sat and Vic opened the laptop and ran the Delta operator through the plan for the LZ and the ingress route towards RV 2. Ned nodded, happy with the call and stood, clapping Vic on the shoulder.

'Okay, Agency man. Let's do this.' He walked over to the remainder of the team who had gathered near Dwight's sleeping area and were talking in low voices as the comms operator ordered the helicopters inbound. Ned briefed the team and ran through some basic contingencies in the event that something went wrong. He had no doubt that it would; no plan ever survives contact with the enemy, but he and his guys had the skills and the experience to adapt to any circumstance, regardless of how poor the odds in their favor. He finished by ordering a comms check and joined the team as they confirmed and checked their radios were working and connected with each other. Dwight held up both hands with fingers splayed and Ned nodded. *Ten minutes to choppers.* He looked around to make sure Vic had seen it and saw the CIA officer wave in acknowledgement.

As the rest of his team made their final preparations, Ned checked the power level on his NVGs and was happy that there was more than enough to last through the night. He and his team were using the older model GPs; the Ground Panoramic Night Vision Goggles that had been in service for several years now. He remembered when these four-monocular devices had been cutting edge technology and the amazing difference he'd noticed when he'd used them on missions in Somalia and Libya. Now, you could buy them from Amazon or eBay if you had thirty thousand bucks to blow. But that was why his team were using them; plausible deniability. If they were dropped or taken from an injured or dead Delta, the US government would point out that anyone could have bought this equipment and allow the finger of suspicion to drift towards the Israelis who wouldn't be above carrying out this type of operation. He ran through a series of further checks on his weapons and ammunition, testing the security of the suppressors on his carbine and pistol, studying the pins on the grenades, heeling the rear of his magazines with his hand to ensure the rounds were seated fully in order to minimize the likelihood of a stoppage. He stood, put on his helmet and fitted the NVGs on the bracket, pulling down the alien-like tubes and adjusting the relief to his eyes. He had just completed this when the muted sound of the helicopters reached him. Ned turned to face the direction from where the noise was emanating but saw nothing in the darkening sky. He knew they'd be close; the heavily modified Black Hawks emitting far less noise than their conventional model. Grabbing his gear, he loaded up and began walking towards the Landing Zone they had nominated for the lift. The rest of the team were already making their way there and he could see Steve and Ryan, the guys who'd pulled security at the LZ, talking on their radios, updating the pilots. The choppers were louder now, and Ned looked up to see Vic had fallen into step with him as they climbed the small, rocky slope to the LZ. Neither man spoke, each content with his own thoughts. When they reached the small plateau, Vic split from him and walked over to the line of men kneeling in the cover of the rocks, all watching the area around them for any sign of activity. Ned carried out a head count to ensure everyone was present before he joined his own group. Through his earpiece he heard the pilot talking to Dwight and confirming that he had them visual. The Night Stalkers were the only pilots who routinely flew in darkness using NVGs and they did it well. The noise was much louder now as the first bird descended and Ned braced himself for the rotor wash and debris shower that was imminent. He felt the blast of air and dirt shove him from behind and a brief moment later, a reduction in noise as the rotor speed was slowed. Through his radio he heard Randy give the order for Team One to mount up and several moments later a message from Randy telling him that Team One was complete and airborne. Ned acknowledged and was showered with dust and small stones once again as the Black Hawk took off. He knew it would move away and act as mutual support for the next chopper which he could already hear starting its own descent. Another debris shower then he heard the call from the crew that they were clear. Ned sent out his own call and stood, turning towards the helicopter and falling in as last man, his team jogging towards the beckoning crew member stood just outside the open doorway. Ned waited until his whole team had boarded then pulled himself in, dropping his main pack at his feet and grabbing a seat. The door was closed, and the helicopter began to lift, gaining some altitude before turning away from the face of the mountain and contouring along the valley.

Ned listened to the updates from the pilots as they coordinated their journey and looked for any signs of problems ahead. It wasn't a long flight to the Iranian LZ, but he could sense a tenseness in the voices of the flyers, the curt replies and minimal radio traffic a sure sign of men utterly focused on the mission. And Ned couldn't blame them. Who would want to be a Black Hawk pilot captured by the Iranians while on a secret CIA mission? No, in their shoes, Ned knew he'd also be pretty tense. When Vic had identified the LZ, Ned had been impressed. With such little choice available, the CIA man had found a halfway decent spot that put a lump of mountain between them and the Iranians that should cover the noise of the choppers as they landed. The pilots had agreed it looked like the best option available but had also advised that if the teams came running out hot, it might be the only spot that they could use as the extraction LZ. Nobody liked this; it was always prudent to use a different LZ for extraction than the one you used for ingress. Your enemy could have watched you land there and just be waiting until you returned, ambushing men and machines and destroying any realistic chance of escape. But sometimes you just had to work with what you had. And this was certainly one of those times. He looked up from his reverie as a call came from the lead helicopter: They'd just entered Iranian airspace.

He knew from the planning that they had around fifteen more minutes until the LZ and felt the adrenaline coursing around his body. He never lost this; that excitement when he and his guys crossed the line into enemy territory, reliant on nothing more than their own abilities and judgements to make it out alive. The thought took him back to other countries, other borders, other enemies, and again, the question came to Ned about how much longer he could keep this up. He was almost forty-two years old and while still strong and fit, injuries took longer to heal, more of the younger guys were pushing his ass in the gym and he knew that if he wanted any semblance of a relationship with his daughters, he couldn't keep disappearing for months on end.

His train of thought was interrupted by the two-minute call from the pilot. Ned looked up to check his guys had heard the message and watched as they gave the thumbs-up in acknowledgement. They began adjusting packs, tac-vests, straps and weapons and in no time at all, the helicopter dropped in a rapid descent towards the LZ. Ned leaned forward as the crew member opened the door, the frigid air blasting him and the noise of the rotors unnaturally loud. He pulled down the tubes of the NVGs, his world now the familiar green-hued panorama that he'd experienced on so many other operations. The supporting helicopter confirmed that the LZ looked clear and Ned's helicopter dropped even quicker, his stomach rising as the pilot descended as fast as he could safely achieve it to get them on the ground and away before the enemy could react. The crew member was leaning out of the door and relaying the distance to the ground to the pilots in a flurry of rapid speech as the bird continued to drop. Ned tensed himself just in time as the helicopter hit the ground a little harder than he'd expected, bounced, then settled, the crew member out the door and giving the command to disembark.

Ned and his team clambered out of the static helicopter and jogged a small distance from the bird where they lay among the rocks and took up positions, ready to defend the choppers against anyone who came to investigate. He heard his helicopter depart and the second team arrive, the dust and wind blast showering his back. The second helicopter departed seconds later, and Ned waited, the silence absolute after the noise of the helicopters. He stood and walked over to where Vic was propped up behind a rock, covering an area to his front. On hearing Ned's approach, he looked up, smiling as the identity of his visitor became clear through the green filter of his NVGs. Ned extended a hand and pulled Vic up before giving him a huge grin.

'Welcome to Iran, Agency man.'

16

ZAGROS MOUNTAINS, IRAN

Zana waited while the operator studied the glow of the screen in front of him. After almost a minute of silence, the younger man looked up at the General.

'All mice are deployed and functional, sir.'

Zana nodded and indicated that the operator should take his place back in the section. He was pleased that all of the three sensors, or *mice* as they were affectionately called, had survived their drop-offs and were working, sending their signals back to the operator. Zana knew it was only a matter of time before the small devices started picking up the movements of the traitor Ardavan. As he made his way back into the file of men, Colonel Hashemi fell in step with him.

'General, I must insist that you allow me to call my superiors and update them with our current situation. We cannot keep them out of this any longer or we will both be killed for treason.'

Zana glanced at his VAJA counterpart, his sneer unseen in the dark of the night. Of course, the VAJA man wanted to get the higher-ups involved; that was the way his organization worked. But they were a *security* organization, not a fighting one. They had no faith in anything other than their own sense of importance and stifling bureaucracy. He could hear the fear in Hashemi's voice, real concern that if they didn't apprehend Ardavan, it would be the hangman's noose for all involved. But Zana wasn't concerned about the hangman's noose because he wasn't going to fail. He was so close to Ardavan that he could almost feel the traitor's filthy neck between his hands. He reached out and gripped the VAJA Colonel's shoulder.

'Stop worrying Hashemi. We're close now. Very close. The traitor will be in our hands and on a helicopter back to Palang within the hour, on my honor. Forget your dark thoughts about the noose and think of the rewards that await you as the VAJA officer who caught an American spy.'

The Colonel shook his head. 'General… please, we *must* call Tehran. I insist!'

Zana stopped walking and leaned in towards Hashemi until their noses were almost touching. His voice was low, but the menace and threat were evident. 'Don't ever question me again Hashemi or the hangman's rope will be the least of your worries. We've almost got the traitor and I don't want to lose any more time arguing with you about this.' He turned on his heel and told the Major to get them moving again.

Hashemi swallowed and felt the trembling in his legs. General Shir-Del was an intimidating man and Hashemi had no doubt that he believed they would catch the traitor. But Hashemi wasn't so confident. Ardavan had already shown skill and cunning when he'd lured the Quds trainees into his ambush and he was still ahead of them, still *free*, in the darkness of the mountains. The VAJA officer shook his head then began walking towards the departing line of hunters whose forms were already being absorbed by the deep cloak of night. On top of everything else, the last thing he needed was to become separated from them and lost in this unforgiving place.

The only sound from the file of men was the occasional clatter as small rocks and shale were displaced by feet and went skidding down the steep slopes. The cold was more apparent now that night had arrived, small clouds puffing from the mouths of the hunters as their breaths condensed in the frigid air. Zana almost collided with the man in front of him as the file came to a halt. He made his way around the individual and walked to the front of the formation where he saw the Major and the signaler discussing something. Seeing him approach, the Major directed the signaler's attention to Zana. The young Quds technician waited until the General was beside him before speaking.

'Palang just identified an unknown transmission from this area. Quick duration but longer than the rest. They've sent some coordinates that put it very close to where we are now sir.' At this, the Major joined them and pointed out on the map where Camp Palang had told them that the transmission had come from. Zana felt his adrenaline surge. If the Palang assessment was correct, they were less than fifteen hundred meters from the CIA's whore. He slapped the signaler's back and grinned, his white teeth contrasted against his dark face.

'Good work boy, good work. Major, let's increase the pace. I want the gap closed so we can finally get this filthy pig who has sold his faith to the American dollar. Keep an eye on what the mice tell us and see if we can't triangulate him even better.'

The file of hunters continued with their advance through the dark mountain passages, their pace quick and every man more alert as they closed the distance with their target. Hashemi was stretching his gait as much as he could, struggling to keep up with the super-fit Quds trainees. His breathing became ragged and he silently cursed the General and his insistence on chasing down the traitor personally. With Tehran's help, they could have flooded the mountain with troops and VAJA officers, giving the traitor not one square inch of free terrain. But no; here he was like a damned donkey, struggling with his load and going over on his ankles in the loose rocks and ice under his feet. He glanced over his shoulder and saw that Captain Dabiri was almost staggering as he too, fought the effects of the pace, altitude and load he was carrying. Neither man had spent any time in the countryside let alone the mountains and Hashemi moaned as his thighs burned in protest ascending a small rise. The Quds men gave no indication that they even registered the change in terrain, maintaining their blistering pace as they strode up the incline.

Zana glanced back and could barely make out the VAJA officers at the rear of the pack. His lip curled in a sneer as he watched them struggling up the rise, their legs buckling underneath them as they strained to keep pace with the formation. A part of him was enjoying the men's suffering, relishing the pain the officers were experiencing that was no doubt bringing them down from their lofty positions as the Republic's guardians of security. *Security!* These idiots had no idea what keeping a nation secure really meant. Zana and his fellow Quds operatives had been keeping the Republic safe for decades, removing threats and enemies abroad *before* VAJA had come into existence. He spat his disdain onto the rocky track and turned his attention once more, back to the traitor Ardavan. Less than a kilometer and a-half and Zana would have him. He whispered to the man in front to pass the message forward to pick up the pace. It was time to finish this.

Hashemi could feel his legs buckling beneath him as his muscles finally surrendered to the fatigue and refused to drive him forward, his gait now a series of staggers and stumbles on the loose rocks of the small track. His mouth was wide open and his breathing loud and rasping as he attempted to suck in as much air as possible to feed his oxygen-starved muscles. But it was to no avail. As he leaned forward to climb another small rise, his legs gave way and he tumbled to the ground, yelping in pain as his body slammed against the sharp rocks. Moaning in agony, he rolled over and shrugged himself loose from his pack just as Captain Dabiri reached him. The Captain bent over and stretched out a hand for Hashemi to grasp but Hashemi could see that the Captain didn't have the strength or the balance to haul him to his feet. He waved the hand away and closed his eyes, sucking in huge gasps of air as he ran his hands over his legs, convinced that he had broken something in the fall. His quick inspection seemed to indicate that there were no significant injuries, but he had neither the energy nor motivation to pick himself up off the ground. He could hear Dabiri trying to say something and opened his eyes to look at his subordinate.

'Colonel... I can't see... the rest... the men... can't see.'

Hashemi groaned as the significance of this statement hit him: General Shir-Del wouldn't wait for them. He was too close and too invested in the hunt to even consider coming back to find them. No, the General would carry on with the mission and then come back for them when he had captured Ardavan. They were on their own. Hashemi struggled to a sitting position and placed his hand on Dabiri's shoulder.

'The General won't be coming back Dabiri. He's too close to Ardavan to give up the lead. We have to think about ourselves now and not just about our current situation. Take your pack off and rest for a moment.' He watched as the Captain shrugged off his pack and lowered it to the ground before sitting on it and turning his attention back to Hashemi. The Colonel continued.

'I am going to call Tehran. This madness has gone on long enough. I am sure General Shir-Del has the Republic's best interests at heart, but I think he has become blinded by obsession and hasn't considered the consequences if the traitor escapes.'

The Captain nodded and pulled his hood up in an attempt to ward off the biting wind. 'Yes Sir. I completely agree. If we don't tell Headquarters now it might be too late.'

Hashemi pulled off his gloves, reached into an internal pocket of his jacket and retrieved his phone. He powered the device up and waited for several moments, his face illuminated by the light from the yellow screen, before uttering a string of profanities. Dabiri looked up.

'What's wrong Sir?'

'The signal is too weak to... no wait, it's getting better. Not quite there but it might just go through.' With that, Hashemi stood, accessed the contact he was looking for and made the call. He smiled as it was answered after only several rings and he spoke into the handset, giving his name and asking to speak with General Khadem. His smile faded as he found himself repeating his request several times. He swore again as he terminated the call, moved a few steps up the mountain and tried again. This time he managed to at least get his request through before the signal dropped and he stared at the handset, watching the fluctuating connection strength. He looked at Dabiri.

'Come on, let's get to the top of this slope and see if the signal improves. Leave the packs here, we can always come back for them, just bring your weapon.' He turned and led his subordinate up the loose scree of the slope, checking the status of the phone every so often.

He knew that once his call went through, he and Dabiri could expect to see their VAJA colleagues within a couple of hours and this whole mess no longer any part of their responsibility. He just needed to get one call through to his General to make this happen.

Zana hurried forward and knelt beside the signaler as the younger soldier looked into his eyes.

'Another transmission Sir, well... several transmissions to be accurate, but coming from behind us, the way we came.' The signaler paused and shook his head. 'There's no way the traitor could have doubled back and fooled us again, is there General?'

Zana opened his mouth to order the soldiers to turn back when the thought came to him that the signaler was right; there was no conceivable way that Ardavan could have achieved this but if not Ardavan, then who had sent the transmissions? A heavy feeling in his stomach took root as he considered the possibility that the Americans were now on the mountain and coming at them from the rear. He stormed his way to the back of the file to sound Hashemi out regarding this matter but stopped short when he saw that there was no sign of the VAJA men. He turned to the last soldier who was stood watching him.

'Where are the VAJA officers?'

The soldier indicated with his head back down the steep slope they had just ascended. 'They began falling back some time ago General. I pushed them along as best as I could, but they are weak and unaccustomed to the mountains. I haven't seen them for some time now.'

Zana swore and was about to head down the slope himself when he stopped as the realization struck him that it wasn't Ardavan or the Americans who had sent the transmissions. It was Hashemi. He had called

Tehran. The General's rage burned in his chest at the betrayal. He turned back to the soldier.

'Tell everyone to remain here until I come back.' Without waiting for an answer, he strode down the steep track, his fury lending him strength and energy as he headed back towards the VAJA officers. He had only descended a hundred meters or so when he heard the voices carrying up the hill towards him. His lip curled in disgust at the men's lack of tactical awareness. What if he had been an American CIA team looking for them? *Idiots.* As he closed the gap, he saw the outline of the two security officers as they clambered up the slope. Zana waited until he was only a matter of a few feet in front of them before he spoke.

'Hashemi. What's the problem? Why are you so far behind? And where the hell are your packs?'

Hashemi gave an involuntary start as the General's presence surprised him. 'General Shir-Del… I… we fell behind and I hurt myself… so…'

'Stop whining man. Who gave you the authority to just give up and sit down like a couple of lazy children?'

Hashemi felt his anger rise. 'General, as an officer of VAJA I am obligated to inform you that your madness is now coming to an end. I have called Tehran and am making them aware of our situation even as we speak so you will shortly be relieved of your responsibilities. I'm sorry General, but this insanity must come to an end.'

Hashemi's use of the present tense was not lost on Zana. 'What do you mean *making them aware*? I thought you said you'd called them?'

Hashemi sighed. 'I did, but only managed to get through who I was and who I needed to speak with before the signal dropped. That's why we're still climbing this infernal mountain, to look for a better signal.'

Zana smiled. 'Let me help you with that.'

The four gunshots echoed around the mountain and the two VAJA officers tumbled back down the steep slope, their bodies bouncing, spinning and cartwheeling as their momentum gathered before they disappeared over the edge of a precipice. Zana lowered his carbine and shook his head in reaction to the ringing in his ears. With a final glance in the direction of the precipice, he turned and began to make his way back up the mountain, his stride strong and confident as he returned to the small column of men awaiting him. He saw the Major rushing towards him, his rifle ready in the shoulder but lowered once he identified Zana.

'General, we heard the shots and I came to…'

'Fine, Major. Everything is fine. Turns out Ardavan wasn't our only traitor but I'm happy to report that he is our sole focus once again.'

The Major looked uncertain and gazed past Zana into the darkness beyond. Zana grabbed the younger officer's shoulder and leaned in until their faces were almost touching.

'There's nothing to see Major. They're dead. They were traitors. Now, let's finish what we came here to do. If you heard the shots, then so did Ardavan and the last thing I need is for him to gain any further lead on us. Understand?'

The Major gave one final glance back down the slope before nodding.

'Yes General. I'll get the men moving right away.'

With that, the Major jogged back to the front of the file and before long they were making rapid progress as they focused once again on the capture of their quarry. Zana felt no regrets at killing the VAJA men; they'd chosen their own fate the moment they'd decided to call their Headquarters. He'd told them in clear terms that even a child could have understood. But they'd opted to ignore his warning and were dead because of their weakness and lack of faith in him. Well, neither of them would make that mistake again, that was for sure. As he leaned into another steep incline, Zana looked up as he felt something on his face. *Snow.* He smiled as he realized that this might help them track Ardavan easier. Jogging to the soldier in front of him, he told him to pass the message forward to open up the pace even further.

It was time to end this.

17

ZAGROS MOUNTAINS, IRAN

The snow stung Karim's face as a strong gust of wind buffeted him. He'd given Vic the signal at RV 2 and the CIA officer would now know Karim needed his help. Leaning into the steep incline, he kept his stride wide, powering up the rocky slope determined to maintain the lead on his pursuers. Glancing back at Affan, he saw that the boy was keeping up, arms pumping as he propelled himself up the hill. Karim knew that he had to get as much distance as he could under his belt to help the Americans when they came. Vic had made it clear during their planning of the exfil that they had to plan for the worst which was that the US would not sanction a military operation into Iran but probably *would* give permission for a brief incursion to get their Asset out. And that's what Karim had to assume was happening now. So in reality, despite his pursuers, everything was going according to plan. The only thing that hadn't been factored in was the deployment of the sensors ahead of them. But as he had no way of identifying where these were, Karim's only option was to keep going and hope that they either missed the screen completely or were extracted by the Americans before the Quds could react to the sensors' alerts.

Turning back to check on the boy, Karim froze as something caught his attention in the darkness below. He ignored the boy's grunt of protest as he bumped into him and remained focused on watching the area where he'd thought he'd seen something. *There!* He growled as he recognized immediately the faint glow from a set of night-vision goggles. The fact that he could see this, however faint, meant that his hunters were very close. He cursed as the realization struck him that his pursuers would be on top of him within the hour. Karim's mind raced as he explored what possibilities were open to him. He couldn't just hope to outrun them; they'd already shown that they could maintain an impressive pace. No, he needed to slow them down again. Tie them up for a while in order to give him a chance to get ahead. He turned back to face the boy.

'Affan, I need your help. Here's what we're going to do.'

He briefed the boy and watched his reaction as he took Karim's instructions. Despite the fact that Affan would effectively be the bait for his trap, he could see that the boy was unfazed by the risk. Karim took him gently by the shoulders.

'Listen. I am asking a lot of you. I know this and if you can't do it, I will understand. But if you agree to it, there is no backing out. Once we set this in motion, it's all or nothing, do you understand me Affan?' He watched as the boy nodded solemnly and pointed to the pistol holstered on Karim's thigh.

'I understand sir. Just show me how to use the gun and I will be ready.'

Karim smiled softly in response to the boy's courage. He removed the pistol and showed Affan the basics that he would need to know in order to fire the weapon. He removed the magazine, unloaded the weapon then made Affan run through the drill several times before he was satisfied. He made the pistol ready again and handed it to the boy.

'That's it. All you do now is point and shoot so don't touch that trigger until I give the signal, understand?'

The boy nodded and stood looking at Karim, the pistol large in his small hands. Karim patted his shoulder then set off among the rocks, stopping every so often to secure a chem-light to a rock along the way. This would be Affan's route out of the area once he had finished his part. The boy would follow the trail of lights, collecting them as he went, before meeting back up with Karim. For his part, Karim intended another ambush but with a view to luring more of his hunters in and levelling the playing field a little. He needed to give his pursuers serious pause to provide him and Affan as much time as possible to get ahead. When he'd finished marking Affan's escape route, Karim made his way down the mountain and towards his pursuers, slowing his progress in order to remain undetected. He gave a small grunt of triumph when he identified the ravine that he'd been looking for. He'd remembered crossing it earlier with Affan and as soon as he'd worked out a rough plan, knew that this gully would be perfect for his requirements.

He threw off his pack and retrieved three items from it, before closing the flap and putting it back on. In the green hue of his night vision goggles, he surveyed the ravine for a moment before heading uphill and emplacing the first of his devices, an M18 Claymore mine. The Quds used this American model in favor of the Russian ones that conventional forces were issued because of the better reliability of the M18. With the Claymore set, Karim unspooled the line and walked backwards across the rocky ground to a position slightly above the emplaced mine. He put down the remainder of the line and the firing device, broke open an infra-red chem-light and marked the spot, ensuring that only the tip of the light showed. He picked his way between the rocks to another spot further downhill and repeated the procedure before carrying out the same action a third time. He then made his way back up to the shelter of a large rock above the herder's track and removed his small flashlight with the red filter and waited.

It was the clatter of a small rock skipping down the mountain that alerted him first. Peering around the cover of his own rock, Karim felt his pulse accelerate as he watched the lead man striding down the track. Throwing himself back into cover, Karim pointed his small torch up the mountain and turned it on, moving it around in small circles. The response was instant as the shot from the pistol shattered the silence. Below him, the Quds operatives began yelling commands and directions. Several bursts of rifle fire raked the mountain, green tracer smashing off rocks and ricocheting in crazed directions. Affan, as briefed, let off a shot every couple of seconds in the general direction of the hunters and from below, Karim could hear the orders given for a team to head up and outflank the shooter. He nodded to himself. His plan was working. Keeping as low to the ground as he could, Karim made his way to the first claymore and positioned himself to see into the gully below. Bullets were still being fired up the mountain from the hunters below, but Karim recognized that this was the fire support from the herders' track attempting to pin the shooter down while their flanking troops moved into position. Karim had picked the spot because he knew that the ravine would be irresistible to flanking troops, providing them cover as they closed on their target. His thoughts were interrupted as the first of the troops made their way up the gully, followed closely by the others. Karim counted eight men before he picked up the firing device and hit it three times in rapid succession. The explosion was loud and briefly lit up the small area, but Karim was already on the move, slithering his way between the rocks to the second position. The shouting and screaming behind him was the only indicator he needed that his strike had been a success. On reaching the second claymore, he barely had time to pick up the firing device before the first of the retreating soldiers staggered down the slope below him. He allowed five men to pass before detonating, the lethal projectiles of the claymore taking out another three men. Again, he was up and scrambling through the rocks to the final location and made it just as four soldiers burst out of the ravine below him. He closed his eyes, struck the firing device and flinched at the explosion which was much closer than the others had been. Opening his eyes, he dropped the firing device and brought his carbine up on aim, turned on the laser sight and trained the infra-red beam on the survivors as they stumbled below him. His suppressor dulled much of the noise, but he took nothing for granted and once the last body had struck the ground, he was off, snaking his way between rocks as the weight of fire from the hunters on the track scoured the side of the mountain. He could hear the shouts and although he couldn't identify specific words, the confusion and panic were evident as the fire support group tried to determine what was going on. Karim was breathing heavily, gasping in deep intakes of air as he powered his way back up the mountain, determined to make good on the chaos below. After some time, he reached the point he'd marked earlier and pulled the chem-light from the rock just as Affan burst into the small clearing. Karim nodded and held out his hand, taking his pistol back, putting it into the holster and accepting the bunch of chem-lights from the boy. He brushed snow from the boy's hair and lifted up his night vision goggles so that Affan could see his face.

'Well done Affan. Very well done. Now we need to move.'

He noted the boy's wide eyes and chest heaving with exertion but also the small nod of acknowledgement. Karim pulled his NVGs back on and studied the area in front of him for a brief moment before striding out, intent on getting as much distance as he could between them and the Quds Force, capitalizing on their panic and chaos while it remained.

Which wouldn't be for much longer.

18

ZAGROS MOUNTAINS, IRAN

Ned looked back at Vic and nodded. 'Sounded like explosions and gunfire to me.'

Vic brought the infra-red binoculars up to his face and scanned the mountain ahead of him once again. 'I've still got nothing.'

The men were quiet as Vic continued to watch the area where they'd heard the explosions and gunfire emanating from. As faint as it had been, he was pretty confident that it had been the sound of automatic weapons. Which meant that Seven was indeed, being chased through the mountain passes by a hostile force. He lowered the binoculars and sat next to Ned.

'Okay, we gotta start looking at the real possibility the Asset's coming out very hot. He knows my visual and to keep coming towards it, so we just have to make sure we keep the bad guys at bay until we've got him.'

Ned nodded. 'And until we get to the LZ.'

'Yep. This might get... what did you call it earlier? ...challenging.'

Ned gave a small laugh. 'Might do brother. Might do. But hell, let's face it, that's why we're here. Wouldn't be as much fun otherwise, would it? What do you think about support options?'

Vic was quiet for several moments as he considered the question. 'I think we will need to be in really deep shit before Washington gives the okay for aerial assets over Iran.'

'That's what I thought. Okay, so it's just us chickens. Plan?'

'Still the same. We'll keep moving forward, hopefully get to Seven quickly, hold off the hunters and scoot back to the LZ.'

It was Ned's turn to remain silent as he pondered the CIA officer's statement. 'Good plan Vic, so long as they don't call up the cavalry and bring in air support. That's when it will get *challenging*.'

Vic laughed and slapped Ned on the shoulder. 'Couldn't have said it better myself. Come on, let's get going before this snow starts covering us up.'

The men got to their feet and joined the rest of the team, heading off in single file, weaving between rock formations and boulders as they made their way east. Wiping the snow from his face Vic's mind raced as he tried to find a better way out of their predicament. Conducting a fighting withdrawal through mountainous terrain for over three kilometers was not his idea of a great exfil plan but it was all he could come up with. When he'd last checked in with Bill, the Station Chief had been very clear about the limited options Vic and the team would have for support; Washington had no appetite to start a ground war with Iran, Asset or no Asset. That said, the fact that Seven had identified CONUS as the target for a Quds operation was a factor that couldn't be dismissed. Vic just hoped that this might sway the decision makers if the shit really hit the fan. He looked up as the man in front of him slowed and leaned into Vic to whisper.

'From Dwight, he's getting multiple hits on communications ahead of us, still thinks it's person to person.'

Vic nodded and the Delta soldier moved back to his place in the line. Frowning as he thought about the statement, Vic again wondered why the comms signatures that they were picking up were local and low projection, no sign of a transmission that would indicate any messages being relayed out of the area. He still couldn't figure out why this might be. Everything he knew about the Quds and VAJA told him that there was something really off-key with the way the hunt for Seven was being conducted up here. Standard practice would be for the Iranians to flood the mountains with troops, cutting off every conceivable escape route. But they hadn't. And since the arrival of that first couple of helicopters, no aircraft other than the drone had been picked up. *What the hell are they up to?* As his foot skidded on a patch of ice, Vic shook his musings from his head and sought to concentrate on the route ahead.

Ned scanned the area ahead of him with the thermal-imaging scope but saw no heat signatures and dropped it to dangle from the cord around his neck. He pulled down the tubes of his NVGs and increased his pace to catch up with the man in front. He'd been vigilant since hearing the gunfire, well aware that the claustrophobic nature of these winding passes they transited would give them very little warning of an approaching enemy. Hell, they could literally bump right into each other before anybody had a chance to react. As he walked, he stretched his neck and grimaced, the dull throb of the old injury a regular companion. The doctors had removed all the shrapnel but the trauma to the muscles and tendons in his neck had taken some time to heal and whenever it was cold and damp, the legacy of the injury came back to remind him how lucky he'd been.

131

Four years before, an RPG from some other fucking fanatic group in Niger. The tough, armored Toyota Land Cruiser not quite tough enough to deflect the Soviet warhead. A neck and arm full of shrapnel, the screaming of the interpreter, the confident commands of his team, the stink of burning leather seats, his blood hot as it poured down his arm and soaked his shirt. But he'd been lucky. Farouk, the interpreter, not so. Poor kid had died in agony, screaming and sobbing for his mother even as the team medic tried to staunch the blood pouring out of him. And Big Mac; paralyzed from the waist down where the shrapnel hit his spine. Ned remembered the incident as much for Cathy's reaction to it. He'd had his share of knocks and bumps before, but she'd taken that one badly. It was the only time he'd ever heard her mention the fear she had of him dying in some god-forsaken place she couldn't even pronounce and leaving her and the girls alone in the world. He'd said all the right things and recovered much faster than the Doc's prognosis, but he'd always remembered her reaction.

And here he was, in the mountains of Iran on a deniable operation with nothing to say that he was an American soldier. Being wounded and captured here would be as bad as he could imagine. Torture and interrogation would be immediate. Then the public humiliations; paraded in front of the world's media, driven in a cage around the streets of Tehran. Then, as the US government couldn't claim him as one of their own, he'd be hanged. Publicly. A last humiliation for a fierce and proud warrior. His earlier thoughts about his family came to the fore once again and Ned found himself feeling emotional. *What the fuck am I doing to them? How long can I really expect them to put up with this?* The thought of his family being briefed by some anonymous State Department official or a Pentagon representative

132

that their husband and father had been arrested in Iran and they could probably expect to see some very tough things was almost more than he could bear. A calm descended upon him and with it a sense of resolve. *This is it. After this, I'm done. I'll stretch out that stint at Bragg and use the time to find something in the private sector.* Ned knew he wouldn't struggle for work; almost all former Delta guys were doing pretty good in the private sector. But a lot of that work revolved around private security, practically doing the same dangerous shit for a lot more money but with none of the support network from the Big Green Machine: the US Military. He thought back to the Benghazi incident where the US Ambassador and some former Special Ops guys working for GRS had been killed. If he was leaving Delta, he didn't intend merely switching his uniform for a polo shirt and some khakis and calling himself a *consultant.* No, he needed something sustainable, US-based with maybe some travel but not excessive. This was about his family now. He'd had his time, cutting around the globe taking care of business. It was their time now. A smile came to his face as he imagined Cathy's joy when he broke the news to her and the girls. The feeling he experienced as he pictured this scenario was enough to convince him that he was doing the right thing. Nodding to himself in affirmation, Ned pushed the thoughts to one side and focused on the task at hand. There would be plenty of time to enjoy his decision, but it would have to wait until he was back on safe ground, away from these mountains and the threat they were walking directly towards. He strode forward and tapped the man in front on the shoulder to get his attention. When the man turned, Ned leaned in and whispered. 'Pass to front man, break at the next available spot.' As the message went forward, Ned passed it along to the man behind, ensuring the team was aware of what was happening. Back in line, Ned's earlier decision came back to dominate his thoughts and he recognized that it was a defense mechanism kicking in, his brain telling him how much he was going to miss this, miss being the guy responsible for getting his team in and out of bad places without losing any of them. He shook his head and opened his pace up, determined not to be distracted from the current mission. The rest could wait.

As point man, Randy scanned the area around him with the TI scope and saw no heat signatures. He walked forward and climbed a small pile of rocks, removed his pack, sat down and aimed his carbine out towards their direction of travel. Behind him, he could hear the soft sounds of the rest of the team as they took up positions of cover while they grabbed a power bar or cold drink. He wiped the snow that was accumulating on his face and scanned the area again, but still nothing. Reaching into his top pocket, he pulled out a Clif bar and wolfed it down, the cold and the physical exercise fueling his hunger. His eyes continued to scour the area in front of him, well aware that the enemy could pop up out of nowhere in this morass of passes, ravines and gullies. Not that he could see all that much, the snow and the dark combining to restrict visibility to the minimum. But still, something was always better than nothing and his regular sweeps with the TI scope would pick up anything alive that was moving through the area. Finishing off the last of his bar, he scrunched the wrapper up and stowed it securely in his pocket, the habit of leaving no trace in their operational area practically muscle memory now. Randy rubbed his eyes as a wave of tiredness swept over him. He was tired all the time these days and gave a rueful grin as he considered the impact age was starting to have on him. His mind was drawn back to the young Ranger he once was, staggering between checkpoints on the Long Walk; the grueling forty-mile ruck march during Delta selection. Back then he'd survived on little to no sleep, like all of them had, determined to get through Selection and make it to the Operators' Training Course. Now here he was, barely thirty-five years old and tired and grumpy like an old man. He knew, of course, that he was fine, that it was just the non-stop tempo of operations that was catching up with him. That a couple of days out of the field, a few *brewskis* and a dip in a swimming pool and he'd be good as new. He smiled as a memory of a break he'd taken last year came to mind. Him, Chuck Stevens and Ned grabbing a couple of rooms at the Grand Millenium in Sulaimaniyah and hitting it *hard*. Chuck had almost been kicked out of the hotel for his constant marriage proposals to the receptionist. *Fuck, that was funny.* They'd had a great couple of days before heading back across the border and straight into hunting the ISIS leadership that was starting to fragment and escape from Syria. His smile faded as he recalled that it was little more than a week after their return that Chuck was killed. ISIS sniper on the front line near Raqqa. One shot, clean through the head. Chuck wouldn't have known a thing. *Was probably still thinking about that hot receptionist when he'd been hit.* Randy sighed and did another sweep with the scope, but the area was still clear. He heard a sound behind him and turned as he felt his leg being patted. He smiled as he saw Ned's big grin in the faint green glow of the Master Sergeant's NVGs. Ned spoke quietly.

'Okay Red let's get moving. Quicker we get this fucking Asset off the mountain the happier I'll be.'

Randy nodded and shrugged on his pack, shuffled down the small rise and took his position at the head of the file, facing forward. Several moments later a tap on his shoulder told him that the team was ready. Without looking back, he pulled down his NVGs and walked off into the night, followed by the rest of the squad who maintained a small gap between each man. After some time, Randy slowed the pace as he negotiated around a large rock formation that blocked their route. Once he had cleared it, he took a knee a short distance in front of the obstacle and waited until the whole team had cleared it before leading them forward. He continued his sweeps with the TI scope and was grateful for the comfort the device provided him when natural visibility was practically zero. The snow and the darkness conspiring to conceal the landscape around them.

Which is why even the last man to negotiate the rocky obstacle hadn't seen the cylindrical object with the small antennae poking out of the snow, despite almost placing his hand upon it as he scrambled over the boulders.

19

ZAGROS MOUNTAINS, IRAN

The white noise in Zana's head refused to dissipate, a constant hum of static as he looked at the sight before him. Nine bodies laid in a single file to the side of the track, the snow already beginning to shroud the silent forms. Nine bodies. Nine of his men killed in one engagement by the traitor Ardavan. *Nine.* And more casualties who were combat ineffective. Including the dead and wounded from Ardavan's first trap, Zana had lost more than half of his men to the American spy. The humming in his head continued until slowly, his senses returned, and he looked around him. His men were in shock, staring fixedly at the corpses of their dead colleagues that they had just recovered from the side of the mountain. Friends and fellow operatives that only half an hour before, had been alive like them. He caught the Major's eye but got no response other than a blank stare and a slight curling of the lip. Zana felt his shock turning to anger and welcomed the healthier emotion. Drawing his pistol, he strode down the path until he was directly in front of the Major and the rest of the men. He let the pistol hang loose by his side as he tried to catch each man's gaze.

'Enough. They are dead. They cannot get any more dead. But each second we waste mourning their passing gives the traitor who killed them a better chance of escape. Let their deaths not be in vain. Let's catch the man who did this and see him hanged in Sabalan Square, pissing his pants and kicking his legs like a frog.' He paused as he surveyed the men's reactions. One or two of them gave sidewards glances at their peers, looking for reassurance but Zana was heartened to see the majority of the men nodding in agreement. He'd hoped to retain their loyalty. They were, after all, Quds Force and Palang trainees at that. He pointed the pistol in the direction that Ardavan had disappeared into. 'We have to go, and we have to go now before the traitor gets away.' He frowned in annoyance as the signaler stepped out of line.

'General, Sir…'

Zana growled. 'Whatever it is, it can wait. We need to move.'

'But General, it's…'

Zana closed the gap in two strides and thrust his face into that of the younger soldier.

'Are you deaf? Did the explosions affect your hearing or your brain? I said move, so let's move.' He spun on his heel but was halted by the soldier's persistence.

'General Sir. I am sorry but this is very important.'

Zana turned back to face the signaler and cocked the hammer back on the pistol as he tilted his head to one side. 'Very well. Tell me what is so important that you are determined to see the traitor escape from us.'

There was a brief silence as the signaler looked over at the Major before he answered in a trembling voice.

'It's the *mice* General. The sensors. We've got activity from one of them.'

Zana beckoned. 'Show me.'

The radio operator held up the small device so that the General could see the screen clearly.

'Here Sir, two minutes ago, multiple individuals passed this sensor.'

Zana nodded. 'How many?'

'At least ten, possibly twelve.'

Zana studied the screen and pointed to the picture of the map that was displayed. 'How far?'

The signaler studied the screen for a moment. 'Approximately three kilometers.'

Zana cursed and turned away as his mind assimilated the information. He would guess that the traitor Ardavan had probably made a good kilometer in distance since they'd walked into his trap. That meant he was closing in with his American masters much quicker than Zana and his Quds operatives could hope to. He thought about calling Tehran, getting the air support that would bring the matter to a swift end. Unless he requested immediate support, the traitor would escape.

He had failed. Zana could feel the eyes of the men upon him as he pulled his Sat-phone out and powered up the device. He was just about to access the contacts list when a thought came to him. As he let it run its course, he could feel his excitement building. Maybe he didn't have to involve Tehran after all. Maybe, just *maybe*, he could still bring the traitor in himself. Or at least with a little help. He walked out of earshot from his men and dialed a number from memory. It was answered within three rings and he smiled at the rough, deep voice on the other end of the line. In his best Russian, Zana replied to the voice.

'Sergeii, it is Zana. How would you like to kill some Americans?'

20

SIRWAN, EASTERN IRAQ

Sergeii Antonovich terminated the call and looked down at his notes in the light of the small table lamp. His breath fogged in the frigid air of the unheated tent, but the cold did not bother him. Russia was far colder than Iraq. He ran his hand over the cropped bristles that grew in sparse clumps on his balding head as he came to terms with the Iranian's information. If Zana was correct, there was a CIA team currently operating illegally in Iran, trying to collect an Asset on his way out. And that team was a short helicopter ride from Sergeii's current location. A very *short* helicopter ride. The Russian rested his chin on his hands as he considered his options. He knew he was going, that much was clear, but how? And who should he take? He couldn't talk to Moscow about this; would never get the approval but as head of Wagner Group Security operations in the region, Sergeii had a lot of autonomy over the actions of his men. And vulnerable Americans? Too good an opportunity to pass up. He fingered the scar above his eyebrow as his mind drifted back to the Conoco massacre he'd barely survived.

After he'd recovered from his surgeries in Moscow, Sergeii had sworn that he would find a way to hurt the Americans, *any* Americans, for the death of so many of his men. As soon as he left hospital, Sergeii had contacted his connection at the FSB and asked what the hell had gone wrong at the Conoco plant. His contact told him that Moscow had made it clear to Washington that the approaching troops were Russian and not ISIS, but the Americans had chosen to engage anyway. His anger had risen as the memory of the massacre returned and the dozens of men Sergeii had lost that day. There had been a few moments during the battle when he was sure they were going to win, but the American air support had ended that with a lethal finality. He'd been struck by shrapnel in his head and chest and knocked unconscious, waking hours later in a field hospital before his repatriation to Russia. A small mercy some might say but for Sergeii, the horrors and humiliation of that day remained ingrained in his mind, a mental movie that ran and ran, unprompted, every day since. With no wife or family to keep him in Russia, he had volunteered to return to Iraq with Wagner and was promoted for his loyalty.

Sergeii had been a decorated soldier with the 45th Spetsnaz Airborne Brigade when he'd been approached by a Colonel from the FSB and asked if he would volunteer to deploy on a sensitive mission abroad. Of course, in Russia the term *volunteer* isn't quite the same as in western countries, no real notion of choice being factored into the word. So Sergeii had joined several hundred other soldiers who, on paper at least, left the military to work for a private security company; Wagner Group. In truth, the company was a mere flag of convenience that enabled Moscow to deploy military forces under the guise of stabilization security personnel. And it was working. Even the salaries were good. But the fighting could be tough, ISIS surprising many hardened Spetsnaz soldiers with their fanatical zeal and willingness to die. But Sergeii loved it. Loved being part of his motherland's expansion across the globe, clawing back the influence that the mighty Russia once had before the puppet Gorbachev destroyed it. But the Conoco massacre had left Sergeii with a thirst for vengeance that he had yet to sate. Revenge for lost friends and colleagues slaughtered by bloodthirsty Americans. He looked down at his notebook and formed a plan in his mind.

***

As he walked over to the main operations tent, Sergeii knew who he would be taking with him. Good, trusted men who felt the same way he did about the murders of their colleagues. The pilots too, could be trusted on such a sensitive mission having proved their discretion many times before. But there was no time to waste; he had no doubts that the CIA team would stay in Iran any longer than was absolutely necessary, so he knew he was on a clock. As he ducked under the flap of the tent, he saw Gregor and Pasha and nodded to both men.

'Pasha, go grab Viktor and Arkady and the pilots. We need to be airborne in ten for a quick mission into the mountains.'

Sergeii did not wait for a response but opened a laptop up and accessed a mapping screen, keying in coordinates until he found what he was looking for. He looked up as several men entered and he turned the computer screen so that they could see it.

'This is where we are going. Yes, it is Iran. Yes, it is the mountains. And yes, there will be an engagement. But gentlemen, it is an American team we are hunting. Twelve of them. An American CIA team trying to get an Asset across the border. We won't get another chance like this.'

There was a moment's silence until one of the pilots spoke.

'What about air defenses Sergeii? Won't the Iranians send aircraft to intercept us?'

Sergeii shook his head. 'No. I am in communication with the Iranian General on the ground who has asked me for our help.'

He could see the mood among the team lighten instantly. The prospect of hunting Americans with the blessing of the Iranians now one to look forward to. Sergeii pointed at the digital mapping and continued.

'But we have very little time. The General gave me the last known location of the Americans which was *here*, but that was ten minutes ago. However, we know they are heading east and on foot which means if we insert *here*, we have a good chance of ambushing them.'

He looked up at the men and was pleased to see the nods of acceptance of the plan. Looking down at his watch he continued with his brief.

'Okay. Five minutes to prepare then be at the helicopter. I would of course, love to take more men but the soldiers and pilots in this room at the moment are the only ones that I trust with such a sensitive mission. I'll brief full details on the pad, so move your arses and see you at the helicopters.'

The men scrambled from their chairs and exited the tent, jogging back to their own accommodations. Sergeii knew they would all be ready in time. Like him, they were all former Spetsnaz and their weapons and equipment would already be packed for a rapid move. He made his way back to his own tent and donned his winter jacket and tactical vest before shrugging on his pack. There was little to no weight in the pack, only the means to survive for a short period should something go very wrong. But he didn't anticipate anything going wrong. Hunting Americans who were conducting an illegal operation in a nation that was giving Sergeii their permission to do so was nothing short of a gift. While Sergeii was well aware that his small team was outnumbered, they were one of the most experienced special forces teams on the planet in his opinion. Each man had seen action in the Caucasus, Chechnya, Ukraine, Syria and Iraq as well as countless clandestine operations abroad on behalf of the FSB. Hardened combatants but also intelligent men capable of independent thought and action. And they would have the element of surprise on their side. The CIA team would, like all Americans, place a heavy emphasis on technology whereas his men preferred old-fashioned soldiering skills to close with the enemy. And with Pasha on the sniper rifle, the Americans would not know what was happening until it was too late. With a last check of his equipment, Sergeii strode out of his tent and jogged towards the helicopter pad where he could hear the whine of the *Krokodil*, the Mi-24 gunship, the reptilian nickname a reference to the camouflage scheme of the aircraft. A sturdy and reliable beast, Sergeii had used this model for most of his military career and the pilots he had chosen were second to none, experienced, confident and extremely capable.

As he arrived at the pad, the rest of his team jogged over to join him. He nodded at Pasha as the sniper patted his Chukavin rifle with its fitted suppressor. Sergeii knew that the rifle had been modified to fire the high-powered Laupa rounds and was sure they would be grateful for this in the hours to come. One of the pilots walked over and discussed the landing site options with Sergeii, eventually reaching an accord that would place them in the Americans' path but out of sight and, hopefully, earshot. They discussed the exfil options and settled on a different site several kilometers east of their insertion point. The pilot returned to the helicopter and climbed aboard as Sergeii briefed the team on the insertion plan then carried out a radio check with each of them. With nothing more to say, Sergeii led the group to the open door of the helicopter and waited until they had all boarded before getting in himself. The co-pilot closed the door and Sergeii pulled on the headphones, listening to the pilots talking to one another. The co-pilot informed Sergeii that their intelligence officer had confirmed that there were no other aircraft expected in their airspace for the duration of their operation, from the Iraqi side at least. As the helicopter lifted into the air, Sergeii closed his eyes and went through his usual routine of running through the entire operation in his head, imagining every possible scenario and what he would do to achieve it. He considered some of the problems they might encounter but again, there was nothing unique to this situation that he and his men had not experienced at some point before. The last thought relaxed him, and he leaned back against the seat and stretched his neck, feeling the helicopter gain speed as it accelerated away from the camp.

He had almost drifted to sleep when the co-pilot gave the one-minute warning. Sergeii looked at the rest of the team and saw them pull off their own headphones and replace them on the backs of their seats. Each man patted their equipment making sure nothing was loose, unfastened or had fallen open during the flight. Sergeii did the same and had just finished when the co-pilot strode past him and opened the door, a freezing wind attacking the passengers almost instantly. Sergeii activated his Night Vision Goggles and adjusted the relief until his sight picture was clear. The co-pilot leaned out of the door and gave an elevation countdown to the pilot pulling his head back in just before they hit the ground with a soft landing. Sergeii was first out of the door and sprinted towards the cover of a cluster of rocks where he knelt with his carbine aimed in front of him.

145

Several seconds later he heard the increase in noise from the helicopter and he was buffeted from behind, almost falling forward from the gust as the machine became airborne once again. In the silence that followed, each of his team scrutinized the area around them for any sign that their approach had been compromised. After a few minutes had passed, Sergeii spoke into his mic.

'Let us kill some Americans.'

21

ZAGROS MOUNTAINS, IRAN

Karim could feel the sweat running down his back as he hauled his body up and over the boulder pile that blocked their way. At the top he paused, sure that he had heard something over the blustering wind, before turning and lowering his hand to the boy. Affan grabbed it and Karim pulled him up, turning back to the route ahead the instant the boy was steady on his feet. He was breathing heavily, struggling to suck in enough air to replenish his fatigued muscles. Karim had no idea of how much time he'd bought them with his last trap but whatever time they had, he needed to ensure they made the most of it. They ran where they could, jogged where able, and stumbled and staggered between rock formations and boulder clusters as he set a relentless pace. The snow was falling heavier now, and Karim knew there was a balance to be had between progress and recklessness. With such poor visibility, if either of them broke an ankle or leg, they were as good as dead. Risking a quick glance back at the boy, he was once again impressed by the orphan's tenacity. Karim could see that the boy was utterly exhausted, but he was keeping up, his small limbs buckling under the strain and effort, chest heaving with exertion. For a brief moment, Karim forgot about their plight and was overcome with a wave of affection for Affan, so keen to escape the hell he'd left behind that he would practically run himself into the ground. *Incredible.* He turned back and scanned the route ahead with his NVGs, picking a path between the rocks, keen to keep moving.

From memory, he knew that the map showed a small plateau ahead of them before rising again into a series of small slopes. When he reached it, he increased his pace to take advantage of the rare piece of level ground. As he jogged along what he assumed was the herders' path, he noted with dismay that the track was all but invisible due to the accumulation of snow. Without the track to guide him, he would have to pick the path of least resistance and hope that it was the same route the track followed. He gave regular glances behind him to confirm the boy was keeping up and was gratified to see the waif pushing through the pain and exhaustion he was undoubtedly experiencing. Looking back to the route ahead, Karim saw that they had crossed the small plateau and were once again among slopes and inclines. He slowed the pace and leaned into the first climb, feeling the burn in his thighs as he attacked the slope. Karim wasn't sure how long they could maintain the punishing pace but knew that it was their only chance.

After they'd ascended a third rise, Karim turned to the boy and waited for him to catch up. He pressed on Affan's shoulder and sat down among the rocks. Pulling out his water bottle, he took several deep swallows then passed it to the boy. He used the opportunity to study the orphan and watched as Affan tried to calm his breathing to allow him to drink. Even beneath the bulky jacket Karim had given him, he could see clearly the rapid rise and fall of Affan's chest. But they had made good progress. Yes, the pace had been punishing but they could expect to come across Vic and the Americans at any moment. The thought that his ordeal was almost over gave Karim real hope. The disappointment of General Shir-Del and the shame he would experience would be too much for the General's professional pride, if he lived long enough to feel it. Karim had no doubt that once he succeeded in escaping with the Americans, the General would have to fight very hard to avoid the hangman's noose. Karim waited until he saw that the boy's breathing had recovered before he stood and extended his hand, pulling the youngster to his feet. He lifted his NVGs and leaned in close.

'Affan, you have the strength of a leopard and the heart to match. We are almost there. At any time from this point onwards, we will meet some men. These are my friends and they have come to help us. Do not be afraid. They are here to get us out of this country, something we both want very much, yes?' He smiled at the surprise in the boy's eyes before clapping him on the shoulder. 'Good. Let us begin the final part of our journey my little leopard.' Karim turned and strode out once again, his step lighter as he anticipated his reunion with Vic. He patted the pocket of his jacket to check that his torch with the red filter was still there. It was important; the arranged signals between him and Vic were a series of flashes from their filtered torches and neither would commit to the pick-up if the signals were wrong or not given.

The next rise was steep, and he skidded as the ice underfoot robbed him of purchase. Cursing, he slung his carbine around his back, freeing up his hands and using them to assist him as he scrambled over the sleek rocks. As he bridged the crest of the slope, he was buffeted by a gust of wind that drove the snow hard against his face. He lowered himself to the ground and scanned the area before him, but the visibility was poor. Sighing, he stood up, ready to continue then dropped immediately back down into the cover of the rocks, reaching behind him and pulling the boy down with him. His pulse quickened as he scrutinized the area in front of him for another glimpse of what he had just seen.

The unmistakable sight of a muzzle flash lighting up in the darkness.

22

QUDS FORCE, ZAGROS MOUNTAINS, IRAN

Zana smiled as the signaler repeated the statement.

'The Bear is engaging the Americans.'

The General turned and slapped his Major on the back, a huge grin dominating his face.

'There you are Major. We have the Americans fixed in place thanks to my Russian friends. Get us moving and keep the pace fast; I don't want Sergeii having all the fun!'

The Major returned the smile and barked several commands before turning and leading the small file of men through the snow-covered rocks. His confidence had returned as had his thirst for vengeance for the death of his men. For a moment back there, he had doubted the General's ability to deal with the traitor Ardavan and felt a brief flush of shame at his lack of faith. Now however, they were back on track to finally finish what they started and he for one couldn't wait. He had already decided that if they caught Ardavan alive he was going to use the knife on him. Give the traitor the death he deserved for the slaughter of the Major's men. Long, slow and excruciating. Ardavan would beg for death. The Major pushed the pace as much as he dared in the treacherous conditions, feet skidding and slipping on the ice-covered rocks underfoot. As he gripped his carbine closer to his body a small smile crossed his face as he looked forward to seeing the face of the traitor when he was finally held to account for his crimes by the razor edge of the Major's knife.

Zana pounded up the slope, almost bumping into the back of the man in front of him in his haste to cover the ground as quickly as possible. With the Americans pinned down by Sergeii's team, Zana and his Quds squad could close with the enemy while the Americans were distracted. His adrenalin was pumping, and he found himself becoming frustrated that they couldn't move faster but knew that the Major was going as quickly as he could in the conditions. As they clambered up a steep slope, the man in front of him slipped and would have tumbled down the side of the mountain if Zana hadn't grabbed him and arrested his fall. The younger soldier flashed a grin of thanks and continued scrambling up the rise, as intent as Zana to avenge the death of his comrades. The General felt a welling up of proprietary pride at the dedication of his young soldiers, ready to give their lives to take down a traitor.

When they crested the top of the slope, the Major called a halt while the signaler shuffled back to Zana.

'General, more news from the mice. Two people, higher than us in a west-north-west direction approximately one hundred meters.'

Zana turned his head to face the direction the signaler had given him. *One hundred meters?* That was nothing. In clear conditions, Ardavan could be watching him now. But these were not clear conditions. The wind and the snow had reduced visibility to several meters so even with night vision optics, the traitor couldn't see any more than they could. He turned back to the signaler.

'Tell the Bear to continue to close with the Americans but that we will be engaging a separate target on his left flank. I will communicate with him further when we have killed our traitor.'

He watched as the signaler relayed his information then pause as he received a reply. In Russian, he requested the message to be repeated before turning to the General with a look of surprise and happiness.

'General Shir-Del, Sir. The Bear has killed two of the Americans.'

23

TASK FORCE GREEN, ZAGROS MOUNTAINS, IRAN

Randy crawled over the rocks and boulders, reached out a hand and hauled the body of his fellow operator from the top of the small slope where only seconds ago, the tall Virginian had crumpled to the ground, felled in mid-stride. Randy hadn't known what had caused it, but he'd seen enough men die to recognize the difference between a fall and death from a bullet. He dragged Buck's body closer to him and yelled as he saw the side of the man's face was missing, a hollow mess of blood, bone and cartilage in its place.

'FUCK!' He keyed the mic. 'Buck's gone, Buck's gone. We have hostiles, direction unknown, distance unknown. Possible sniper, I repeat, possible sniper.'

As he listened to the call from Randy, Ned was already running towards the cover of a small mound of rocks when the man in front of him collapsed without warning. Ned cursed and threw himself to the ground, crawling the last few feet to the crumpled figure. He grabbed Mike by the strap of his tac-vest and rolled him over, staring at the giant exit wound in the soldier's neck.

'Mike's gone, Mike's gone. Confirm sniper. I say again, confirm sniper.'

Around him, his men were throwing themselves into any cover they could find, covering their arcs of fire, desperately seeking the enemy who had just killed two of their team. Ned looked around as someone landed beside him.

'Fuck Vic. This ain't good man. This is not good.' He looked out over the rocks before dropping back down again and calling it on the radio. 'We have two KIA, repeat, two KIA. Anyone else hurt?' The replies came quick and clear and to his relief there were no further casualties. Vic slid closer to him.

'Who is it?'

Ned sighed and shook his head. 'Mike and Buck. Gotta be a sniper. And a sniper with a fucking thermal scope at that.'

'I'm sorry Ned. So fucking sorry.'

'Let's leave that for later, we're in the shit now and need to get out of it.' He keyed his mic again. 'Does anybody have a fucking clue where the shooter is firing from?' The negative responses echoed one another until Randy replied.

'I saw Buck go down and I'm gonna call left flank above us.'

'Okay, let's start there. Get the Thermal Imager up and running, see if we can ID any movement. Dwight, you picking up any signals we can DF?'

There was a pause before his comms guy looked for anything they could lock on to and Direction Find back to the enemy.

'Yes Ned, but it's weak, no transmission to… wait. Got it. They're close, very close. Got a bearing and location to within ten.'

'Good. Get with Randy and put some fucking pressure on them while we prepare extraction.' When he received the reply, he turned to Vic. 'Okay, we need to get ready to extract under Randy's covering fire. We take the bodies out with us. We've brought the bags, so we take turns carrying them and providing cover. It'll be a tough schlep back to the LZ but there's no other choice.'

Vic shook his head at the sudden loss of two Delta operators so soon into the mission. He hadn't known the guys to any great degree but knew their team-mates would be devastated at the loss. He also knew that they'd save that devastation for the appropriate time. He'd seen it before, where the anguish of death and loss was compartmentalized, shoved into a little locked box in the operator's head while they focused on completing their mission. His thoughts turned to his Asset. There wasn't a hope in hell of getting Seven out now, if indeed he was still alive. No; the focus had to be on their own extraction and survival. A sniper with a thermal-imaging scope was a force-multiplier; an individual disproportionately more effective than a platoon of soldiers, even in the reduced visibility of the snow. He looked up as Ned spoke.

'Randy and Dwight's gonna rain down some grenade fire on their position on my call. Let's get Mike and Buck ready for the off.' He repeated his intention over the radio and detailed individuals to tasks. The men stayed low as they set about stripping their dead comrades of weapons, ammunition and equipment and distributing the items among the team. The bodies were secured in the bags quickly but with consideration for the friends and team-mates they once were. Ned gave a nod to Randy as the operators assigned to the bodies knelt, ready to lift once the grenade team started their work. Randy returned the nod and he and Dwight put the M320 grenade launchers into their shoulders. Ned waited until the dull retort of the first grenade being fired reached his ears before giving the command. 'GO. GO.

GO.' He took point and led the team out of their cover just as the first grenade exploded and a brief flash lit the night sky on the slope above them. A steady rhythm of explosions continued as he and his team carried the bodies back towards the LZ. He pushed the pace as much as he dared, taking into account the weight that his guys were carrying between them over treacherous ground, but they couldn't hang around. That fucking sniper would be the end of them if Randy's grenade stomp didn't work.

There was nothing like the comforting knowledge of knowing your enemy's head was burrowing into the ground under a weight of grenade fire while you were on the move. Looking over his shoulder, Ned saw that the guys carrying the bodies were keeping up, their heads lowered as they propelled themselves out of the killing zone. He faced forward again and strode out, taking advantage of a level area to increase the pace. By his reckoning they had some distance to go before he felt confident enough to bring the birds back in. He keyed his mic as he jogged at the head of his men.

'Dwight, you picking up anyone else out here?' His concern was that the sniper who had engaged them was part of a larger group and he had no idea if they were heading towards or away from them. The reply came after several moments.

'Nope. Nothing since those last transmissions.'

Ned grunted, the statement giving him neither comfort nor concern. His thoughts strayed to the bodies of his two dead operators and their families. He pushed them to the back of his mind to focus on the task at hand; getting him and his team the hell out of the shit. He was wondering how long Randy and Dwight would keep the grenade fire up for when a shout from behind caught his attention and he turned in time to see one of the operators who was carrying a body collapse. *Fuck*!

He threw himself to the ground and crawled several meters to the cover of a large rock as the calls came over the net letting him know everyone's status. The missing voice was Rick, Ned's go-to guy for all things explosive's related. Ned swore under his breath even as he looked for a way out of their predicament. Rick must have been taken out by a sniper, his sudden collapse identical to Buck and Mike's. His mind racing, Ned considered the possibilities. Either they had been engaged by another sniper or the same one who had taken out Mike and Buck had moved position and was tracking them. He needed to talk to Randy.

'Hey Randy, we got bad times here man. We have another KIA and looks like a sniper again. You guys get anything on BDA?' While he waited for the reply, Ned hoped that the Battle Damage Assessment, the BDA, would at least tell him their grenade stomp had killed some of the enemy. His earpiece crackled as a transmission came through from Randy.

'Nothing Ned. Visibility to shit and thermal not picking anything up. We're coming in on your six now.'

Ned turned his attention back to the area in front of him, scanning the rocks and boulders for any signs of movement. He was now down three guys and could see a terrible reality fast approaching. Carrying two dead comrades out was difficult enough but three was going to really hinder them and present an easier target to whoever was picking them off. *Fuck*. But he'd been here before, stranded in hostile territory and unable to take his dead Operators home. He hadn't liked the decision then and didn't like it now. But he had to think of the living, not the dead. With a sigh he lowered his head and spoke into the mic.

'Dwight, Randy. Prep *Red Pete*, I say again, *Red Pete*.'

There was a moment's silence before the replies came in. It was a terrible thing to ask them but each man on the team understood the necessity. This was one of those defining characteristics that separated Special Forces' Operators from the conventional military: the ability to shut off emotions and sensitivities and deal with the task at hand. And burning the bodies of your dead friends and colleagues with Red Phosphorous, or *Red Pete* as they referred to it, was a horrific task. But Ned had no choice; carrying three bodies out would render his team almost combat ineffective and incapable of taking the fight to the enemy. If they stood any chance of making it to the birds, they would have to close and kill with whoever had been picking them off. And fucking fast.

He crawled back from the small rise and looked over to see Randy and Dwight placing the body bags together and stacking the Red Phos grenades in preparation. He felt the sting in his eyes as the raw emotion hit him and he shook his head to rid himself of the distraction. *Later.* Looking around their position, he saw Vic had the thermal binoculars and was scanning the area to their right flank where the sniper threat had come from. Ned had to come up with a plan to get them out of here but whatever it was, they needed to eliminate the threat first. His mind became calm as he ran through a course of action that would put his guys back on the offensive, taking the fight to the enemy. Face set in grim determination, his plan became clear and as he keyed his mic to brief the team, he knew he wanted only one thing from it:

No more dead brothers.

24

ZAGROS MOUNTAINS, IRAN

Sergeii dropped to the rocks beside Pasha and patted the sniper on the back to let him know he was there. He was breathing heavily after his sprint across the open ground and he swiped at his face, smearing blood across his forehead and wincing as his gloved hand brushed the torn gash. The grenades had surprised them, and he'd barely escaped, rolling over and over away from the impact zone but still catching a sliver of the lethal projectiles on his forehead. Gregor and Viktor hadn't been so lucky. Viktor killed outright as a grenade exploded right beside him and Gregor's head shredded by a combination of metal and rock fragmentation. Sergeii hadn't even had the time to strip his comrades of their weapons and ammunition. Arkady limped his way into their position and applied a dressing to a flesh wound on his leg before settling into a defensive crouch, weapon aimed in the direction of the Americans. Sergeii pressed his face up against Pasha's ear and whispered.

'Give me some fucking good news.'

The sniper remained completely still as he replied in his customary monotone.

'Three dead Americans. Soon to be four.'

Sergeii patted his back. 'Good work Pasha. Even the numbers up a little more and we'll move in.'

'Of course.'

Sergeii shuffled backwards until he was close to Arkady. 'How's the leg?'

Arkady shrugged his shoulders as he replied. 'I have had worse. Hurts but no real damage.'

'Good, good. Pasha will take out as many of the Americans as he can before we close on them. If I was them, I'd be trying to call in my extraction. My Iranian General informs me that he doesn't think they will risk any air support, but they will call in helicopters to pull them out. We need to finish them before that happens. My Iranian friend would like some prisoners if possible, but we will see how that goes.'

Arkady nodded his understanding and Sergeii sent an update to Zana, letting him know there were three less Americans wandering his mountains. No doubt the General would be pleased with that message. He turned back to Pasha and sidled closer.

'What are they doing?'

'There's been no movement for a while now. They will be looking for a way out that won't expose them to me. They have three bodies to carry and this will be a big problem for them.'

Sergeii grunted. The Americans were too soft when it came to their colleagues. A Russian would leave a dead comrade on the battlefield, the former warrior now little more than a heavy piece of meat that could no longer contribute to the fight. The Americans were too sentimental, but Sergeii was relying on this, knowing that the burden of their dead colleagues would ultimately mean death for the rest of them. Well, *almost* the rest of them. Zana was adamant that he needed prisoners and Sergeii was beginning to see the value in this, the humiliation to the Americans a far more powerful blow than a handful of dead deniable soldiers on an Iranian mountain pass. His mind was made up: Prisoners were no longer a nice to have. They were his priority. He tapped Pasha on the shoulder.

'Arkady and I are going to move closer on their right flank. We'll pressure the Americans to start moving and you can pick them off from here. I need prisoners, so see if you can just wound a couple of them.'

The sniper gave a soft grunt of understanding without moving his focus from his target area. Sergeii nodded to Arkady and the pair began a slow crawl over the uneven, snow-covered ground giving a wary glance now and then towards the Americans' position. In his mind's eye Sergeii imagined himself as his grandfather, closing with the Germans over the freezing rubble of Stalingrad. His country's enemies had always underestimated the strength and determination of the Russian people, the Americans merely the latest to be guilty of this. And Sergeii was only too happy to be the messenger of this error to the Western imperialists. Revenge for the savage defeat he and his Wagner comrades had received at the hands of American airpower fueled his motivation. The knowledge that he would not face any American aircraft tonight boosting Sergeii's confidence that he would destroy the American soldiers and humiliate their nation.

He stopped to adjust his NVGs when a whispered transmission from Pasha came through.

'*There is movement to the right of their location, but I don't have a clear shot. Moving my position now.*'

Sergeii replied with two clicks on his pressel switch to let his sniper know he had received the message. He gave Arkady the hand-signal to hold, and saw his colleague take cover with his rifle pointed towards the Americans' location. Sergeii narrowed his eyes as he tried in vain to identify any movement through the green glow of his optics. His earpiece buzzed again.

'*Am in position now and acquiring target. Wait… target acquired and taking shot.*'

Sergeii stared hard towards the Americans' location and heard the faint retort from Pasha's rifle and a second later a brief flash from the area where the Americans were taking cover. He assessed Pasha's bullet must have travelled through its target and ricocheted off the rocks, causing a spark. He grinned to himself at the thought of the Americans realizing they were being cut down one by one and that there was nothing they could do about it. He congratulated his sniper.

'Pasha, well done. We are moving in now to close.'

He began to move but had only gone several meters over the jagged rocks when he paused and sent his message again, having heard nothing from his sniper. When the silence came a second time, Sergeii began to feel uneasy. He gave a quick radio check to Arkady to confirm his equipment was working and received a clear reply. He really wanted to move in on the Americans now while they were dealing with the chaos of a further casualty, but his gut told him that something was wrong. Sergeii's instincts had been proven right on too many occasions for him to ignore them and he spoke into his mic again.

'Arkady, you wait here and cover me. I am going to check on Pasha as he is not responding to my transmissions.' Arkady replied instantly and Sergeii made his way back across the ground that they had just covered. When he reached the spot where they had left the sniper, he saw that Pasha wasn't there but remembered that he had altered his position in order to acquire the American target. Sergeii knew that Pasha wouldn't have gone too far to achieve this and raised himself up on his knees, scanning the area around him.

Within seconds he spotted Pasha lying behind his rifle, focused completely on his targets. Sergeii shook his head slightly in admiration and crawled over to Pasha, softly calling to let him know he was approaching. The sniper maintained his vigil and Sergeii shuffled his body alongside Pasha's and patted his colleague's back.

'Tell me we got another one, Pasha.'

When his statement wasn't acknowledged, Sergeii repeated it a little louder. He frowned as the silence remained and raised himself on his elbows, leaning in closer to Pasha's face. Sergeii gasped when he saw the shattered forehead and the concave hollow of the sniper's skull that had been hidden from his approach. Pasha had been shot in the head as he lay behind his weapon and had never moved since. Sergeii's rage flooded his senses and he grabbed the big rifle from the sniper's dead hands, turning the weapon towards the Americans and looking into the thermal scope. He snapped his head back and gave an involuntary cry of disgust as he pulled lumps of flesh and gore from his eye socket, remnants of Pasha's face that had splattered into the receptacle of the rifle's optics. He leaned forward to scoop the visceral matter out of the eyepiece when the rifle was snatched from his hands by an unseen force and catapulted into the rocks beyond. Sergeii felt his palm stinging before the realization dawned on him that the weapon had been shot from his hands. His eyes widened and he threw himself to the ground, rolling fast, away from where he had just been kneeling. A loud crack near his head confirmed that the Americans were hunting him, and his adrenaline surged with the familiar excitement of being in close combat. He didn't even feel the sharp rocks stabbing him as he rolled and tumbled over them back towards Arkady, hearing his colleague calling his name. Sergeii reached Arkady and saw the puzzlement on his face, but he wasted no time, crawling into cover and pointing his weapon towards the Americans' position. He felt Arkady slither alongside him.

'Sergeii, what the fuck is going on?'

His breathing was ragged, and he willed himself to slow it down, calming and relaxing his body before replying.

'The Americans got Pasha. Straight through the head. They must also have a thermal scope.'

There was a brief pause where all Sergeii could hear was his breathing and the gusting of the icy wind.

'So what do we do now Sergeii?'

Sergeii Antonovich narrowed his eyes and curled his lip as he replied.

'Change of plan Arkady. We take no prisoners now. We kill them all. Every last one.'

25

ZAGROS MOUNTAINS, IRAN

Karim waited for several minutes before he crawled back from the rocks where he had been observing the shooting on the slope to his front. The deteriorating weather had not allowed him to see clearly enough to identify exactly who was fighting who and his first thought had been that Zana had sent a team of Quds ahead and they'd encountered the Americans. As all he had to go on was muted muzzle flashes in the dark, Karim questioned his initial assessment. The sporadic nature of the shooting was not how the Quds would take on an American force. They would employ their standard flanking maneuver, using a heavy weight of fire to suppress the Americans while a team made their way to close with them. *No, this is different.*

He made his way back to the boy and sat where he could see the waif's face clearly. Affan looked up to him, his wide eyes filled with questions. Karim shook his head and leaned in until their heads were touching.

'I don't know exactly what is happening, but I think my American friends are meeting some resistance. We need to help them.' When the orphan made no comment, Karim continued. 'I need you to stay here again and wait until I come back for you, yes?'

The boy shook his head and Karim gripped his shoulder.

'Listen; our only way out of these mountains and this country is with my American friends. They don't make it; *we* don't make it. That is the truth.' Karim handed his pistol over to the boy. 'If anything happens, use this. Do what you did before; point it at the middle of a man and squeeze the trigger. Move a few meters away, hide and wait. I will find you. Understand?' He watched as the boy dropped his head and gave a slow nod of resignation. Karim patted his back. 'Good, good my little *Palang*. I won't let you down. I'll be back as soon as I can. Stay here, stay hidden and stay warm.' He rose and turned to leave but looked down as his hand was gripped. He covered the boy's hand with his own and met the pleading, wide eyes.

'It's okay Affan. I will be back, I promise.' He pulled his hand loose, lowered his NVGs and made his way in a crouch across the open ground, keeping larger rocks between himself and the shooters. Karim wanted to get close enough to identify their numbers and, if possible, who they were, before he engaged. He didn't think there were many, as there would have been much more shots being returned but he needed to be sure. Karim lowered his body position as he made his way closer to where he had last observed the shots being fired from. Taking care with each foot placement, he stalked over the uneven ground, scanning all directions to avoid being surprised or ambushed. He paused as his foot connected with a hard object that moved and made the sound of metal colliding with rock. Looking down, he saw a large rifle, a sniper's rifle made even longer by the suppressor fitted to the end of the barrel. As he studied it, he saw the shattered stock near the cocking mechanism and understood why it had been discarded. It was also clear to Karim that this was not a Quds' weapon. He recognized the make and model and knew for certain that no Iranian unit used such a rifle. But that begged the question; whose was it?

A soft sound caught his attention and he lowered himself onto his stomach, slowly moving his head to scan the area where the sound had emanated. It took him a few seconds but then he saw it; two men moving slowly, like him, among the rocks and snow on their stomachs. Karim could see they were trained by the way only one man moved while the other covered him. But they weren't Iranians, he knew that for sure. While the question bothered him, he put it out of his mind. It didn't really matter who they were, they were trying to kill Vic and his team and Karim had to do whatever he could to make sure that didn't happen.

Now that he had slowed down from his race across the mountain, Karim could feel the chill on his body as the keen wind drove the snow against him. He kept his focus on the area where he had last seen the two men, the odd fleeting glance of shadows among the snow flurries his only confirmation that the figures were still there. Stalking towards them, he took great care with his foot placement, not wanting to trip or fall in any manner that might alert the men. He settled his breathing as he moved, his training kicking in as the muscle memory of closing with a foe in close quarters took over.

Skirting around a large rock that loomed in front of him, he dropped quickly to the ground as he almost walked straight into the back of the men. At barely two meters in front of him, he could even hear snatches of their whispered conversations, brief bursts of speech that drifted to him on the wind. He strained to hear the words as he covered the men with his carbine but couldn't identify what they were saying. Risking a brief glance at the ground in front of him, He placed a gloved hand down and, bringing his focus back to the stationary men, crawled forward to within a meter then stopped and brought the rifle up on aim. As he placed first pressure on the trigger, his eyes widened as a fraction of the conversation reached his ears and with it, no more doubt that these were the enemy.

Karim didn't need to use his optics at this range and looked over the length of the rifle as he pulled the trigger and killed his first Russians.

26

ZAGROS MOUNTAINS, IRAN

Zana saw the small flashes and raised his carbine up, aiming in the direction of the activity before cursing and lowering the weapon. He had no idea who was firing at who and spun on his heel to address the signaler.

'Who is that? Get Sergeii now and ask him to identify his location.'

He watched as the signaler keyed his mic and spoke in Russian. He repeated the query and receiving no response, asked again. The young Quds operative looked up at Zana and shook his head.

Zana cursed aloud and strode to where his Major was crouched behind the cover of some rocks observing the area where the muted muzzle flashes had come. Dropping beside him, the General leaned in closer.

'What do you think Major?'

His Major answered without taking his eyes from their target area. 'One shooter. Suppressor. Looked like two targets up close but I cannot be sure.'

Zana stood and stared hard at the darkness beyond the swirling snow as his mind assimilated the facts. One shooter, taking on two targets. Up Close. *Ardavan*.

He leaned down and grabbed the Major's shoulder. 'Get up. It was Ardavan doing the shooting. Come on man, we have him. We have the snake.'

He turned on his heel and made his way back to the signaler as he heard the Major giving hushed commands to his men, splitting them into sections to flank the vile traitor and finally bring an end to the hunt. He barked at the radio operator. 'Anything from the Russians?'

The young operative shook his head. 'Nothing General. I have been trying but nothing is coming back.'

Looking back towards where he believed the traitor Ardavan to be, Zana wondered whether the two targets that the Major had seen shot at close range were the reason for the Russians' radio silence. He sighed as he came to terms with the fact that his Russian ally was in all probability dead in the snow not twenty meters from where he stood. A sound caught his attention and he turned to see a file of his men make their way up the slope while a second section lined out with spaces between each man and moved directly towards where Ardavan had been. Nodding with determination, Zana opened his stride and caught up with the line, taking a position on the end as they walked forward, weapons ready. After some time, he heard the call in his earpiece from the flanking section above them. They were in position and waiting.

Other than the wind, Zana heard no noise, the discipline and training of his men such that even when closing with the enemy for the kill, no conversation was necessary. As the driving snow stung his face, the General stared hard at the area in front of him, willing the traitor to appear from the white maelstrom. He really wanted Ardavan alive, wounded maybe and suffering great pain, but he couldn't give that order to his troops. Ardavan was well trained and had significant operational experience, evident in the way he had lured the hunter

171

force into not one but two traps. No, he was not to be underestimated and Zana was unwilling to risk losing Ardavan again by ordering his men to aim to wound and not to kill.

His thoughts were interrupted as the man to his side dropped to the ground and took up a position aiming to his front. Zana mimicked the soldier and pointed his carbine through a gap between two rocks as he waited to find the reason for taking cover. A moment later he heard a quiet whisper in his earpiece from his Major.

Body ahead.

Another quiet command was given, and two men crawled forward from the line, disappearing into the swirling clouds of snow. Several minutes passed before a further message came over the airwaves.

Come to our location.

The soldiers on the line stood up and advanced forward. Zana saw the two men who had gone in advance kneeling and studying a body that was sprawled over a scattering of sharp rocks. As the Major deployed his troops around the area to secure it, Zana approached the body and placed his carbine on the ground. With exaggerated care, he took hold of the upper torso of the corpse and eased the head and shoulders up in small increments, studying the ground underneath. Satisfied that it had not been booby-trapped, he flipped the body over and studied it. The pale face, poor complexion and dark hair gave him some hints that he might be looking at a dead Russian and a thorough study of the man's clothing, weapons and equipment confirmed it.

Zana shook his head, picked up his carbine and looked for the Major. He saw the officer deep in discussion with the signaler and made his way over. The Major looked up as he saw him approach and pointed down the hill behind them.

'The mice are picking up a lot of movement down there General. More than four people we think.'

Zana looked in the direction the Major had indicated and frowned as he tried to work out what was going on. They could be Americans, or they could also be Russians as Zana didn't know how many men Sergeii had brought with him. It could even be Ardavan with his American handlers, escaping the mountains as Zana was stood trying to figure things out. He made up his mind.

'Major, bring the flanking section down from the high ground. We move towards that group. I suspect it is the Americans, but we will soon see. Come man, no time to lose.' He noted the brief hesitancy on the Major's face, but it was fleeting, and the commands were soon relayed across the radio. Despite his confidence that they would catch the traitor, small elements of concern were beginning to creep into Zana's thoughts. The fact that the traitor had managed to ambush his force twice was unexpected. But now there was also a dead Russian who Zana knew would have been one of Sergeii's best. Increasing doubt gnawed at the General's confidence. If Ardavan had managed to link forces with the Americans, the Quds were going to have a serious fight on their hands. With their depleted numbers, Zana knew that they needed the element of surprise on their side with which to balance the odds in their favor.

Some quiet activity to his rear made him turn and he saw the flanking section had joined the main body of troops. The Major took hold of the officer in command of the other section and briefed him quietly. Both men then made their way to Zana and he leaned in as the Major spoke.

'What's your plan sir?'

Zana indicated with his head to the slope below them. 'We make our way down there, slowly and quietly until we see what we're dealing with and then, well then we'll just deal with it.' Allowing no time for questions he nodded to the Major. 'Get the men ready. We move in one minute.'

The Major began speaking quiet commands into his mic and around them, troops moved into formation ready to deploy. After only thirty seconds, the Major turned back to Zana.

'We are ready General.'

Moving as one, the line of Quds operatives stalked down the slope, each man careful of his foot placement even as they strained their eyes to see what was in front of them. Soft, quiet commands over the radio were the only disturbance to their advance and Zana felt his stomach tighten in anticipation of closing with the enemy. He was aware, as all the men probably were, that the enemy could have the upper hand in this dark snowstorm but equally, Zana and his men could be on top of the Americans before they were even noticed.

The Major gave a glance along the line and could only make out the vague features of the soldier next to him, the remainder of the line lost in the dark and the snow. It mattered little; his men's training and discipline meant that he didn't need to see them to know they were doing their jobs. He turned his attention to his front again and tasted the metallic tang of adrenalin as the prospect of close combat approached. He almost yelled in surprise as a figure rose up before him, appearing from the depths of the swirling snow like a *djinn*. His training and muscle memory kicked in before the shock set in fully and he raised his carbine up on aim.

Major Amadi frowned as his carbine was pushed up higher than he had intended, and his eyes and mouth opened wide as a lance of agony in his back took his breath away. As he dropped to the ground, he could feel himself being supported and struggled to comprehend what was happening even as he coughed hot blood from his mouth onto the snow around him. Hands lowered him to the ground, in an almost tender fashion and he began to choke as he drowned on the blood filling his lungs. His last thought as panic and terror flooded him was that he was going to die alone on this freezing mountain. With a last gasp of breath, the Major's eyes fluttered closed and his spasming ceased as the snow began to settle on his now peaceful face.

27

ZAGROS MOUNTAINS, IRAN

Randy wiped the blood from the knife as Deke rolled the body into a small dip between the rocks. With the amount of snow that was falling, the corpse would be covered in no time. But Randy didn't have the luxury of waiting around to watch that happen. He needed to take down as many as he could and as quietly as he could to give the Team a fighting chance at getting out of these fucking mountains. Deke gave him the hand signal and they began moving towards the Iranian line again as it advanced down the slope. They half-jogged, half-walked in a crouch until Deke signaled that he had sight of the line. Without the need for words or communication, Deke loped off on the flank as Randy identified the shape of an Iranian through the snow. He moved fast, knowing that if they were communicating on their radios, at some point soon, someone was going to notice they were down one of their guys. Taking a deep breath, Randy casually walked into the position on the line where the guy he'd killed would have been. He noticed the figure to his left wave in acknowledgement and he returned the gesture, gratified to see the man return to facing forward. Content that the ruse had worked, Randy dropped back a little and angled his approach until he was directly behind the man. A brief moment later Deke jumped up in front of the Iranian and Randy closed in to capitalize on the diversion. In one fluid movement he thrust the blade deep into one lung while reaching around and pushing the man's carbine up into the air. Keeping hold of the weapon as the man collapsed against him, Randy pulled the knife out then stabbed hard into the other lung, cursing as the blade was deflected by a metal buckle but correcting quickly and thrusting the knife in at a higher point. As the body collapsed fully into him, Randy lowered the carbine, pulled the knife out and jammed it behind the dying man's throat, cutting forward in a sawing motion until the blade broke free of the windpipe.

Satisfied with his kill, he wiped the knife on the move, catching Deke's nod through the green glow of his NVGs. *One more. Let's do one more.* They were closer to the line this time and caught up quickly. Again, Deke stalked off ahead and to one side while Randy closed in behind the shadow of the man at the end of the line. They repeated the same tactic and it worked as well as the other two. As he pulled out the knife and lowered the body, Randy could feel this man was lighter than the others and figured him for a youth or a younger soldier. *Whatever.* Young or old, a finger on a trigger did the same job. Whoever he was, he knew what he was getting into when he came up here. Looking up, he gave the hand signal to Deke that they were done. He would have no problems with working his way along the line taking them out one by one, but you could push your luck too far. As he and Deke took up the empty positions on the flank, he removed a couple of grenades from his tac-vest and motioned to get Deke's attention. Deke confirmed he had seen and understood, and Randy pulled the pins, clasping the fly-off levers tight and took a long look up the line of soldiers. While he couldn't see beyond the man to his left, he had a good idea of the level of the line. With a last look at Deke, he turned back and one after the other, threw the grenades in a high arc to land just ahead of the advancing troops. As one, he and Deke propelled themselves to one side, running down the slope to the position where Ned and the Team were waiting. Randy was smiling as he raced down the treacherous slope, only half in control of his progress as he leapt rocks and slid on shale. They'd made it farther than he thought they would when the dull concussions reached them. Without looking back, both men skidded to a halt by a row of large boulders then scrambled over them, dropping into a natural hollow below, landing on their backs.

Randy looked up, breathing heavily but still smiling as Ned reached down and held out his hand.

'Welcome home brother.'

28

ZAGROS MOUNTAINS, IRAN

Sergeii Antonov slumped against the rock and allowed his body to slide down until he was sat resting against the cold stone. His breathing was loud and ragged as he shrugged off his small pack, growling at the fire of pain that engulfed his entire left side. Tearing open the pack, he pulled out his medical kit and opened the Velcro fasteners. He worked fast, hands shaking, knowing he had already lost a significant amount of blood and could not afford to lose much more. Gritting his teeth and turning awkwardly, he poured the sachet of QuickClot over bleeding holes in his back, hoping the granules were covering the wounds that while burning him with a visceral intensity, were too far around his body for him to see. He groaned and threw his head back, teeth clenched hard, the tendons in his neck straining beneath the skin as he absorbed the pain. After a moment, he opened his mouth and gulped a series of quick, shallow breaths as wave after wave of agony assailed him. Reaching back to the pack he pulled two field dressings and proceeded to dress his wounds, uttering loud curses as they opened and closed with his exertions. Panting from his efforts but satisfied he could do no more to stem the blood loss, he packed his medical kit away and pulled his rifle back onto his lap.

Shaking his head in disbelief, Sergeii struggled to come to terms with the fact that he was the only survivor from his team. Feeling the cold snow settle on his face he realized that survivor might only be a relative term: If he couldn't get off the mountain soon, the combination of blood loss and exposure would render him as dead as his comrades on the slope above. Anger began seeping into his thoughts and with it the shame of having been surprised and bested by someone he hadn't even seen but had killed Arkady and severely wounded Sergei from very close range. He wondered if it had been the Americans or Zana's little traitor. Snorting with derision at his own self-pity, he realized that it didn't really matter who it had been, he was fucked either way.

Sergeii looked down at the carbine resting on his lap and knew he had to move. And soon. But he could imagine the agony awaiting him as soon as he made the first move to stand up. Taking a deep breath, he pushed himself up, using the rock as support. His eyes widened and a scream erupted from him as he felt the wounds tearing open under the dressings. Head clammy with the sudden onset of sweat, he leaned into the rock and hyperventilated as waves of nausea engulfed him. He moaned and shook his head to ward off the assault. Sergeii was no stranger to pain and had a high threshold to withstand it, but this was different. He knew from experience that these wounds were serious: Three bullets into his back, below the lungs but certainly into the region of the kidneys and other organs. Knew also that the rounds would have bounced around inside him, tearing, shredding and destroying everything in their path. Calming his breathing, Sergeii looked up and towards the east where they had arranged for the helicopter to come back for them. *Them*. There was no longer a them. Only him. He didn't know if he could make it that far, but he knew he had to try while he still had the strength to do so. Gripping the carbine, he straightened up and one small step at a time, began walking, every foot placement sending a coil of agony around his body. His breathing was ragged but he forced himself to concentrate on his steps, watching his feet move, careful not to over-extend or trip on the rocks under his feet.

He settled into a labored cadence, a controlled stagger, head down and focusing on the ground to his front. Oblivious to everything around him but the top of his boots as they carried him across the deepening snow, taking care with each step to place a foot down before moving the next one. Slow but steady. He knew that a fall or a slide here would probably be the end of him. After some time, Sergeii realized that he had been moving down the mountain, his fixation on his steps clouding him to his navigational change. He grunted with surprise that he hadn't noticed this. He was usually very much aware of exactly where he was and which direction he was headed. In truth, it mattered little; he was pleased with his progress and being a hundred meters lower than he thought he was didn't constitute any significant problems.

It took some time before he realized that he wasn't feeling so much pain anymore and had been in an almost trance-like state, hypnotized by the cadence of his footsteps through the small snowdrifts. This was a bad sign and he tried to focus on his wounds, encouraged his brain to find the pain, make him feel something to confirm he was still alive, not merely an entity walking in a snowbound limbo. He was about to reach around and give his back a rub when he heard the voice.

Sergeii stopped and cocked his head to one side, panting and rasping for breath. He swayed as he listened hard for a repeat of the sound. When there was nothing after a minute or so of waiting, he decided he had imagined it and was preparing to start walking again when the voice returned, closer, louder and with it, complete confirmation of who he was dealing with. His stomach spasmed as he lifted the carbine up and aimed it towards the disembodied voice in the snow just as it spoke again, the unmistakable twang of the American mid-west.

Okay, I'll take point but we gotta beat feet gentlemen.

Sergeii pulled the butt of the weapon tighter into his shoulder and pushed the selector to automatic. He didn't know how long he could sustain standing upright with a weapon kicking into his shoulder but was determined that if these were his last breaths to be taken, he wouldn't die alone. When the dark form loomed out of the snow in front of him Sergeii squeezed the trigger and a burst of fire hammered into the shapeless form in front of him.

29

ZAGROS MOUNTAINS, IRAN

Ned shouted as he saw Randy drop to the ground and at the same time flinched as the unmistakable buzzing of rounds zipped past, close to his head. He dropped to one knee and brought his rifle up, firing controlled bursts into the area where he had seen the muzzle flash. Beside him another figure knelt and began firing into the darkness and whirling snow. Ned felt a pat on his shoulder and moved his aim to one side as one of the team darted past him, grabbed a hold of Randy and dragged him back behind them to the safety of cover. Ned stood, spun on his heel and ran back to the cover of the boulders they had only left moments before. He reached the medic who was cutting Randy's jacket open and attending to the wounds. Cursing, Ned stooped to look closer and spoke.

'Well?'

The medic ignored him as he continued with his ministrations, then glanced up as he leaned over and grabbed a chest seal from his pack.

'Not great. Bad wound where the round entered just under his armpit, but this should stop the lung collapsing. Big bleed from his brachial but got the tourniquet holding that. Took one into the pelvis that's got me worried, think there's already internal bleeding.' He paused and looked over his shoulder for a brief moment. 'Who the fuck is that? The Quds? We need MEDEVAC now or Randy won't make it.'

Ned nodded and stood, talking into his mic. 'Speak to me. What we got out there?'

Soft acknowledgements came over the net telling him pretty much what he already knew; someone had shot them up and disappeared back into the snow. He balled his hand into a fist and swore quietly before looking around and walking over to Vic who was kneeling with Dwight, working with the comms.

Ned looked down and saw Vic had noticed him. The CIA officer stood and leaned in closer.

'I'm calling for EVAC. We can't sustain this Ned. We need to get the fuck off this mountain before none of us make it.'

Ned shook his head. 'You really think Langley will authorize the birds back into this shit-storm? Not a chance my friend, we either make it to the LZ or we don't make it anywhere.'

'No. I haven't asked Langley. I have Mission Command, Ned. I've ordered the birds back in myself. Got confirmation a minute ago. They'll come in even though it's hot. Dwight's giving them our location and thinks they can hold a hover at about four feet to keep rotor clearance.'

Ned looked at the CIA officer for several moments. 'That's a ballsy call my friend.' He looked behind him for several seconds before turning to face Vic again. 'But you're right; we need EVAC now, even though we got unknown hostiles very close. If they take down one of the choppers...'

Vic stood and looked Ned in the eyes. 'So let's make sure they don't.'

'What about the Asset?'

Vic shook his head. 'He's either dead or as good as. Best case scenario is he's taken advantage of all of this and has been making good ground to the border. But I seriously doubt that. This is a determined force that's chasing him and they're not giving up.'

Ned dropped his head on his chest and sighed. 'It kills me that good men have died here, and we don't have anything to show for it.' Looking up, he caught Vic's eye. 'Must be getting old, expecting it to be any different. Okay, so we hold here until birds are inbound then clear the perimeter. You good with that?'

'Yep. Let's keep it simple and get off this damned mountain.'

Ned walked off to brief the team as Vic knelt beside Dwight, looking for an update on the helicopters' progress. He knew Ned was right; if the enemy took down a chopper it would be a huge propaganda coup to say nothing of the death of the pilots and crew. Hell, it might not even take enemy fire to do it. Landing in a snowstorm at night on a treacherous mountain was inviting all kinds of problems. But this is where the Night Stalkers came into their own. Vic had seen them land in worse. Not much and not often, but still worse.

Dwight informed him that the birds were twenty minutes out and Vic stood and made his way towards Ned who was kneeling beside Randy and the medic. Ned glanced up as he approached and Vic stooped, bringing his face close to Ned's ear.

'Twenty minutes.' He looked down at Randy, saw how pale the face was against the dark fabric of the sleeping bag he was cocooned in. His eyes were closed, and Vic couldn't discern any breathing. He was just about to say something when the medic turned his attention from the intravenous line he was setting up, and back to his patient. He cursed and darted forward, ripping the sleeping bag open and tilting Randy's head

185

back. As the medic dropped and blew two hard breaths into Randy, Ned was already in place to begin compressions when the medic sat up slowly and waved Ned away. Ned lifted his NVGs from his face and stared hard at the medic before nodding and pulling the sleeping bag over Randy's lifeless body. Sitting back on his haunches he rubbed his face with his hands then looked at the medic with the question evident in his eyes.

The medic shook his head. 'Internal bleeding. Just too much on top of the lung damage Ned. I'm sorry man.'

Ned nodded, his gaze unfocussed as he thought about the friend he had just lost and what he was going to say to Laura. A sound brought his attention back to the present and he saw the medic shaking out a body bag. Ned stood and walked over to check if the rest of the team who had made it this far had anything to report. He needed to get his mind back in the fight. Leave the emotions for later.

Vic watched Ned walk away and couldn't imagine what the Delta soldier was going through. His team slaughtered on a deniable operation in the mountains of Iran. A lot of soldiers in Ned's position would lay the blame for the deaths at the feet of the CIA; another fool's errand for the spooks ending in the deaths of their friends and colleagues. But Ned was a professional. Knew that these were the risks and that it was his job to accept them and make the operation happen. But he was also a human being, affected and influenced by the same factors as any other person, including the deaths of close friends and colleagues. The difference was that Ned and men like him could lock those emotions down and release them later in a time and place of their own choosing. Well, that's how the theory went at least. Vic was reminded of some of the older Paramilitary Operations Officers from Ground Branch who had mentored him at the Agency and the heavy baggage and mental scars they had carried after decades of operations like this one. Sighing, he pulled out his Sat-phone and looked in vain for any contact from Seven. He wasn't surprised. The earlier assessment he'd given to Ned, while pessimistic, was in all likelihood the most accurate. Seven was being pursued by one of the most effective terrorist organizations in the world, and they were taking the hunt personally. Hell, he could already be dead, and the Iranians were now just trying to get the cherry on top of the cake; a covert team of American Special Forces on a deniable operation. He felt a twinge of doubt as the thought of the incoming helicopters came to him. They could not afford to have either of the birds taken down, their extraction relying on them. But he couldn't second guess his decision now, the call had been made and the plan was in motion. Far from perfect, granted, but driven by their circumstances. This prompted a memory of one of the legends of Langley that came back to him, a homily delivered as part of a presentation on paramilitary operations. The lecturer had spent thirty years in the field, running deniable operations in every theatre of conflict that the USA had been involved in during that time. Referring to decision making in the field, his gruff, gravelly voice and straight talking had held the trainee officers' attention.

'A perfect decision in the field? It exists. And do you know what it is? It's the decision that works, people. No matter how dangerous, creative, off the wall… questionable. If it works, it was perfect. You will always be judged by shiny asses back here from the comfort of their corner offices and the genius of hindsight. You can't think about that. You've got to think in the now. What works now? What do I have to do to get my ass and the asses of the team out of here right now?'

The honesty of the delivery and the instructor's pedigree had struck a chord with Vic and he'd had cause to remember that one small vignette several times through the years as he'd found himself in sticky situations.

Like this one.

30

ZAGROS MOUNTAINS IRAN

Karim landed beside the boy and thrust his hands out as Affan raised the gun in reflex, disarming the youth and sending the pistol spinning onto the ground, clattering over the rocks. The boy's wild eyes and look of terror changed to almost comical relief and he lunged at Karim, throwing his arms around him and holding him tight. Karim hugged the boy back hard, surprising himself with the depth of his own emotions. After several moments he released his hold and gently pushed Affan away from him. Even in the darkness, the whites of the boy's eyes were prominent, and Karim ruffled his hair.

'I told you I'd be back, Affan. I would never leave you little *Palang*. Never.'

The boy nodded and wiped his eyes with his sleeve as Karim leaned forward and picked up the pistol from the ground and jammed it back into his thigh holster. He stood and made his way to his pack which he shrugged into before picking up his carbine and looking back at Affan.

'Let's go. There are too many people on this mountain for us to stay still. Keep close Affan.'

With that, he led the way, carbine on aim as he picked a route across the treacherous, snow-covered rocks. His mind returned to the men he had just shot. *Russians.* Clearly General Shir-Del was taking no chances in his efforts to capture Karim. But it added another layer of risk and complexity to an already difficult situation for Karim. *How many Russians are there? What technology are they using? More importantly, other than the two he had shot, where are the rest?* His brain raced as he tried to consolidate his thoughts. The original plan was as good as dead. Between the Americans, the Russians and the Quds' operatives, the mountain was turning into a chaotic battleground, compounded by the snow and darkness. Karim knew his only choice was to keep moving east towards the border and hope that he could somehow slip through the lines of those hunting him. He had no doubt that they would have positioned a blocking force of some kind ahead of him, but he would deal with that problem when he came to it. He threw a quick glance over his shoulder and felt a paternal pride as he saw Affan walking fast, determined to keep up with him. The pride changed to concern when he reminded himself of the dire situation that they found themselves in, the thought of anything happening to the boy filling him with anger. He shook his head and focused on the area in front of him, scanning for any movement, knowing that they only stood a chance if, as he had done with the Russians, Karim was able to kill them first.

He thought about the information he was carrying, concealed in small thumb-drives in the toughened case secured in the inside pocket of his jacket. When he'd initially discovered he could access the files on the computers at Camp Palang, he knew he had to get the information to Vic. Knew that the lives that would be saved would be worth the danger and risk he would be under. But it hadn't been as easy as he thought. All the files were read-only and each time they were opened, a record was logged of who had accessed them, at what time and for how long. Also, there were no ports for external devices to be inserted where the files could be copied. He'd initially considered doing it the old-fashioned way, with a notebook and pencil but this would have been time-consuming. He'd then had the idea to film the files, record the screen in front of him as he read the contents. Using a small camera, he'd done just that, accessing the files only now and then and recording the contents to the hard drive of his camera. He downloaded this content onto the thumb-drives that he stored at his exfiltration cache. To cover his tracks, he wrote exercise scenarios based around the information he had read on the files, a plausible cover story for his activities should anybody question him. But no one had.

And here he was, dragging a boy across a mountain, pursued by Iranians and Russians as he tried to make it to the safety of his American Handler. A situation he'd never imagined in his life that he would find himself in. And *should* never have found himself in. But when a CIA officer had slipped him a slim file across the table of a Beirut café, Karim's life had changed forever. The information in the file providing him with the only motivation he'd needed to turn on his masters and join forces with his country's most hated enemy. He'd had no doubt that the information was true. Yes, the files could have been doctored, manipulated and designed to be authentic but Karim had known just by reading them that they were real. The timeframe, details and wording convincing in their authenticity. And the CIA hadn't needed to go to any great lengths to snare Karim; they had him cornered the moment he sat down in that café in Rue Hamra. They'd known that he was either going to work for them or disappear into one of their Black Sites around the globe for a lengthy interrogation. But the information had been enough. The initial spark of anger within him soon a blaze of rage and fury that fueled his prime motivation for turning:

Revenge.

After a lifetime of believing his parents had died in a terrible accident, Karim had learned the vile truth from the contents of a slim folder given to him by a CIA officer in a café in Beirut. That the accident had been a state-sponsored cover-up to hide the massacre of dozens of civilians by a team of Quds Force convinced they had discovered an Israeli spy. That when their 'spy' had gone to ground in the factory, the workers had protested the local man's innocence and refused to give him up. Locked and barricaded the doors to prevent the Quds from getting their man. The decision had been made to kill everyone inside, take no chances that the 'spy' had accomplices that the Quds were unaware of. Kill all the rats while they were trapped in one location. According to the file, the Quds had intended using the massacre as an example to other, unpatriotic individuals of the consequences they could expect. But Tehran had balked at this; the murder of over seventy people based on little more than a suspicion, too harsh even for their appetites. The possibility that such a massacre could actually encourage rebellion rather than quell it fueling the necessity to cover the atrocity up with a banal story about a tragic accident where all lives were lost. Witnesses to the incident were arrested and killed to deter the threat of the real story spreading. And it had worked. Karim and, he assumed, the other living relatives of those killed in the factory completely believing the glorious Republic's version of events.

A strong gust of wind buffeted him and brought his attention back into the present. He had to keep moving, make fast progress east in the hope that the General and his hunters would drop the pursuit at the border. Unlikely, he knew but even slim hope was better than none. Karim's thoughts turned to Vic and what the CIA officer would be doing to help Karim's exfiltration. The possibility that Vic was already dead entered his head and he began exploring his options if this turned out to be the case. Karim would have to make it into Iraq and then find a way of connecting with US Forces in the country in order to get his information into the right hands. He couldn't trust the Iraqis, knew from experience the networks and support that Iran had established at every level of that country's infrastructure. But all that would come later; he and the boy needed to make it off the mountain and into Iraq before anything he'd thought about became even a remote possibility.

A quick glance over his shoulder satisfied him that Affan was keeping up and again, a respect for the boy's tenacity and endurance sent a wave of affection coursing through Karim. And with it a renewed determination to keep the boy safe and the only way he could do that was to get him into Iraq where the attributes he admired most about the orphan would stand him in good stead. Give him the chances he would never have in Iran. As his head swam with contingencies and back-up plans to ensure their survival, Karim realized that he needed to know one way or another if he had any support left on the mountain or if he and Affan were alone. Looking ahead, he spotted a cluster of rocks and made his way towards them, making sure the boy followed.

Karim knelt and removed his backpack, pulling a small mobile telephone from one of the pouches. He pressed the power button and looked around as the device booted up, remembering how close he had been able to get to the Russians and wary that his adversaries may pull the same trick. Looking back at the phone he stabbed at a series of keys and watched as the satellite connections came online and the call was initiated. He put the phone to his ear and listened to the dial tone repeating over and over. After some time, he sighed and was about to terminate the call when an American voice punched through the cloud of static and made him smile with its remark.

'I can't believe you're still alive.'

31

ZAGROS MOUNTAINS, IRAN

General Zana Shir-Del raised his face to the swirling snow, opened his mouth wide and screamed to the skies beyond the darkness. Rage, grief and frustration in equal parts fueled his bellow as it echoed around the rocks that he and his remaining operatives were taking shelter amongst. As he lowered his head to the cold rock face, he surrendered to the dejection that flooded him. *Eight.* He was now down to eight men. Eight survivors from a force of twenty-five. Seventeen of his Palang trainees and staff now seriously wounded or cold corpses on the slopes of the freezing mountains. He'd severely underestimated the traitor Ardavan, had not been prepared for the astonishing attrition the former Quds operative had been able to inflict upon Zana's forces. And with the help of the Americans, the traitor was as good as gone. They'd succeeded in pinning Zana and the survivors to the side of the mountain, the Quds' operatives in panic and disarray as grenades exploded among them and they tried to determine what was happening and who had been hurt or killed. By the time Zana had taken charge and all troops were accounted for, even he was stunned by their losses. And shocked at the brazen way some of his best men's throats had been slit as if they were nothing more than *halal* goats and left to freeze on the cursed mountain. He'd ordered that the dead remain where they fell, unwilling to risk the sacrifice of any more of his men to booby-trapped bodies or watchful Americans monitoring the corpses through the scope of a sniper rifle. Having led his small band of numbed survivors to the shelter of the rock formation, the full impact of their loss had been immediately apparent in their lack of numbers.

His self-pity was interrupted by an insistent tapping on his shoulder and Zana looked up to see the signaler trying to get his attention. He took in the younger soldier's countenance of exhaustion and shock before asking him what he wanted. The signaler cleared his throat and indicated with his hand to the glowing screen of the device he was holding.

'It's one of the mice, General. Very strong signal showing two people, moving initially but now static almost on top of the sensor.'

'Show me.'

The signaler turned the screen so that Zana could see the display. As he watched, the younger man interpreted the diagrams and symbols on the screen, explaining and emphasizing the relevance of the message.

'They are only twenty meters over there sir, and still in the same position.'

General Shir-Del looked in the direction the signaler had indicated, willing his eyes to pierce beyond the veil of driving snow and darkness. His apathy receded as a cold hatred took hold, clearing his mind and allowing him to focus. *Two people.* Could it be the traitor Ardavan and his companion or was it more likely to be the Americans? He wasted no more time on the question, the answer being of no significance to his decision. Americans or Ardavan, he was going to kill them. The blood of his brave Quds operatives would not be the only drink that the mountain took from him this night. Turning to the band of huddled forms sheltering among the rocks, he stepped closer and barked at the dejected group.

'Stand up straight and listen to me. We have underestimated our opponents and we have paid dearly. We have lost our brave, loyal colleagues to the traitor Ardavan and the American whores who came to claim him.' He thrust his arm out and pointed into the darkness. 'But only twenty meters away and hiding among the rocks just as you are, two of our enemy believe themselves safe. Believe that we are done, defeated, running away from them even as our comrades' bodies freeze on the earth around us.' He paused and leaned in, making eye contact with each individual. 'But we are not done. We are not defeated, and we are not running away. We are going to make our way over to those rocks and kill whoever is there, Ardavan or Americans, it doesn't matter. What matters is that whoever is there killed our comrades in cold blood, and I will not leave this mountain alive while the opportunity exists to avenge them. I would rather die with honor, avenging our brave warriors, than live with the worm of shame in my heart for the rest of my life if we don't do this. And I know each and every one of you feels the same way.'

There was silence as the men stared back at him but he could see his words had got through to most of them; their backs a little straighter, their eyes meeting his where moments before they would be lowered and focused on their feet, chests pushed out a little farther. He gave them no time to reconsider or re-evaluate.

'Let's go. One line, close together, each man only an arm apart. We walk till we meet them then we start shooting and we don't stop until these snakes are dead. Follow me.'

With that, he grabbed the signaler and raised his eyebrows in query. It took a brief second for the younger man to understand the General's meaning but then he got it, checked his screen one more time and nodded at his superior officer.

'They are still there. Same place and direction.'

Around Zana, the remainder of his diminished force closed up and formed a line, staring into the darkness, awaiting the final word from their leader. Zana nodded to himself, shouldered the stock of the carbine into his shoulder and stepped forward.

'With me.'

His men either side of him, Zana strode in the direction the signaler had indicated, the visibility limited to a mere body-length before them. He knew they could literally stumble upon their quarry but also knew that he had the upper hand; he *knew* where his quarry was, but the quarry didn't know where Zana and his men were. A touch on his elbow brought his attention back to the signaler who indicated with his hand a slight change of direction and then held up his fist before spreading the fingers out twice for the General's benefit. Zana understood: *ten meters*. He felt his adrenalin surge with each step and could now make out the rock formation in front of him as he brought the carbine up on aim, bent his knees slightly and continued forward. The rocks curved naturally downhill and Zana followed this contour around one of the larger boulders and was just about to glance over his shoulder to check on the progress of his men when a body loomed out of the darkness immediately in front of him. The fraction of a second that it took to overcome his startle response was quicker than that of the other man, and Zana squeezed the trigger and felt the recoil in his shoulder as the rounds left the carbine and tore into the unidentified individual in front of him, propelling the body back into the darkness and out of sight.

32

ZAGROS MOUNTAINS, IRAN

With one arm, Karim half-dragged, half-leaned on the boy. He choked and sputtered before spitting a thick stream of blood out of his mouth and onto the rocks beneath him. A ricochet on a rock face sent splinters of stone into his cheek and he recoiled from the stinging sensation, too high on adrenaline to fully register the pain. Their pursuers were close, so close he could identify individual voices as they closed on him and the boy. Only the darkness and falling snow stopped the hunters from seeing where their quarry was running. His breathing was becoming more ragged; wet, heavy rasps as his oxygen-depleted body struggled to balance intake with requirement. They were in deep trouble. He was badly wounded and knew he wouldn't see the hour out, had seen enough men with similar wounds over the years to diagnose his own without false hope or pity. Had he been alone he would have turned and faced his pursuers, taken as many of them with him as he could. But he wasn't alone. He was with the boy.

As they careened over rocks and skidded on ice, Karim risked a glance at the orphan. Affan's face was the very definition of terror; wax-white even in the poor light, eyes wide and the mouth a yawning rictus sucking in as much air as he could to feed his exhausted muscles. They couldn't sustain this for more than a few minutes and Karim knew this was nowhere near enough. He reached into one his pouches and removed the fragmentation grenade, almost falling as he struggled to adjust his balance. He didn't ask the boy to stop, merely used his teeth to pull the pin before lobbing the grenade behind them. With the five-second delay and the cover of the rocks around them he knew they would be safe from the lethal shrapnel when it exploded but it should give their pursuers something to think about. It seemed to Karim that they had only taken a couple of steps before the flash and bang erupted behind them and he heard the shouts of their hunters. But he and the boy were good. Affan, to his credit, not even acknowledging the distraction. But it was only a temporary delay to the inevitable. Karim knew the General was too close to give up now. He had the taste of his prey and was beyond the point of recall, only a matter of time before Karim and the boy lay dead at his feet.

But that didn't mean they had to make it easy for him.

Karim pulled on the boy and forced him to stop. Affan stared at him, wild-eyed as he shook his head and reached out to grab Karim's blood-soaked arm. Karim ignored the boy and retrieved the last two grenades from his pouch, pulling the pins from each and clasping them tight in his fists. He turned with difficulty, emitting an involuntary yelp as a lance of pain assailed his chest and lungs. With his good arm he lobbed the first grenade in a high arc into the darkness then repeated it with the second, the *ting* of the fly-off levers pinging into the darkness barely audible above his labored breathing. Moments later, two consecutive flashes followed by muted concussions confirmed the grenades had worked. Whether or not they'd had any effect on his hunters however was something he couldn't know. No matter. He'd only wanted to buy time. He knew that whatever time he'd bought would be very short; even if he'd wounded them, the General would force his men to close for the kill regardless of casualties.

Karim grabbed Affan's arm and indicated with his head that they should move. The boy needed no further prompting and supported Karim's weight by ducking under his arm and slinging it over his bony shoulder. They moved as fast as they could over the treacherous ground, falling and recovering, each tumble an agony for Karim to endure. As Affan tried to haul him up after a particularly heavy fall, Karim shook his head.

'No more, little leopard. No more.'

The boy shook his head, eyes watering and thrust his arms forward to grab at Karim's jacket but he swatted them away, wincing at the effort.

'Affan, no. I can't. I am dying and won't make it any further.' He sucked in some cold air and grimaced at the fire in his chest. His breathing became heavier and his head began to drop. Breathing in through his nose, Karim lifted his head back up and made eye contact with the boy who had dropped to his knees and was openly weeping, shaking his head in denial. Karim felt tears well up in his own eyes and a sadness consume him at the thought of leaving the boy alone. Fighting the greyness at the edges of his vision he leaned forward until their foreheads were touching.

'Affan, you can live. You *will* live and that is an order. Otherwise everything we have done is for nothing. But you must help me now, quick and without questions. Take my pack off and follow everything I tell you to do. NOW boy! You need to hurry.'

The shock of the raised voice spurred Affan to move and he helped Karim remove the pack, cringing at the man's groans of agony. Karim gave the boy specific directions and Affan removed the claymore mines from within the pack and helped Karim unspool the command wires. Karim showed the boy how to unfold the legs and position the devices securely among the rocks. He ensured Affan placed the blasting caps in the detonator wells before ordering him to conduct a final check of the mines. Karim took the ends of the wire that the boy passed him and inserted these into the firing mechanisms, leaving them ready but with the safety in the 'on' position. He coughed again, his body racked with spasms and blood pooled in his mouth before trickling out and running down his face. His head drooped but he hadn't finished with the boy. Drawing on his final reserves, he lifted his head and pulled Affan closer to him. When he had the boy's ear at his mouth, he spoke without pause, determined to get the information out before their hunters stumbled upon them. When he'd finished, he gave the boy a small sack, dropping items that Affan would need before loading the pistol with a fresh magazine, cocking it and depositing it on top. He handed the sack to Affan and felt his throat constrict as he watched the tears streaming down the boy's face. Karim pulled the boy's head to his shoulder and leaned his face into the boy's hair as his own tears ran down his cheeks. A sound to his left broke his sorrow and he thrust the boy away from him before grabbing the claymore firing mechanisms.

'Go little leopard. Go and live. Make all of this worth something. Be the man that would make me proud to have known you. Go boy. GO!'

Affan had seen something move in the darkness and, taking a last look at the only man who had ever shown him kindness, screamed his grief into the wind, picked up the small sack and ran into the darkness. Karim watched him go and felt his body slump as his responsibilities were now over. He'd given the boy a fighting chance and that was all that he could do. His vision blurred as he reached for the firing mechanisms and he had to concentrate hard to get them in his hands without dropping them. His eyes narrowed as he tried to focus on the safety switches, but he managed to move them to the 'off' position just as several men loomed out of the darkness. They didn't see him immediately and it was only when the lead man let out a yell of surprise that the others noticed Karim slumped against the rocks. When he didn't move or react, they moved closer, carbines on aim as they shuffled forward. Karim felt the greyness colonize his vision and knew he was close. Without moving any other part of his body, he depressed the handles of the firing mechanisms firmly, sending the electrical charge along the wires to the lethal devices. The explosions of light and sound assailed Karim and he fell sideways onto the rocks but felt no pain. As he lost consciousness, the last sounds he heard were the muted screams of his hunters and as his breathing stilled, his last thought was that the little leopard still had a chance.

33

ZAGROS MOUNTAINS, IRAN

Zana clambered to his feet and fired a burst from his carbine into the darkness where the explosions had come from. Without waiting for his men to recover, he screamed, eyes ablaze with fury and strode forward firing short bursts as he went. As a swirl of snow cleared, he saw the body collapsed at the base of a boulder pile and he turned his weapon and emptied the remainder of his magazine into the traitor Ardavan. He released the empty magazine while pulling a full one from a pouch, placed the new mag on the weapon and released the working parts forward before firing a further three rounds into Ardavan's chest. He stopped, lowered the weapon slightly and scanned the area before focusing his attention back to the body of the traitor.

Zana walked slowly forwards, weapon up and alert for any reaction but he saw immediately that Ardavan was dead, the position of the body and the darker shade around the chest of the jacket telling Zana as much. As he studied his former subordinate, the General felt a mix of emotions: Rage with Ardavan for his duplicity and treachery, relief that he had finally brought the traitor to justice and could now contact Headquarters, and... something he couldn't quite define. A lack of satisfaction. A desire not sated. He brushed it off and turned his head as one of his men stumbled towards him. He saw it was the signaler and the man's face was covered in blood. He saw Zana looking at him and raised a gloved hand to his head.

'My head Sir. Something from the explosion hit me.'

Zana nodded. 'Scalp always bleeds a lot. Looks worse than it is. You'll live. Now, help me search this viper and see what he's carrying.'

The signaler stared back the General for a moment, angered but not completely surprised by the officer's utter lack of empathy. He shook his head then moved towards the body as the General began opening the pockets on the dead man's jacket.

Zana cursed Ardavan's name as he rifled through the clothing, scrunching the pockets, collar and seams for any concealed items that the traitor may have secreted. But beyond standard pieces of kit he'd expected to find, there was nothing. Frowning, he turned his attention to the tactical-vest and backpack, rooting through every pouch and cavity but again, finding nothing out of the ordinary. He stood as several more of his men staggered into the area, nursing wounds and injuries of various severity. He failed to notice the fear and dejection that the remnants of his force emitted from their wan faces, his sole focus now on scouring the area around Ardavan's body. It took him several minutes before his eyes picked out an anomaly among the drifts of snow and he dropped to one knee to study it.

A footprint. Recent and not Ardavan's. This was smaller and the tread of the shoe different from the traitor's field boots. Zana could now see a very faint trail leading from this print and knew that Ardavan's companion was still alive and making good their escape. He stood and barked at the huddled survivors.

'Let's move. The traitor's companion is running. Come now, let's get this bastard and finish this thing once and for all.' He turned on his heel and strode out but stopped when he heard no sounds. Looking back over his shoulder he saw that none of the men had moved and were stood still, eyes lowered. His anger erupted and he spun to face them.

'I said MOVE! Get those weapons up and follow me. This bastard is getting away and I don't have time for your shit.' His anger turned to genuine surprise when again, none of his charges responded to his order. Zana's lip curled and he turned his carbine upon the gaggle of cowards.

'You will all lift up your weapons, get into file and follow me now or by Allah's will, I will cut you down where you stand.'

After a moment, the men glanced at each other and Zana relaxed as he saw the weapons being brought into the shoulders and no longer held like women's handbags. His satisfaction was short-lived as he saw that each man's rifle was pointed at him. His eyes widened in disbelief. He had *never*, in all his years as a leader of men, witnessed anything so outrageous. He barked again.

'Point those fucking guns away from me and fall in line. NOW.'

A young Captain spoke up, his voice wavering as it competed with the gusting wind and snow. 'Enough General. It is over. Many of us are dead, the rest are wounded, and you have your dead traitor. So, it is enough. If you want anything else, then do it yourself. We are calling Headquarters for medical recovery.'

Zana growled and took a step towards them but stopped in shock as the Captain fired his weapon, the bullet passing close enough to Zana that he heard the buzzing as it zipped past his ear.

'That's far enough General. One more step and we will kill you. Leave your corpse on this forsaken mountain for tomorrow's crows. You have betrayed your Unit and your Headquarters with this personal obsession, and we will tolerate no more.'

Zana's finger curled around the trigger as rage clouded his mind, vengeance for this final betrayal the driving thought foremost in his mind. He didn't care about dying, had never been frightened by the prospect, but he'd be damned if he was going to be killed by a mutinous mob of cowards. As his senses returned, he looked back in the direction the footprints led and made up his mind. Lowering his weapon, he addressed the forlorn group.

'As you wish. I will hunt and kill the traitor myself. But I will return, and you will all be punished harshly for this. *Very* harshly. You have brought great shame to your country and your families this day and you will live to regret it. But you have all made your decision as I have made mine. Stay warm you nest of vipers and I will see you all again soon.' With that, Zana turned and strode into the gloom, head low, straining to follow the tracks that grew fainter with every flurry of snow that filled the indentations. He cast aside the behavior of his mutinous troops and applied his entire focus to the task of tracking Ardavan's accomplice. The mutineers could wait.

He would deal with them on his return.

34

ZAGROS MOUNTAINS, IRAN

Ned Kelly lowered the thermal scope and slid down from the small rocky embankment until he was lying beside Vic.

'If I had to guess I'd say that was your boy fighting his way out. I picked up around five signatures closing in on something before the explosions then lost them as they went into dead ground. Some more shooting, then quiet for a while then a single shot. Nothing since then. But they are only fifty meters away Vic, really close man.'

Vic nodded at the Delta soldier's summary.

'I don't know what the hell to think Ned. It could have been Seven, but I haven't been able to raise him since his last contact, so we don't have any way of knowing. Our pressing problem is the inbound birds. We need to make the LZ as safe as we can and that means we have to clear these assholes out of here.'

'Yeah, I know. Okay, let's stop wasting time. I'll take one other and go forward for a sneak and peek. You stay here with the rest and monitor the birds' ingress. I'll update with what we find. Good?'

Vic nodded again and made his way up to the crest of the small rise, scanning the area through his NVGs while he listened to Ned briefing the team over the comms. Ned called Lopez forward and then gave the call to say they were moving out. Other than the wind around him, everything was quiet as Vic continued his vigil, almost praying that the enemy would walk into his sights and make his job easier. Kill them all before the choppers arrived. Experience told him that this was very unlikely, that they'd be fighting a tough battle right up to their extraction but still, a man could hope. His earpiece crackled softly as a transmission from Dwight came through: *Birds inbound ten minutes.* Ten minutes. Vic felt a gnawing apprehension in his stomach at the thought of the imminent arrival of the helicopters into a hot Landing Zone. Had he made the right call? Was it really worth the risk of losing two aircraft loaded with the highest specification of technology and equipment?

Vic switched his focus back to scanning the dark terrain before him. He could second-guess himself all night, but the truth of the matter was that they were combat ineffective, and the mission now had to be a recovery of the team and their dead colleagues. He thought about Seven and wondered if there was the slightest possibility that he was still alive. Alive and being dragged back to the stinking cells of Evin Prison for the first of a stream of endless tortures and interrogations. Vic hoped Seven had died, quick and clean and before any of the Quds had got to him. A far more preferrable end for a brave man who'd sacrificed everything to try and get his information to Vic.

Vic still had no idea what the information was: CONUS target but no what, where and when with which to initiate any action against. He could only hope that other assets, both technical and human, would throw something up to give the Agency a fighting chance. His thoughts drifted again to the cluster of body-bags in the center of the small defensive position they were holding. Good, brave men who'd given the ultimate sacrifice on a mission that would never be publicly acknowledged. And then there was Seven; either dead with the snow and rocks as his eternal companions or severely wounded and on his way back to Tehran for interrogation. This happened from time to time with assets; they lived dangerous lives, a precarious balance between collecting actionable intelligence and not revealing their true role. Risks were taken and sometimes these risks were too much and the asset was caught. Vic didn't take it to heart; he'd liked Seven, admired the man even but at the end of the day he was an intelligence asset, a means to an end. Sure, Vic felt some sadness, but he'd lost assets before. Sometimes the agent just stopped showing up and answering communications and was never seen or heard from again. Other times, their exposure and punishments were made very public in order to deter others who may have been approached by the Agency or were thinking about approaching them. It was the nature of the work. You could like and respect your agents but as an intelligence officer, you never became too close to them.

Vic thought about the Iranians currently trying to kill them and was still puzzled as to why no reinforcements had come to flood the mountain and trap the American team. He wondered if weather was a factor and that the Quds had decided to send a small elite cadre of individuals to hunt down the Americans. If that had been the plan, it certainly wasn't going well for them. He hoped Ned and Lopez would locate the Iranians so that they could try and deal with them before the arrival of the birds.

***

Ned slithered over the ice-covered rocks and raised his head in increments as the voices to his front carried to him on the breeze. Through his NVGs he could see a huddle of around five individuals, rifles slung over

211

shoulders as they sat hunched close together for warmth. Creeping closer, he saw now that they were Iranians dressed in cold-weather clothing and well-equipped which suggested that they were Quds. He also noted that many of them were wounded, dressings and bandages now visible from his close range. He felt Lopez slide into position beside him and he dropped his head onto his arm and whispered to his fellow soldier.

'Five or six. No sentry. Most wounded. But well equipped and at least one big radio.'

He watched Lopez nod slowly before replying.

'You go left into cover, I'll take 'em straight on and you mop up the runners. Good?'

Ned patted Lopez on the arm in affirmation and crawled on his stomach until he reached a small group of boulders. Using these as cover he rose to his knees and looked over at the Iranians, now only barely visible. Slinging his carbine back to the front of his body, he cupped his mic and spoke softly into it.

'In position.'

He received two clicks in reply from Lopez and a moment later he watched as the tall Texan strode into the clearing and opened fire. Much of the sound was muted from the suppressor but Ned could hear the rifle as Lopez fired small bursts of automatic that shredded into the sitting Iranians. Screams of shock and pain soon drowned out any other sounds and as Ned watched, several of the Quds made it to their feet and were scrambling over rocks in an attempt to escape the killing zone. Two of them tried to return fire but Lopez had them before they could take proper aim and the men dropped to the frozen ground, weapons unfired. The soldier with the radio on his back made it over a boulder pile and was running towards Ned, oblivious to the Delta man's presence. Ned lifted his carbine up as the young soldier began screaming something unintelligible into

212

the night. Taking aim at the head, Ned fired a quick burst and saw the signaler catapult over a knee-high rock where his body came to rest in a crucifix-like position. Lopez was beside Ned a fraction of a second later looking into the darkness beyond. Ned followed his gaze.

'You any idea what he was yelling before we took him out?'

Lopez nodded. 'Took the Farsi course last year. He was yelling *General, General.* What the fuck you think that means?'

Ned pondered the question before answering. 'Think that means we might have us an Iranian General out here with us. Real VIP for a shindig like this. Come on, let's take a look and see if we can't introduce ourselves to our special guest.' He moved forward, carbine in the shoulder, knees bent and focused on the land in front of him through the green hue of his NVGs. The last thing they needed was to stumble into a position of Iranians and lose the initial firefight. He thought back to all the information they'd picked up through the night and was sure that even if there was a General out here somewhere, he couldn't have many more men with him. According to Ned's rough calculations, and having heard no indication of reinforcements, there could only be a couple of Quds operatives left out here, four at the most. But he didn't take this as granted; there could be more of them. He was also cognizant of the time going by and wanted to be done with this before the birds arrived.

It was Lopez who spotted the faint indentations in the snow and identified them as recent tracks. Ned agreed and the pair followed the trail, Lopez studying the footprints and leading the way with Ned covering his colleague and scanning the area around them. Lopez began moving faster and Ned knew that these tracks must be fresh ones, easier to see and follow. They'd covered a fair distance in a short time and Ned was going to suggest changing roles with Lopez when the Texan dropped to the ground and gave the hand signal for enemy ahead. Ned lowered himself to the ground and lay next to Lopez, weapon aimed in front as he saw movement ahead. While he watched, the movement took the form of a man, arms moving up and down. Ned was just about to squeeze the trigger when another person materialized out of the snowy gloom and appeared to be fighting with the first man. Ned chewed on his lip as he attempted to interpret the scenario before him.

What the fuck is going on now?

35

ZAGROS MOUNTAINS, IRAN

Zana stared in disbelief at the disheveled child before him. *This* was the snake Ardavan's companion? This... *child*? The General took several seconds to get over his surprise but remembered that child or not, he was probably carrying whatever Ardavan had given him to take to his American masters. Zana still couldn't quite accept that this waif was Ardavan's travelling companion. Would have thought him a little young to be carrying out acts of treason against the regime. But traitors came in all shapes and sizes and he really shouldn't have been so surprised that Ardavan's accomplice was a child. The boy was scrambling on the ground where he'd fallen after trying to outrun Zana. He was having difficulty getting to his feet and Zana was about to stride over and haul him up when the boy managed to stand and face him.

Zana assessed that he couldn't be more than twelve or thirteen, his scrawny frame, hollow cheeks and sunken eyes telling the story of an impoverished background. He was dressed in a man's jacket, probably Ardavan's, but of interest to Zana was the sack that the boy held tight in his hands, knuckles white as he grasped the bag as though his life depended on it. Which Zana acknowledged that it just might. But he didn't have time for any more assessments. He slung his carbine around so that it dangled from the sling and rested against his side. He pointed at the sack.

'Give me that now and you may live.'

The boy remained motionless, nothing to indicate he'd even heard the directive. Zana growled and raised his voice.

'I said, give me that bag and I might let you live. NOW!'

This time the boy started at the shout and shivered but still did not comply. Zana took two quick strides and backhanded the boy in the face, grabbing the bag with his other hand as the waif fell to the ground. Zana opened the back and felt inside, pulling items out and examining them before discarding them on the snowy ground. Food, a water bottle, gloves, bandages. The General tipped the sack up but nothing else fell out of it. He dropped the bag and turned his attention back to the boy, grabbing a handful of his jacket and hauling him up until his face was mere inches from Zana's own.

'Where is it?'

The boy said nothing. With a speed that belied a man of his years, Zana's head was a blur as he thrust his forehead into the boy's face, letting him drop as the child recoiled from the shock of the head butt and collapsed in a heap. Zana leaned over the boy, grabbed his hair and yanked backwards until he was looking into the blood-covered face.

'I will ask you one more time: Where is it?'

The boy coughed and blood poured freely from his crushed nose. He tried to say something, but Zana couldn't hear him.

'What? Speak up, I can't hear you boy.'

He leaned in, tilting his head to one side to get his ear closer to the boy's mouth. Instantly he was in agony

216

as his ear erupted in utter pain and he screamed, thrusting the boy away and with him, the better part of Zana's right ear in his mouth.

The General bellowed and brought a hand to his ear, lips curled back in disgust and disbelief as he felt the sticky mess and the space where his upper right ear should have been. His crazed eyes turned to the boy who was spitting the bloody detritus out of his mouth as he scrabbled backwards over the rocks. Zana was on him in an instant, pummeling the boy's face and head as he screamed his rage, arms pumping up and down as he rained his blows on the child. The boy was doing his best to cover his head, but Zana's assault was relentless, and he completely overpowered the waif. After some time, he paused, lowering his fists and breathing heavily as he watched the boy's head flop to one side. His rage still unsated, Zana took a step back and was about to kick the boy into life when another thought came to him. He'd missed the opportunity with Ardavan, but he wouldn't miss this one.

The knife.

Even if the boy was close to losing consciousness, the pain of the knife would bring him back. Zana knew this from experience, had conducted the same technique on several unfortunate individuals over the years. But this was different. *This* was going to be enjoyable. He would take his time, draw the torture out. Get what he needed but he wasn't going to cut it short. No. If Ardavan couldn't pay for his crimes then his young accomplice would settle the account. Was only fair. A faint smile reached the corners of his mouth and he wiped the blood that started to run between his lips from his wounded ear. He spun the knife in his hand, grasped the handle and looked up to show the boy what was coming.

Zana's mouth dropped open as he took in the sight of the pistol barrel aimed between his eyes, the gun impossibly large in the child's hand. Before he could think another thought, the boy pulled the trigger.

Affan waited a moment before walking over to the man's body and looking down at it. The man was lying on his back and his eyes were open, blood running from the hole in his forehead and pooling in the right socket. Affan was sure he was dead but had never killed a man before so he gripped the pistol with both hands, aimed as best he could through his swollen eye and pulled the trigger again. His ears were still ringing from the first shot but this one was also very loud. When he closed his eyes the imprint of the flash remained. He patted his chest and squeezed at the pocket, ensuring the small package that Karim had given him was still there.

When the man had caught up with him, Affan knew he couldn't outrun him so had feigned a fall in order to get the package and the pistol out of the sack and conceal the items on his person. And it had worked. He had survived. Broken nose, broken teeth and his head felt strangely light, but he had survived. His eyes watered as the shock of the situation kicked in and how close he'd come to being killed and failing Karim. But he hadn't failed and thought Karim might even be proud of him. He was about to pick up the items on the ground when a flurry of movement erupted from the snow and he brought the pistol up, aiming it at the man who was pointing a rifle at him.

Ned paused for a beat as he realized he was looking at a kid. But this thought was swiftly followed by the realization that the kid was pointing a big pistol at him. With a fraction of a second with which to assess the situation, Ned acted on instinct. He knew Lopez was covering him from behind, so Ned lowered his carbine, allowing it to hang from the sling. He opened his arms out wide to show his benign intentions.

'Whoa kid, whoa. Hey there, why don't we put the gun down huh? I'm not going to hurt you, you understand?' The gun was unsteady and wavering, but Ned could see this was due to its weight and the kid's terror. 'Come on buddy, nobody needs to get hurt here, just lower the gun.' With still no response, he wondered if he should try to get Lopez to talk to the kid, but he could see that it would only take the slightest thing to set the kid off. Ned patted his chest with his hand and smiled as wide as he could manage.

'Friend. Me, friend. Amigo, compadre, good guy.' The boy was struggling to keep his hands from shaking and Ned could imagine getting shot by accident if this went on much longer. He shook his head in frustration as he tried to find a way to resolve the situation without putting a bullet into the kid. He patted his chest again.

'American. Me… American… understand?'

He watched as the boy tilted his head to one side and finally spoke, a quiet voice, heavily accented English, shaky and stuttering with fear.

'American? American?' The boy pointed at him with his free hand and Ned smiled and nodded.

'YES! American. Me American.'

The boy lowered the pistol, but Ned remained still, not wanting to spook him. He was about to ask the boy for the gun when the child spoke again, and Ned's mouth dropped open in astonishment.

'Vic. Take me… Vic.'

36

ZAGROS MOUNTAINS, IRAN

Vic Foley looked from the boy back to Ned and addressed the Delta Master Sergeant.

'He said *what?*'

Ned shook his head. '*Take me to Vic.* That's what he said. Couldn't believe my ears, didn't realize you ran Assets that young.'

Vic was examining the scrawny child in front of him as he replied. 'Erm… we don't. This is not my Asset, Ned. Lopez?'

The tall Texan came forward. 'What do you need?'

'Ask the kid who the hell he is and how he knows my name. Oh, and what the hell he's doing out here.'

Lopez nodded and squatted down until his face was level with that of the boy's. In soft tones he spoke with the waif, introducing himself and relaying Vic's questions in a gentle manner. The kid's face was a mess of swelling and blood, but Lopez could still see the fear apparent. There was a small pause before the boy replied, his small face grimacing at the pain from his shattered mouth. When he'd finished, Lopez nodded and turned to Vic.

'Says a man called Karim rescued him. He's been helping this Karim guy fight the evil men who tried to stop them meeting Karim's American friend.' Lopez paused and gave a glance back at the boy before continuing. 'Says Karim is dead, body not far from here. But before he died, he gave the kid something and told him that he had to ask to be taken to Vic. This Karim guy taught him to say it in English.'

Vic moved towards the boy and slowly placed his hand on the trembling shoulder. 'Okay, tell him I'm Vic and ask him what it is he has for me.'

Lopez interpreted the request and the boy responded by unzipping the top of his jacket and rummaging inside until he pulled out a small, rectangular object and handed it to the CIA officer. Vic looked at the object and saw that it was a case of some sort, metallic and with a dual-button release mechanism. He applied pressure to the buttons and the top of the casing separated from the bottom with a soft click. Taking great care, Vic removed the lid and studied the contents of the small case. Four USB thumb-drives were seated in molded depressions in the base of the case. He shook his head in wonder. Seven had come through. The man had died on a freezing mountain due to the information he'd been carrying but he'd still made sure that he got it to Vic. He turned back to Lopez.

'Tell the kid he's done an amazing job. Amazing. Get him cleaned up and see to his injuries as best you can, I want to get these out over the comms now. Birds inbound in less than five, so we need to work fast.' He turned on his heel and began striding towards Dwight but stopped and looked back at the boy.

'Lopez, what's the kid's name?'

There was a brief conversation and Lopez looked back at Vic and grinned.

'Says his name is *Palang*. That's Farsi for leopard.'

Vic returned the smile and nodded at the boy. 'Well, that works for me. Thank you for your courage, *Palang*.'

With that, he hurried over to Dwight to get the contents of the drives uploaded and into the system. Even if the team had trouble making it out, at least the information would get to the right people. He dropped to one knee and spoke quickly, directing Dwight as the comms specialist set up the SATCOM to link with the encrypted laptop. Vic punched in his access codes and the machine booted up instantly. He placed the first of the drives in one of the ports and initiated the download. The task was complete in under five seconds and he repeated it with each drive until he'd finished, stored the drives back in their case and secured the case in one of his interior pockets. Turning back to the laptop he fired a quick missive to the analyst department where Seven's information was assessed and disseminated and signposted them to the location of the information he had just uploaded. It would have been flagged as incoming Flash Traffic from Operations anyway, but Vic didn't want to leave anything to chance. He looked up as Dwight tapped his shoulder.

'Birds in two.'

Vic nodded and packed the laptop away as Dwight disassembled the SATCOM gear and stowed it away. Ned jogged past and pointed.

'I'll bring the chopper in. Lopez is dealing with the bodies and Deke's pulling security. Gonna try to find some level ground around here.'

Vic waved in response and walked over to where the boy was sitting hunched against some rocks, chin tucked into his jacket in an attempt to stay warm. Vic sat beside him and using hand movements and sounds demonstrated as best he could, a helicopter coming in to pick them up. After the initial confusion apparent in the boy's expression, he saw the message eventually sink in and the kid nodded his understanding. Vic could hear Ned talking to the pilots and now heard the hum of the rotors as the sound drifted in and out of hearing range, carried on the gusting wind. He listened as Ned described the LZ to the pilots and his recommendation that they leave the back of the helicopter hanging over the steep ledge as he didn't think the slope they found themselves on would accommodate the bird's full size. Vic understood and had seen this done several times before and was sure it was nothing new to these pilots. The sound of the rotors was now stronger and continual, and he heard the pilot confirm he had visual on Ned's signal. Deke informed them that he had no hostile activity present and the pilot acknowledged as the first bird came into the LZ under Ned's guidance.

While it was adjusting its landing on the treacherous slope, Ned nominated the guys he wanted to get on the first chopper and directed them to take the dead with them. Vic watched as Lopez and his detail picked the bodies up between them and ferried them in shifts to the helicopter that was still invisible to Vic through the dark and snow. It was under a minute when he heard Ned transmit that the first bird was clear to go. The Delta Master Sergeant then called everyone else in for the next lift. Vic turned to the boy and motioned for him to get up. When he stood, Vic put his arm around the kid's skinny shoulders and jogged towards the LZ, eventually sighting Ned's Infra-Red chem light that he was swinging in a loop to guide them in. As Vic and the boy arrived, Ned indicated with his hand where he wanted them to wait and tapped the back of his head several times. Vic understood the message and reached to the back of his own helmet and clicked on the Infra-Red strobe that the pilots would see as they descended. He looked up as another two figures joined them, Deke giving him the thumbs-up to let him know everyone was in. Deke then relayed this to Ned and the bird was called in. Vic covered the boy's eyes with his hand and lowered his head as the sound of the rotors became loud.

37

ZAGROS MOUNTAINS, IRAN

Sergeii smiled and looked up into the dark sky and driving snow. *Yes; there it is again.* He could hear it better now. His pick-up was coming. His beautiful *krokodil*, the king of Russian helicopters, was coming to pluck him from this freezing mountain. To take him back to the barracks where he was going to drink and maybe go into town, enjoy himself in that little whorehouse where he and Vladimir had once… His smile turned to a frown of confusion as he couldn't remember who had called the helicopter in and why they had done it. Weren't they supposed to finish this route march and get the trucks to bring them back? He coughed, deep hacks emitting a bloody spittle from his mouth leaving a pink, frothy residue in the corners.

The agony in his chest cleared his mind and Sergeii remembered exactly where he was. This was no Spetsnaz training exercise in the Urals. There was no nearby town, let alone whorehouse. There was no transport, helicopter or otherwise coming for him. He was on the side of a freezing mountain in Iran, the sole survivor of a team of exceptional soldiers. And he was dying. Knew he'd lost too much blood and could feel his lung collapsing as the air leaking into the cavity deflated the organ like a punctured soccer ball. He wouldn't have long to wait; the dreams and hallucinations becoming longer and more realistic. Hell, he could still hear the imaginary helicopter from his last daydream. This brought a sad smile to his face and he leaned his head back against the rock, closing his eyes once more, surrendering to the inevitable.

His thoughts ran together; a miasma of memories and recollections of friends, fighting, wars and women. He remembered Julya, the receptionist from Lviv he'd initially ran as an informer but had soon found far more pleasurable in bed. She had incredible red hair and he tried to remember her face but couldn't concentrate because of the noise from that bastard helicopter. He frowned with frustration as he tried to ignore the imaginary machine and return to the lovely Julya, but it was bloody persistent and…

Sergeii's eyes snapped open and he stared into the darkness with an intensity that had all but deserted him since being wounded. The helicopter was *real*. It was here. And it wasn't his. For several seconds he did nothing but listen, his entire attention devoted to the sound of rotors. And then a gust of wind buffeted him and answered his last doubt. Did he dare hope that Zana and his troops were mere meters away from him? That he could actually survive this? But he didn't have the luxury of time with which to dwell on these questions: That helicopter would take off the instant it was loaded. Sergeii knew what he had to do.

He took a series of rapid breaths, clamped his teeth together and pushed himself up from his seated position. His eyes widened and he screamed as his wounds stretched and opened but he used the pain, exploited the enormous surge of adrenalin that flooded his system. He lurched toward the direction of the rotor wash, staggering on stiffened legs, mouth wide open in a vain attempt to inflate his crumpled lung. The wash was strong now, the snow and small rock particles stinging his face and as he shielded his eyes, he saw movement and identified a group of men jogging towards a black hulk of a shadow that was barely visible against the dark mountain. Several steps nearer, Sergeii halted and stared at the sight before him.

The helicopter was a Black Hawk.

He'd found the Americans.

His expression went blank and his arms dropped to his sides. Without any conscious thought, he reached to his thigh holster for his pistol, but the weapon wasn't there. He couldn't remember what he'd done with it or with his rifle. Assumed he must have dropped them somewhere as he'd stumbled about in a state of semi-consciousness. He opened up two pouches on his vest and withdrew two cylindrical devices. Without dropping his gaze from the helicopter, Sergeii removed the pins from the phosphorous grenades and clamped one in each blood-soaked hand. Maintaining his fixed stare on the aircraft he staggered forward once again, skidding and stumbling on the rocks and ice. Even as the debris from the rotor-wash assailed his face, the Russian did not blink, the bright blue eyes focused on the men clambering into the open door of a Black Hawk helicopter that hung off the edge of an Iranian mountain. He could see that there were only two more men making their way to the door of the aircraft and a warm, calming sensation infused Sergeii as he realized he was going to succeed. Walking forward, he brought his arms up and crossed them over his chest, the lethal cargo clasped in his hands now tucked hard against his shoulders in a vice-like grip.

Sergeii threw one leg in front of the other and began to run toward the helicopter in a stiff, jerky motion, regaining his balance every time his feet skidded or slid.

The last man was climbing into the helicopter as Sergeii reached it and screamed.

A noise shocked Ned and he turned to see a crazed man staggering towards the bird. Ned was positioned awkwardly and tried to bring his carbine up to bear but then saw what the man was carrying. Time seemed to slow for Ned, and he realized several things at once: He wouldn't get his rifle up in time to neutralize the threat. That even if he did, the grenades would probably still take out the bird. And that only he could do something about it. Without pause for further thought, the Delta Master Sergeant leapt from the doorway of the Black Hawk and threw himself at the man. As they collided, Ned gripped the man in a tight embrace but continued driving forward, pulling the man in tight and pinning his arms against Ned's chest. Ned used all his strength to maintain the momentum and propelled the man backward as they stumbled on rocks. The man was screaming something unintelligible in what sounded like Russian and his face was a grotesque mask of rage and pain. Ned could feel him trying to pull his arms free and release the lethal grenades, but the Delta Master Sergeant held fast. He saw the edge of the precipice approaching and knew they were still too close to the tail rotor to risk his plan. Knew that if the Russian loosed even one of the grenades, the damage to the chopper would see it plummet into the chasm below. His throat hitched as the reality of what he was about to do dawned on him and he closed his eyes, focusing his mind on a picture of Cathy and the girls. A sad smile contrasted with the tears rolling down his face and the warm flood of emotion that flooded his senses. Ned shook his head and roared from the bottom of his lungs, tightened his grip on the Russian and powered forward driving them over the edge of the dark abyss.

Vic yelled as he watched the pair fly over the edge of the precipice and into the darkness below. There was a humming in his head as he tried to come to terms with Ned's last actions. Someone was slapping his shoulder, but he ignored them, staring at the void into which his friend had plummeted. There was a brief flicker of light, but it was soon swallowed once again by the darkness. Vic felt his chin grabbed and looked up to see Deke's face close against his own.

'We're moving. Got hostile aircraft inbound. Ned's gone man. Give the order.'

Vic nodded and relayed the order to the pilot to lift off. Ned was gone. Another ten seconds or so and he would have been safe. Safe in the Black Hawk making his way back to Iraq and eventually to his wife and kids. Ten seconds. *Fuck.*

Affan watched Vic as the man's head dropped into his hands and he knew the pain that he was feeling. He too, had felt this heartbreak when Karim had died. The feeling that something warm and sad had flooded into your chest. Affan discreetly noted that the other Americans were also sad. No one was speaking and they were all looking at the floor of the helicopter. He gripped the edge of the seat hard as the helicopter dropped suddenly before swooping back up and weaving its way through dark passes that Affan couldn't see. The man who spoke his language was not in this helicopter so Affan couldn't ask any questions. But he wanted to know. He turned to the soldier next to him and tapped him on the shoulder. When he looked up Affan pointed at the floor of the helicopter, then the front of the machine and spoke.

'America?'

It took Deke a couple of seconds to work out what the boy was asking and when he got it, in spite of everything, he managed a small smile. He stretched out a hand and gave the kid's hair an affectionate tousle. 'No man. America too far. We're going to Iraq. You understand? Iraq.'

The boy nodded solemnly. 'No America. Yes Iraq.'

Affan leaned back in his seat as the warmth of the helicopter and the rhythm of the rotors lulled him into a state of weariness. He didn't know Iraq, but Karim had said he would be safe there and if Karim said it then Affan knew it would be true. As his breathing deepened and limbs relaxed Affan gave silent thanks to whoever was listening for the day he had stumbled across Karim on the cold slopes of a mountain in western Iran.

38

6 MONTHS LATER

TIJUANA, MEXICO

The man finished his *chalupa* with a small sigh of contentment and wiped the corners of his mouth with the paper napkin. His hands he merely rubbed on the thighs of his grimy jeans. Taking out his wallet, he removed several bills and placed them under the plate before standing, adjusting his sweat-stained baseball cap and walking off down the quiet street, his worn cowboy boots kicking up small puffs off dust in the afternoon sun. Turning a corner at the end of the street he saw himself being assessed by an optimistic hooker, but only for a moment as her professional judgement deemed the wiry, dark-skinned Mexican as not having enough money to spend on such a luxury. The man continued along the street, long legs covering the distance with ease, moving aside for other pedestrians, old-school manners prevalent in his actions. He crossed a road and took a quieter side-street to where it met with an intersection which he crossed and made his way into a hot, dusty park, the grass and plants almost as brown as the baked earth from where they sprouted with admirable determination. Taking a seat on a bench that had colonized the only shade from a nearby wall, the man pulled a brown bag from his back pocket, reached inside and removed the cap from the bottle. He took a furtive swig, gave a contented sigh, smiled and leaned back on the bench watching the cars as the passed him. Bringing the bottle up to his mouth again, he spoke softly.

'This is Lopez, Standby, Standby, Standby. That is Victor 1 mobile west from my location. Driver plus three.'

A soft buzz in his concealed earpiece preceded the reply.

Copy that Lopez, Victor 1 mobile. Driver plus three.

Lopez continued to drink regularly from the paper-clad bottle that contained nothing more alcoholic than iced tea, as the updates on the operation came through his earpiece. After around five minutes he stood and began walking through the park until he reached the road at the other end. A shabby grey van that had seen better days pulled up and Lopez waved at the driver before climbing into the passenger seat. To all intents and purposes just another tired, down at heel laborer getting a ride from a friend. As the van moved off, Lopez turned to the driver.

'Where we at?'

The driver continued to monitor his mirrors as he replied.

'We have Victor 1 and looks like they are going straight for the tunnel. Victors 2 and 3 showed up earlier to make sure everything was good, and our intercept picked them up confirming the time over the phones.'

Lopez was quiet for a moment as the van picked up speed. 'So, this is it? It's on?'

The driver nodded. 'Yeah brother. Looks like it's the real deal today. No more dummy runs.'

Lopez reflected on the information. This would be the third time that the Unit had deployed to get these motherfuckers but up until now the only activity the group were carrying out was entering and leaving the United States illegally through a tunnel system in Tijuana. But they always came back. Same journey every time: Entry point a collection of old storage units in the parking lot of an abandoned KFC then under the border to an industrial unit in Otay Mesa, San Diego. While the activity had Homeland Security and the Feds scratching their heads, it was Vic who'd identified that these were dummy runs; rehearsals to identify any problems or issues before they carried out the live operation.

Lopez had been impressed; he'd never worked the criminal gangs. Had done a few operations against the cartels in their backyard but these Barrio 18 boys behaved far more professionally than he would have given them credit for. The gang members had been under surveillance for almost a month and stuck to very strict procedures. They kept their drinking and whoring discreet, didn't frequent the bars and clubs like Lopez and the guys had expected. But Vic had explained that some of the gang were former security henchmen of Marduro, the Venezuelan president, real nasty pieces of work but professional with it. And they were key to the operation; no way were the Iranians going to entrust getting a dirty bomb into the US to a group of Venezuelan *barrio* thugs. No, the Iranians would have hand-picked the crew for this job with the blessing of the Venezuelan president. No doubt about that.

It still amazed Lopez that an operation they'd carried out on a mountain in Iran six months ago had led them directly to a Quds plot to build, bring and detonate a dirty bomb on US soil. The intelligence that had been downloaded from those small drives had been the biggest haul of tactical information ever to come out of

Iran. Targets, personalities, timings, agents, planned operations, ongoing operations. But what had been sobering to them all was the amount and extent of planned attacks against the US, all of which would have been attributed to Islamic extremism. ISIS sympathizers and networks held responsible through the trail of crumbs the Iranians would leave, leading the investigations down a mess of rabbit holes. These were well-planned operations that had been covered in every detail and without the trove of intelligence from Vic's Asset, the dirty bomb attack would have worked.

The Iranians and Russians had been helping prop up Marduro's government for some time, keen to keep a foothold in America's back yard. And when the sanctions bit Venezuela hard, the Iranians had all the leverage they required. The Asset's intelligence detailed the deployment of senior Quds officers to the Central American country and the millions of dollars in gold they 'donated' to Marduro. But the payoff was a steep one; help the Iranians in hitting the *yanqui* neighbors to the north with a blow that would rattle them severely. According to the intelligence, Marduro had actually been happy to provide any support his Middle Eastern friends required as long as there was plausible deniability. The Quds officers had assured the dictator that this would be the foremost consideration. While everyone was on board with punching the great USA on the nose in its own backyard, nobody wanted to be the recipient of its wrath if suspected of involvement. So former members of the regime and the cream of Barrio 18, Venezuela's premier mega-gang, were placed under the authority and direction of the Quds team entrusted with the operation.

The raw materials for the device made their way from the Natanz nuclear facility in Iran through various channels and cut-outs to Venezuela where they were assembled into the viable device. Criminal and cartel networks were exploited to provide safe passage of the bomb to the US border, a loose cover story of smuggling an important person north and staggering sums of money changing hands ensured the route was safe. Then a few weeks in Tijuana conducting rehearsals and making sure they hadn't been compromised. An Iranian officer masquerading as a Trade Delegate visiting Tijuana Province from his embassy in Mexico City oversaw the operation with clinical precision. Vic had briefed the team that this guy was definitely a seasoned Quds officer with overseas experience. The CIA watchers identified that this man routinely carried out counter-surveillance drills and left tells and triggers in his accommodation. A sharp operator leaving nothing to chance. On the US side, the Joint Task Force of CIA, FBI, Homeland Security and DoD had identified a network of Iranians and Venezuelans in communication with one individual who linked the group in the north to the Iranian officer in Tijuana. Again, the drills were good; burner phones, veiled speech, short calls, driving large distances before making contact and constantly switching locations where they called from.

But they were against a Task Force that had been given the Presidential go-ahead to do whatever it took to stop this attack. Unlimited budget, unlimited manpower, every asset made available to them with a mere phone call. The gloves were off on this one. Which Lopez was grateful for. He'd never been a fan of joint task forces and didn't enjoy inter-agency operations. But for Delta to have had any role in this operation within the US, it had been necessary to embrace the union. The *posse comitatus* law that forbids US military to operate on US soil given an exception due to the severe nature of the threat and the inter-agency composition of the task force. It was a non-issue while Lopez and the Delta squadron were operating in Mexico but once back on home ground, they would just have been bystanders. And nobody wanted that, particularly after the loss of their brothers on that damned Iranian mountain at the hands of the same people who were now trying to massacre hundreds of innocent Americans.

He was brought out of his thoughts by the transmission from the surveillance team watching the tunnel entrance.

All Victors present. I say again, all Victors present.

Lopez listened to the acknowledgements and felt the excitement building within him. These fuckers were going to go through with it. Another transmission confirmed his thoughts.

Victor 2 distributing backpacks to six individuals. Three coyotes up front, armed and with radios, three at rear armed and with radios. Mules also armed with assault rifles.

Lopez could see the scene in his mind. The *coyotes*, the guides, leading the way, looking for any problems and clearing the way for the *mules* and their precious backpacks. But they wouldn't find any problems in the tunnel. The tunnel had been entered by a team from Delta and the CIA some weeks before and microphones, sensors and cameras secreted through the entire length of the subterranean avenue. So there was no need to put men in the tunnel, the devices would cover the entire journey of the Venezuelans and their lethal payload.

Lopez imagined the tension building in the Situation Room as the feeds from the drone and static camera systems were relayed onto the array of large screens. All the representatives from the various agencies staring hard at the images before them, willing the Venezuelans to commit to the tunnel. As the van took a left towards the Forming-Up Area, Lopez heard the transmission they'd all been waiting for.

Coyotes and Mules into tunnel. Coyotes and Mules into tunnel.

With that, the driver accelerated and in under a minute they entered a large yard and the gate was hauled closed behind them as they came to a halt. Lopez moved fast, exiting the van and hauling open the side door where he reached in and began donning his assault gear. The lightweight Kevlar protection followed by his Tac-Vest, pouches stuffed with magazines and grenades of varying capabilities. He switched radios to his ATAK-configured system and checked in with Control. The driver joined him, hauling out his own bag and suiting up for the task. The pair then jogged over to a group of similarly dressed individuals who were waiting at the corner of a tall metal fence. They peeled a corner of the fence aside and Lopez and the driver ducked under and through the gap, entering the yard where the entrance to the tunnel was. With Lopez on point, the remaining soldiers fell into line behind him. As he approached the storage unit he spoke into his mic.

'This is Foxhound, are we clear to enter?'

The response was instant.

Yes Foxhound. You are clear, clear, clear.

Without a pause, Lopez led his team into the open door of the storage unit. He maintained a fast pace, carbine up on aim as he entered the darker interior of the unit. Making his way to the back of the room he pointed at a cluster of oil drums.

'Pete, Rusty. Get the cover off the tunnel, Mac and Paulie, first entry.'

The nominated individuals moved around him and took their assigned roles. They'd all seen the footage of how the Venezuelans entered and exited the tunnel and were familiar with the routine. Pete and Rusty maneuvered a gear lever and the cluster of barrels slid smoothly and silently to one side, revealing a hatch in the floor. Through the transmissions from the team monitoring the cameras, the men knew the Venezuelans were far enough along the tunnel that they wouldn't hear the Foxhound team's entry. Pete and Rusty opened the hatch and Mac entered first, descending the ladder into the depths below. Paulie went next and the moment his head was below floor level, Pete and Rusty followed the first pair. The remainder of the team conducted the same drill until all were into the tunnel other than the two who pulled above-ground security. A precaution in case anything went wrong while the rest of the team were below.

Lopez turned at the foot of the ladder and strode past his team, taking point as he clicked the power on his NVGs. He wouldn't use them yet as the tunnel was lit enough to see adequately, but he knew that the lights were going to be cut as soon as the Venezuelans were out on the other side and the team would need their NVGs after that point. The plan was simple enough; the Venezuelans would be allowed to exit the tunnel and make it to American territory before the strike went in. Snipers were already positioned in the industrial unit across the border and head shots was the order, taking these animals down in one concerted action. Leaving no possibility that they could get any communication back to their superiors. After the slaughter, the bomb mechanisms would be retrieved, and the technicians would move in and wire the unit with a sizeable device which would be detonated on the departure of the American personnel. The resulting news coverage would be sure to notice the presence of men in HAZMAT suits, a suggestion that whatever had exploded had contained something nasty. The hope was that when this hit the news, the Iranians would assess that there had been a malfunction of the device components resulting in a premature detonation. And there would be nobody who could challenge this narrative as the directive was clear; no survivors from this engagement. Other teams were already deployed to grab the brains behind the audacious attack before he disappeared into the Tijuana night.

For their part, Lopez and his team were the backstops; holding below ground to deal with any *squirters*; runners who managed to escape the initial assault and ran back into the tunnel. As they made their way along the subterranean thoroughfare, Lopez followed the almost constant commentary in his earpiece. The tunnel cameras had triggered the Venezuelans at the ladder on the American side and the *Standby* call was given to alert everyone to the imminent arrival of the *coyotes* and *mules* and their lethal cargo. Lopez began running, his men following and after less than a minute, saw the base of the ladder ahead of them. He held up his fist to signal the team to stop and spoke softly into his mic.

'Foxhound in position.'

The brief acknowledgement was immediately followed by the sound of gunfire and muted shouts and screams above them. The tunnel went pitch dark as the lights were cut and Lopez and his men flipped down their NVGs, the fifth-generation devices providing an almost as good as daylight view for the men. A clanging above, a shaft of light as the tunnel entrance was opened and a man tumbled down the ladder, landing in an untidy heap on the ground. He stood, staggered for a few steps as he realized he couldn't see in front of him then placed the palm of his hand on the wall and began walking forward as fast as he dared. Behind him, another individual dropped down the ladder and ran into the tunnel before he too, realized he couldn't see. The men began yelling at each other, voices high with fear and alarm, desperate to make progress but unable to see where they were going. Lopez watched as his green laser danced across the leading man's chest and he fired. The frangible rounds he used were designed specifically for use in caves and close urban fighting where conventional bullets passing through a body could ricochet and kill or wound the good guys. The added benefit of the ceramic rounds was that they literally exploded on impact and Lopez could see his rounds tearing hideous holes in the chest of the lead man. The second man tried to turn but Paulie had put four into his back before the Venezuelan had taken even a step. Lopez walked forward, placed the end of his suppressor just above the forehead of the first man and pulled the trigger. He carried out the same action with the man lying on his front before sending the transmission.

'Foxhound, all Targets down, I repeat, all Targets down.'

In keeping with the plan, the Foxhound team picked up the bodies and carried them to the foot of the ladder where a couple of ropes with karabiner clips were lowered. Lopez and his men looped the ropes under the armpits of the dead men and the team above hauled the corpses up and out into the light. They would join the rest of their dead *compadres* in preparation for their second, more public death. When Lopez climbed out of the entrance, he saw that the interior of the warehouse was bustling with activity. Groups of people clustered around in cliques according to role. The snipers loading their weapons into nondescript vans, the specialist technicians removing the bomb mechanisms from the backpacks of the dead Venezuelans, biometric and photography teams documenting the dead. Lopez caught the eye of a man moving amongst the groups and he gave him a nod of recognition and a wry salute.

Vic returned Lopez' salute with one of his own but had no time to spare to engage with the man further. As lead on the operation he had to oversee every aspect of the strike and the follow-up deception operation.

Nothing could be left to chance. But so far, everything had gone according to plan, a fact attributable to the pre-emptive intelligence he'd had from Seven's files. This had provided the Joint Task Force with the ability to deploy surveillance, technical intercepts and full camera coverage of every key part of the Venezuelans' operation. No surprises. And he'd been pleased when the survivors of Ned's squadron were allocated to the Mexico element of the operation. Couldn't have asked for better guys with purer motivation. He looked up as he heard his name called and saw his FBI counterpart pointing at a group of technicians closing the doors of a van carrying the logo of a fictional plumbing company.

'Foley, techs are done, biometrics complete and Delta leaving scene. We need to hustle.'

Vic nodded and jogged towards the roller doors, giving a nod to the FBI Agent at the controls to open the doors. Vic jumped in the passenger seat of the plumbing van and the driver moved off immediately with the discreet escort cars in front and behind them, protecting the inert but contaminated devices sealed within the specialized containers in the rear of the van. They passed a couple of pick-up trucks and another van travelling towards the site which Vic knew contained the bomb squad team who would plant the device in the warehouse and, once all friendlies were off site, detonate it. The area had been cleared and controlled hours before the Venezuelans had entered the tunnel, so the entire complex was devoid of civilians.

Vic's cellphone buzzed in his pocket and he answered the call, talking freely over the encrypted device with the Agency's Deputy Director of Operations, the DDO. The deliberately misleading title allocated to the DDO glossed over her official role as head of covert operations for the entire Agency. The call was congratulatory, the senior officer having watched the entire proceedings from the White House Situation Room alongside the top tier of the nation's government, security and intelligence representatives. Vic hadn't seen a gathering of that magnitude since the Bin Laden raid. He thanked the senior officer for her call and listened as another transmission came through his earpiece.

This is Aztec One. Visual on Tango, and Breach team moving in…

39

TIJUANA, MEXICO

The four men moved as a close unit, creeping along the dusty sidewalk, hunched over to avoid breaking the line of the wall that concealed them from view. Their weapons, helmets and collapsible ladder marking them as something more serious than the criminal gangs who sometimes targeted the area. The street was darker than usual, a fact attributable to the broken streetlights, shot out with an air-rifle earlier that day by the surveillance team in preparation for tonight's operation. The men continued with their silent approach, no words or communication necessary, each man having conducted dozens of these operations in different countries around the globe. A short distance behind them a similar team emerged from the shadows, moving in the same manner and following the same route. This team stopped short, placed their ladder against the wall and two men used the apparatus to negotiate the obstacle, covered by their colleagues who followed them into the garden once the pair had taken a position to cover them. Once complete, this team ran in a crouch to the sanctuary of the deep shadows by the side of the house. Again, without a word of command or communication, they snaked along the wall, weapons ready in the shoulder and disappeared around the corner into the rear of the property.

At the front of the house, two members of the breach team detached themselves from the group and placed the explosive charges to the four corners of the door by the adhesive backing on each small block. The pair left the doorway and joined their two colleagues, backs against the hard cover of the wall of the house. The Team Leader spoke quietly into his mic.

'Standby. Standby.'

A second later the quiet neighborhood was rocked by the explosion and several windows shattered in the near vicinity. Dogs barked and people shouted but the Breach Team was oblivious to this, already through the shredded door frame and moving fast into the house. The Team Leader ducked as a spray of automatic fire raked the wall beside him punching large holes into the drywall. A shadow darted between rooms before he could fire, and he cursed as he relayed the information.

'Fucker's armed and running. Coming your way.'

The Delta Sergeant watching the rear door nodded and aimed his weapon at the entrance. A split-second later the door flew open and a small man in an open-necked shirt stumbled down the stairs, almost tripping in his haste. The Sergeant smiled and squeezed the trigger, watching in satisfaction as the runner dropped to the ground, the Scorpion machine-pistol spinning away into the darkness of the yard. Before the runner had even stopped moving, two of the team were on him, zip-ties, gag and hood, immobilizing the man while the shock of the shot was fresh. They conducted a quick search of his pockets and dropped the items into small bags attached to their belts. The Delta Sergeant stood and relayed the update back to the Team Leader.

'That's JACKPOT, JACKPOT, JACKPOT.'

The Team Leader acknowledged the status and the Sergeant walked over to his men and nodded.

'Get him to the front. Wheels inbound ten seconds.'

His men lifted the prone body of the Iranian between them, moving fast around the corner of the building. The Delta Sergeant studied the ground for several seconds before he spotted what he was looking for. He stooped and picked the rounded beanbag-like object and dropped it into the open bag attached to his belt. While it wouldn't really matter if someone had found the object, the fact that a non-lethal projectile was used in a mysterious incident would alert the Mexican authorities that this wasn't just another beef between cartels or local *narcotraficantes*. As he made his way to the front yard, he reflected that he was glad they'd got their guy alive. He'd initially questioned the wisdom of taking down an experienced Quds operative with a non-lethal round, but the CIA had been insistent; the Iranian was a major intelligence asset and he needed to be taken alive. The Delta Sergeant grinned as he imagined the pain and shock that the Iranian was currently experiencing but however much that was, it was a hell of a lot less than what he was going to experience in whatever CIA Black Site he was being transported to. The Sergeant had accompanied detainees to a couple of these secret prisons around the globe and had seen first-hand the effects on a prisoner when there were no constraints on their captor's interrogation methods.

As he entered the front yard, a van pulled up, side door already open. His guys tossed the gagged and bagged Iranian into the vehicle where he was received by waiting hands that secured him to the floor as the van accelerated away and the door was hauled closed. People were coming out into the street now that things had quietened down. A fat man in a stained white vest scratched at his balls with one hand while filming the proceedings on his mobile telephone. This didn't concern the Delta Sergeant as he knew the techs had already pre-empted this issue and would ensure that no civilian communications would leave the area. Everything jammed until tomorrow morning and all media recordings and transmissions erased as a standard measure. He looked up as two more vehicles sped into the street and he and his team jumped into the first van while the Breach Team took the second. As the vehicles negotiated the tight Tijuana backstreets, the Delta Sergeant looked at his watch. One minute and thirty seconds from crossing the wall to full team exfil. He was satisfied with that. The vans picked up speed as they hit the wider thoroughfares that would get them out of the suburbs and towards the freeways and eventually to the waiting air assets to fly them out of the country.

40

CIA BLACK SITE '*WOLF LARDER*', DJIBOUTI, HORN OF AFRICA

Vic Foley sucked on the juice of the orange segment, relishing the flood of sweetness in the glare of the hot sun. He looked at his watch. *Three hours.* It had only been three hours, but his hopes were high. This would be the twentieth interrogation session in three days for their Iranian guest and Vic hoped this would be it. They were close, he could see that from the condition of the detainee. They already had his real name, background and current operations he'd been involved with, but he was still withholding the vital stuff: What's coming? What is the Quds planning to carry out in the near future? Vic was certain this guy would know. Not everything, but definitely relating to the US. That being, after all, this guy's turf. Ali Rashid, aka, Aban Dirwan, aka… well, it didn't really matter. He had around a dozen aliases depending on whether he was operating under diplomatic cover or not. He'd been assigned the codeword VOLTAGE, which Vic acknowledged was ironic considering the means of interrogation that VOLTAGE had been and was, currently experiencing. But it was necessary. VOLTAGE wasn't just an experienced Quds operator; he was connected by family to the biggest players in the game. And Vic knew that this was why he'd been resisting so hard. But biology would win out in the end. There was only so much pain and torture that the mind would allow the body to endure before the mouth opened and streamed forth with everything the interrogators wanted.

He cut another segment from the fruit and had just taken a bite when the door opened and Sayed stepped out, frowning in the bright sunlight before donning his sunglasses. He took a crumpled pack of cigarettes from his pocket and lit one, inhaling deeply before deigning to dignify Vic by noting his presence. He cleared his throat before speaking in his broken English and menacing gruff baritone.

'Our Iranian friend is talking now. Has remembered his manners and many other things as well. You should speak with him.'

Vic nodded. 'Thank you, Sayed. I am in debt to you once again my old friend.'

Sayed laughed and pointed his cigarette at the CIA officer.

'Fuck debt. Pay me money then no debt.'

Vic laughed as he stood and stretched. 'Don't worry, I have your money. I will pay you when I finish talking with our guest. Clean him up, give him new clothes and take him to the meeting room.'

Sayed nodded and brushed cigarette ash from his beard before flicking the butt of the cigarette into the sand and heading back into the interrogation room. Vic tossed the remainder of the orange into a decrepit oil drum and made his way to the main complex of ramshackle buildings that housed the more secretive elements of the *National Gendarmerie,* of whom Sayed and his nasty gang belonged. Vic didn't like Sayed, but it had to be said, the man got things done. This would be the third time in as many years that Vic had needed the services of Sayed and his crew and he'd never been let down yet. VOLTAGE and men like him were the most effective and prolific killers in the world and while Vic was no fan of torture *per se*, the rules for terrorists such as VOLTAGE had to be different. This man was probably overseeing a dozen or so major operations worldwide at any given time. Relying on international protocols for detainee interviews and adhering to Human Rights' clauses just meant more people died while the evildoers like VOLTAGE exploited the legal loopholes open to them.

Black Sites had been officially discontinued some years ago to satisfy the hysterics of the liberal elite and the pressure from the media. Unofficially however, a small portion of the capability had been retained for selective cases. Vic got it; sanctioned torture of an individual by a civilized, democratic nation *should* shock and disgust people. But the type of person taken to these sites had long ago lost any right to class themselves as a human being. And there was always a clock, a short time in which to get the information before a massacre or atrocity took the lives of innocents somewhere in the world. Vic had worked the Pakistan end of the international plot to bring down two transatlantic aircraft that would have resulted in the deaths of hundreds of Americans. And the lead for that had come from an Al Qaeda go-between the Agency had lifted in Berlin and taken to the *CAT'S EYES* site in Poland for an 'enhanced' interview. And he'd talked. Given up names, phone numbers, communication lines, logistics, the network of sympathizers. The attack was thwarted as a direct result of one scumbag suffering so that hundreds of innocents could live. In Vic's world, that was a very fair trade-off.

He opened the door to the building and entered a small room where he took bottles of water from a fridge and a tub of nuts and dried fruits. As he walked down the corridor, he relished the chill from the air-conditioning while he made his way to the observation room. Vic held a key for this small room, but he made it his practice to leave nothing in here that could come back and bite him in the ass at a later date. The cameras and cassette recorders were all old school; no threat of the contents being hacked or swiped as there would be with modern digital equipment. And after every session with a detainee, Vic took the tapes and left only the analogue recording equipment behind.

He loaded the devices with new cassettes, checked the power was good then turned on the lights for the meeting room. From the one-way mirror in front of him, the meeting room beyond was now illuminated brightly. Vic turned the devices on to recording mode just as the door to the meeting room opened and two of Sayed's crew pushed the detainee inside. They pointed to a chair and the detainee obliged, taking a seat but avoiding eye contact with the men, his head bowed and hands shaking as he placed them on the table. Sayed's men left without a sound and a moment later joined Vic in the observation room. Vic pointed to the camera and recorder.

'All working.'

The men nodded and left the room, their part done. They would sit in the communal room drinking dark tea that was half liquid, half sugar and watching Nigerian soap operas that they didn't understand on a TV with a broken speaker. Vic watched VOLTAGE for several minutes, assessing whether the man had truly broken or was playing for time by pretending he had. But Sayed was good at this. If he said a detainee had broken, then Vic took the Secret Policeman at his word. Nodding to himself, he grabbed the water and snacks and headed into the meeting room. He opened the door and noted that VOLTAGE didn't even look up. Vic could smell soap and saw immediately how much cleaner and presentable the detainee was. Taking the other chair available, Vic slid a bottle of the water and the tub of fruit and nuts across the table.

'Drink. Eat. It's over. No more unpleasantness.'

VOLTAGE looked up, caught Vic's eye for a brief moment before reaching for the water, his hand shaking as he stretched. He struggled to break the seal on the lid and began to cry, shoulders quivering as he sobbed quietly. Vic made soothing noises and made his way round the table, gently taking the bottle from VOLTAGE and removing the top before handing it back to the detainee. VOLTAGE drank huge gulps from the bottle and Vic placed his hand on it, stopping VOLTAGE from tipping the entire contents down his throat.

'Whoa there, whoa. You'll make yourself sick. Take it slow.'

He helped VOLTAGE by taking hold of the bottle and controlling the flow while he placed his other hand on the detainee's shoulder, a soft, almost affectionate touch. When the bottle was empty Vic gave the shoulder a gentle squeeze and went back to his seat. VOLTAGE looked up at him, eyes bloodshot and staring from the shadows of the sockets, hollow and tight from exhaustion. He tried to speak but the sound was merely a garbled sob. Vic held up his hand, maintaining the soft, calm tone.

'Take your time. There's no rush. You've been through a lot.'

More sobbing, as Vic had anticipated. It didn't matter that VOLTAGE's suffering had been under Vic's direction, he was now being shown kindness and compassion for the first time since he was renditioned from Mexico. And Vic would continue to play the part of the good guy with the underlying threat that if

VOLTAGE didn't help him, there was nothing that Vic could do to stop those thugs taking VOLTAGE back out to the house of horrors he'd just survived. But Vic knew that wouldn't be necessary. The shower, clothes, water, food and a kind human being were provided to be the antithesis of what the detainee had undergone. And Vic had yet to meet the detainee who chose to return to his torturers after being treated like a human being again. VOLTAGE looked up at him and cleared his throat.

'Please. I will tell you anything you ask. Please. Do not let those men touch me again. I beg before Allah, do not send me back to them.' His voice cracked and the sobs returned.

Vic leaned forward, forearms resting on the table as he spoke. 'Then don't make me do it. I don't want it, and you don't want it but the only person with the power to stop that from happening is you Aban. Only you.'

Voltage nodded and wiped his face with his sleeves, the arms of the jacket far too long but a deliberate choice, making the detainee feel small even within the clothing he was wearing. He lifted his chin and in a flat voice asked the question Vic had been waiting three days to hear.

'What do you want to know?'

41

8 MONTHS LATER

CIA OPERATIONS' ROOM, LANGLEY, VIRGINIA

Vic Foley shook the hand of the woman and noted the firm grip and eye contact that his superior maintained. The rolled-up sleeves and intense gaze adding to the picture of a senior officer mixing it with the troops. Diana Cahill was something of a legend within the CIA; a senior officer who had cut her teeth on the streets of Moscow and Beirut, survived a car-bombing while operating under Non-Official Cover in Pakistan and been an early champion of the drone program. Her star had been in the ascent throughout her career but her lead on the Bin Laden operation had cemented her standing with both the Agency and the folk that mattered on The Hill. Vic watched as Diana cleared her throat and looked around the busy room.

'Okay. We all know why we're here and what we have to do. Some years ago, I sat in this very room as two helicopters of Navy SEALs crossed into Pakistan airspace to bring retribution to the individual who slaughtered thousands of innocents on our home soil. For that operation to take place required a lot of faith:

Faith that our Case Officers and Analysts had got it right. Faith that the Imagery Analysis Cell were correct that it was an unusually tall, Arabic man who paced the dusty yard of a compound in Abbottabad. Faith that we weren't sending our brave SEALs into a bloodbath from which they wouldn't return.' She paused and indicated with her hand to the array of screens on the wall behind her.

'But today, we don't need faith. Because we have Intel; good, solid Intel from multiple platforms that corroborates what we've always known but could never prove: That the subject of tonight's operation is the most effective terrorist that has been working against us for many years. Far, far more effective than UBL ever was. Up until eight months ago, this terrorist was smart; he only took us on in other people's backyards, killing and maiming our soldiers and allies by proxy. But eight months ago, he directed an operation that would have meant the detonation of a dirty bomb in San Diego. And the game changed.'

The Deputy Director of Operations turned and nodded to Vic. 'Not only did we stop that atrocity, but we managed to capture the brains behind the operation and enjoy several productive interviews with him.' There were some quiet chuckles at the Director's euphemism, and she let them subside before continuing. 'And that's where we got our smoking gun ladies and gentlemen, well... several smoking guns. But that was only the start point. From there we tasked Assets, intercepted communications, maximized surveillance and proved beyond a shadow of a doubt the terrorist's lead in the San Diego attack and several more that are in the pipeline targeting our Armed Forces and Embassies overseas.'

She paused and walked over to a screen that displayed a clear photograph of the target; military uniform, a handsome, masculine face, strong jawline framed by a neat, white beard. The dark eyes cold and pitiless as they glared down at the assembled team dedicated to the demise of their owner. Diana Cahill pointed at the face on the screen. 'Tonight's target, Operation PERSECUTE, is both retributive and pre-emptive in focus. We have not informed Host Nation of our intent nor have we alerted any of our Five Eyes counterparts for obvious reasons. So, there *will* be repercussions; political and diplomatic as well as professional ones. But that will be dealt with by people far higher up the food chain than me. Our sole concern tonight is taking PERSECUTE off the board people and sending the message loud and clear to the world: You hit us, we hit back. *Hard*'

There was a round of enthusiastic applause and the DDO held up her hand and waited until it had faded away before she continued. 'Okay, you've heard more than enough from me so let's get this done. Make us proud, people.' Diana nodded to Vic again before making her way out of the room as everyone took their positions according to role. Headsets were donned, telephone and computer keys typed upon, comms links tested, video feeds brought on-line from the ISR assets which were predominately drone downlinks. The activity was busy but calm, each Head of Department experienced and confident in their abilities, handpicked by the DDO for this very reason. Vic was the exception to the rule; he had no role or input into tonight's activities. He had been invited to the proceedings purely as an observer, an honor bestowed upon him by the DDO herself as a nod of thanks to Vic for stopping the San Diego attack and getting the Intel on PERSECUTE. As a rule, only those with direct involvement in the operation were cleared to be in the Operations' Room during a live op, but Vic was grateful that he would get to see the end result of over a year's worth of work. From the day he'd recruited Seven in a café in Beirut to sitting across from a broken Iranian Quds officer in a Black Site in Djibouti, everything had been leading to this moment. And tonight, he would get to see it first-hand. To see that the deaths of Ned, Randy and the other Delta guys had not been for nothing. That Seven's sacrifice had been worth it.

He looked up as the team monitoring the target aircraft announced that it would be wheels down from Damascus in ten minutes. The drone team acknowledged and confirmed. The Iraq desk provided an update that a vehicle convoy was mobile from the military side of the airport and moving to the commercial side. The NSA guys informed the group that PERSECUTE's and associated cellphones were back up and live feeds from the devices were displayed on a dedicated set of monitors where the contents were rebroadcast in English. Vic read these transcripts with interest, noting that one of the associated numbers was confirming travel arrangements and received an acknowledgement which highlighted how many vehicles would arrive to pick them up. His gaze was naturally drawn to the drone footage of the column of SUVs that were speeding towards the aircraft as it taxied to a halt. One of the NSA technicians pointed to a screen.

'PERSECUTE has been designated vehicle three with one other passenger.'

Vic watched as the drone marked the third vehicle in the line of SUVs and he followed the progress of the red diamond shape superimposed on the roof of the car. The feed from the second drone showed airport staff shadowed by a dozen heavily armed soldiers rushing the steps to the door of the jet. Updates were coming in thick and fast from all elements and Vic felt the familiar excitement within him as the operation was about to reach its climax. The door of the aircraft opened, and the armed soldiers took up positions facing away from the jet as several individuals disembarked and made their way down the steps. The MQ-9 Reaper drone locked and marked the faces of the passengers and on a linked screen to the feed, the identities of the men were displayed with PERSECUTE's details highlighted and enlarged to establish his prominence among the group.

The individuals in the SUVs had jumped out and opened the doors for their distinguished guests. Vic watched as PERSECUTE took a back seat in the third SUV as the earlier text message had stated. Another man joined him in the back carrying a couple of small bags and the doors were closed by one of the SUV team. They waited until the vehicles were all complete with their passengers then the small convoy moved off, driving at speed through the airport and towards a manned exit where armed troops stood ready. The red diamond superimposed on the roof of PERSECUTE's SUV marked him separately from the yellow diamonds on the others.

Vic had been included in the final mission brief and knew that the intended strike area was outside the airport terminal and on an access road reserved for the movement of security forces and visiting VIPs. There was a quick update from the relevant elements to confirm everything was ready and as the convoy picked up speed along the deserted road, the order came from the Operations Center Command.

'Prosecute, Prosecute, Prosecute.'

There was silence in the room, every head turned to the feed from the drone cameras as the convoy of unsuspecting Iranian Quds officers made its way along a quiet Baghdad thoroughfare. The picture on the screen became a bright flash followed by roiling clouds that obscured the activity on the ground. As the smoke dissipated, a burning SUV could clearly be seen. The feed from the second drone had been zoomed in to pick up the granular details of the strike and Vic heard a couple of intakes of breath at the sight of an arm protruding from the twisted chassis of the burning vehicle. Around it, the other SUVs had stopped and were disgorging the passengers who ran to the scene of the strike, shocked and unable to comprehend what had happened.

The NSA comm feeds showed numbers being called from the various cell phones and running transcripts in English kept the room abreast of the conversations. From these messages the panic was evident and an explosive device in the car the suspected means of the killing. A Case Officer from the Iraq desk spoke up.

'From Asset with visual on ground, confirmation PERSECUTE is dead.'

To corroborate this, several of the telephone transcripts were now stating the same information. There was a further silence in the room which was broken by the Operations' Command Center Director clapping his hands. The applause caught on and soon the whole room was filed with the sound. Vic joined in, impressed with a job well done. He looked back to the telephone transcripts in time to see the confirmation from the Senior Quds officer on the ground that their most experienced exporter of terrorism was dead. The second most powerful man in Iran and a man who had dedicated his life to the killing and destruction of Americans and American interests around the globe. A man who had almost succeeded in detonating a dirty bomb on American soil. A man that the CIA computer-generated code had designated PERSECUTE. Vic took a last look at the real name of their target as it dominated the transcript screens:

Major General Qasem Soleimani. Commander of the Quds force of the Islamic Republic of Iran.

42

ONE YEAR LATER

SMITHSONIAN MUSEUM, WASHINGTON DC

The boy looked up at the aircraft suspended from the ceiling with an expression approaching awe. This would be his fifth visit to the Smithsonian and if he had his way, he'd come to this wonderful place every day. There were so many *amazing* things in this incredible place that he was sure he would never get to see everything, no matter how long he lived. And the aircraft he was engrossed with, while something he'd seen on every previous visit, still fascinated him anew every time.

Vic Foley smiled at Affan's undisguised joy and fascination. He turned to the couple sitting beside him.

'How's he shaping up?'

The woman smiled and indicated with her head. 'Look at him; tells you all you need to know.'

The man turned to face Vic. 'He's doing awesome. Learns quick and his English is already really impressive.'

Vic was pleased with Affan's progress. He'd never doubted that Martha and Joe would make great foster-parents for the boy, but the confirmation was welcome. He lowered his voice slightly. 'And the nightmares?'

Martha met his eyes. 'Been months since the last one and even at that, it was pretty mild.'

Vic was pleased to hear this. The boy had been hunted like an animal across a freezing mountain and experienced a brutal beating before killing the man who was intent on killing him. The doctors the Agency had assigned had diagnosed PTSD, but their prognosis had always been optimistic, mainly down to Affan's age. Kids having a better track record of getting through these horrors in time.

When Vic brought Affan back to the States he'd made it clear that he was personally liable for the boy and that the CIA owed the kid and owed him *large*. But his defensive stance had been unnecessary, the Agency stepping right up from the off, all medical and professional assistance opened up to the kid. It had been Bill Howard, his old Chief of Station who had told Vic to touch base with Joe and Martha. Martha was former Agency but left after blast injuries she suffered during a suicide-bombing attack on a hotel in Kabul. Vic didn't know Joe; he was an older guy, former Green Beret who had finished his time in the military and now ran an outfit that introduced disadvantaged kids to the outdoors. Bill had mentioned them to Vic because he knew that they had fostered kids from troubled backgrounds before and would be a safe pair of hands on this occasion where it was even more imperative that the right people were involved. The moment Vic met them and explained the circumstances of Affan's arrival in the US, he knew Bill had called it right. Calm, reasoned, showing empathy rather than sympathy for Affan's experiences, the couple committed immediately to helping the boy. And the change in Affan was plain to see.

The kid had needed several surgeries to the fractures in his cheekbones and jaw, dental reconstruction, and therapy sessions to deal with the mental traumas. But looking at him now, Vic saw a bright-eyed, happy kid enjoying himself at his favorite place. He'd filled out some too; gone were the hollowed eye sockets and gaunt cheeks replaced by a healthy teenager's smiling face. The thick, matted nest of hair Vic had seen in the mountains of Iran was now a glossy, thick mane that framed Affan's face and Vic could already see the handsome young man Affan was one day going to be. He grinned and looked at Joe and Martha. 'You've done a good job. Maybe *too* good. That boy is gonna be a heartbreaker for the ladies!'

Martha laughed. 'That's exactly what Joe said about a month ago when we took Affan to a company cookout and he was *very* popular with the girls.'

Vic walked over to Affan and laughed at the boy's reaction when he saw the CIA officer. Big eyes, huge grin and practically sprinted across the gap that separated them, running into Vic at full speed and throwing his arms around him.

'Vic! Vic! I didn't know you were coming. It's great to see you. Where have you been? It's been too long!'

Vic ruffled his hair and chuckled at the quick-fire questions. 'Hey Affan, how you doing buddy? You look good man. Real good.'

Affan stepped back and looked up at the tall American who had brought him to this country. 'I am good Vic. Very good. Joe and Martha are the best. We went camping in the mountains last week and Joe and I caught fish and we cooked them on the fire then we went in a canoe where we saw a bear on the shore...' He stopped as Vic laughed aloud and put his arm around the youth's shoulders.

'Slow down little leopard. We've got all afternoon. You don't have to tell me everything in one breath.'

Affan grinned back. 'Sorry Vic, but it was the best trip *ever* and Joe says I'm a natural outdoors man. We're gonna do it again in the fall. You should come.'

Although the accent still came through in his speech, Vic noted that it was getting less and less prominent every time they met, and the Americanisms were now common in his conversations. With Affan's dark looks and mild accent he could easily be mistaken for someone of Hispanic descent rather than Iranian. Vic thought again about what this kid had gone through to get to where he was today, and a feeling of pride welled up within him at how far Affan had come and how he was embracing his new life.

They left the museum accompanied by Joe and Martha and made their way to the ice-cream vendor that Affan had declared his favorite ever after his first visit to the museum. As they approached, Vic pressed down on Affan's shoulder to get his attention.

'Affan, I've brought someone here who wants to meet you. Is that okay?'

'Sure. Who is it?'

Vic looked up and nodded at a woman sitting on a nearby wall. The woman stood and walked towards them, a soft smile on her lips as she approached. Vic placed both his hands on Affan's shoulders as he introduced the woman.

'Affan, this is Cathy. Cathy, Affan.'

Affan held out his hand for the woman to shake and she laughed as she accepted it, charmed and amused by the confident adult gesture coming from one so young.

'I'm very pleased to meet you Cathy.'

'And I you Affan.'

There was a moment's silence and Affan studied the woman. She was very pretty but even though she was smiling, there was sadness in her eyes. He wondered who she was and why she had wanted to meet him. A thought came into his head and the words were out of his mouth before he had time to consider their impact. 'Are you the wife of the soldier? The one who died?'

Cathy nodded and felt a hitch in her throat and the tears start to well in her eyes. 'Yes Affan. That was my husband. Ned.'

Affan was silent for several seconds before stepping forward and taking both of Cathy's hands in his and meeting her eyes. 'He was very brave. Braver even than Mr. Karim. You should be very proud of your husband Miss Cathy. He saved our lives.'

Cathy felt the tears streaming down her face and pulled Affan into her, embracing the handsome boy who had the manners and empathy of someone much older. 'Thank you Affan, thank you. I just wanted to meet you for myself. Vic told me so much about you I just had to meet this amazing young man who knew my Ned.'

Vic felt his own eyes begin to tear up and he looked away reflecting again on how adult Affan could sometimes be, his emotional intelligence that of a man in his forties rather than a young teenager. When he'd returned Stateside, Vic had visited Cathy as soon as he could, wanting her to hear first-hand, what her husband had done. He'd kept in touch since, updating her on Affan's progress and how he was adapting to American life. It had been his suggestion that she meet this remarkable boy, see with her own eyes the good that had come from Ned's sacrifice. Martha patted Vic's shoulder, raising her eyebrows in a discreet *are you okay?* gesture. Vic nodded and brought his attention back to the group. He met Cathy's gaze.

'You gonna join us for ice-cream? According to our newest American citizen here, it's the best in the world.'

Cathy laughed again and wiped the tears from her eyes and cheeks. 'I'd love to.'

Affan took hold of Cathy's hand and started walking towards the vendor, telling her that mint choc-chip is the best flavor of ice cream invented and that if she has never tried it before, she should try it today.

Vic took a seat on the wall and watched as the wife of a dead Delta Force warrior was charmed and comforted by an Iranian kid her husband had sacrificed his life to save on a freezing mountain almost two years before. As Joe and Martha joined them, a light-hearted debate about which flavor was actually the best ensued. Vic crossed his arms and leaned back looking up at the sky through his sunglasses.

He thought about when he'd first identified a confident Quds officer running a mentoring program with Hezbollah in Lebanon and wondered if he was worth the trouble. Remembered researching and finding the information that he thought might just sway the officer into accepting Vic's deal. Being impressed by the courage and tenacity that the newly recruited Asset had shown in the field from the start.

And then, when he could have just ignored the information, kept himself out of harm's way, the Asset had chosen to risk everything to get it out. And he had. Risked his life and lost it but in doing so had saved the lives of hundreds of innocent people.

And one boy. One remarkable boy who was going to be a remarkable man one day.

And with that thought in his mind Vic Foley stood and went to join the happy group of people brought together by the incredible sacrifice of two brave individuals on a freezing mountain in Iran.

THE END

Thank you for reading and I truly hope you enjoyed this book. Please, if you have enjoyed it, take the time to leave a review and let others know how much you liked it. Thank you once again.

James

ALSO, BY JAMES E MACK

ONLY THE DEAD

'Only the dead have seen the end of war'

In war-torn Libya, veteran Commando Finn Douglas is forced to commit an appalling act in order to save the lives of his men. Haunted by his actions, he suffers a further blow when he learns that his family has been killed in a terrorist attack in London. Numb with grief and trauma, Finn turns his back on the world of war and killing and flees to an island wilderness to escape his demons.

A team of Military Police are tasked with bringing Finn to justice. But for one of the policemen, the manhunt is a more personal issue; a chance for revenge to right a wrong suffered years before.

When Finn intervenes in a life and death situation, his sanctuary is shattered, and the net tightens. The manhunt becomes a race against time between the forces of law and order and a psychotic mercenary determined to exact his revenge on Finn for thwarting his plans.

For Finn, the world of killing and conflict returns with a vengeance on the blizzard-swept mountains of the island. Only this time there is nowhere left to run.

Only The Dead is a thriller in the tradition of Gerald Seymour and a standout debut from a new British author.

FEAR OF THE DARK

An idyllic Scottish Village…

A small team of rural Police Officers…

A man who won't talk…

When a violent stranger is arrested and refuses to give his name, it is only the beginning. Digging further into the background of their mysterious prisoner, Police Constable Tess Cameron finds that he is a disgraced former Special Forces soldier with a chequered past.

As the worst storm of winter hits the village and communications and electricity are cut, the severe weather is blamed. Tess, however, feels that something more sinister may be responsible for their isolation.

Because the stranger has friends.

And they want him back.

Whatever it takes.

In the darkest night of winter, Tess and her fellow police officers find themselves facing an elite team of killers determined to rescue their leader. And Tess knows that if they are to survive the night, they have only one choice: Fight.

First Blood meets *The Bill* in this exciting new thriller from the author of Only the Dead.

THE KILLING AGENT

London. Cardiff. Edinburgh.

The worst terrorist attacks that the UK has seen.

A country in turmoil, a government in disarray.

Lovat Reid, a veteran covert operator with the Special Intelligence Group, is tasked to help track down the mastermind behind the attacks. With his partner Nadia, an officer from the Special Reconnaissance Regiment, they soon realise that they are dealing with an individual the likes of which they have not seen before.

When another atrocity is carried out, the entire weight of the Intelligence agencies and Special Forces is thrown behind the effort to find the terrorist responsible. But for Lovat, something isn't quite right. Suspecting a dangerous power-play between the agencies, Lovat digs a little deeper into the background of the terrorist suspect.

And is stunned by what he finds.

With a race against time to halt the next attack, Lovat and Nadia find themselves fighting a war on two fronts as they strive to uncover the depth of deception while hunting the master terrorist.

From the killing fields of Kandahar to the back streets of London, the consequences of a secret assassination program are brutally levelled against an unsuspecting British public.

271

SINS OF THE FATHERS

Belfast 1973:

A team of undercover soldiers deploy on an operation into the heart of republican West Belfast unaware of the horrific catastrophe that awaits them.

Belfast 1995:

The IRA struggles to convince their members to maintain the fragile ceasefire. When its London bombing cells are compromised and arrested, the leadership knows there can be only one reason for such a defeat; an informer in their midst. A *Tout*.

As the top echelons of the IRA hunt for the informer, the intelligence agencies continue with their covert operations against the terror group. For Marcus Vaughan, a new operator with the Special Intelligence Group, the dark world of the Dirty War is everything he trained for and more. Running agents and surveillance against IRA targets, Marcus embraces his new calling.

But when the legacy of a long-forgotten operation comes crashing into the present, the war suddenly becomes personal for Marcus. *Very* personal. And as he begins to uncover a web of treachery and deceit stretching back decades, Marcus soon realizes that the dark forces involved will stop at nothing to cover their tracks.

From black operations in the back streets of Belfast to the shadow world of spooks and spies, Sins of the Fathers takes the reader to the heart of the undercover war in Northern Ireland.

LINKS

https://web.facebook.com/authorjamesemack

www.jamesemack.com

james@jamesemack.com

Printed in Great Britain
by Amazon

28670912R00160